THAT WHICH MAY DESTROY YOU

ABDA KHAN

Chiselbury

Copyright © 2025 by Abda Khan

First published 2025

Published by Chiselbury, a division of Woodstock Leasor Limited, 14 Devonia Road, London N1 8JH, United Kingdom

www.chiselbury.com

The moral right of Abda Khan to be identified as the author of this work is asserted.

Cover design by: Indra Murugiah

ISBN 978-1-916556-59-1 (hardback)

ISBN 978-1-916556-85-0 (paperback)

ISBN 978-1-916556-60-7 (epub)

A CIP catalogue record for this book is available from the British Library.

1

R v Miriam Hassan
Birmingham Crown Court
Monday 4 November 2019

Miriam walks lightly up the steep stone steps. They look as battered as she feels; the pounding of feet over the years has turned them into the colour of old dry ash. She brushes her right hand along the stain-smeared cold wall on her way up. Her head hangs low during her slow ascent towards the light. She feels sick, perhaps due to hunger, or perhaps her nerves are getting the better of her. She pushes back down the burning acid that fights to make its way up her throat. *Whatever it is, it will pass,* she tells herself. *It will pass. Everything comes to pass, eventually.*

As she enters the Defendant's box, she lifts her head; the sudden sharp bright light hits her. She closes her eyes for a few seconds, and then she reluctantly prises them open, a little at a time. She scans the room slowly.

Birmingham Crown Court is full to bursting and abuzz with activity. There are teams of lawyers briskly flicking through large folders of papers, frantically making notes at the sides of statements, and busily scribbling in their note pads. Members of the public are settling down for the day in the public gallery, munching on boiled sweets, as they wait in anticipation for proceedings to begin. Local and national journalists are sitting poised to take down all the gory details they hope may emerge from someone's testimony. Miriam's former colleagues are also sitting amongst the crowd; they exchange whispers, still at a loss as to how all this has happened, how she has ended up here, her fate in the hands of a court.

People are present in this courtroom for very different reasons, and from very different walks of life, but they are all here to watch this spectacle unfold.

Miriam catches sight of Nina, who gives her a reassuring smile, as only a best friend can. As her gaze starts to wander, Miriam notices that there are many people she has never set eyes on before. She cranes her neck around further, and she catches a glimpse of two people who she hadn't expected to see in this courtroom today. To her surprise, she sees her father and brother are also present, sitting next to each other, silently. She hasn't seen them, or anyone else, other than her legal team, during her entire time in remand, having refused any visitors. She could not face the prospect of allowing others to see her in that place, in that state. She had assumed that her refusal to see her family would perhaps lead to a resumption of the distance between them. After all this time, now, in the most desperate moment of her life, they have come, and that is what counts. Her brother looks straight at her; the corners of his lips curl up a little, and he gives her a small nod of the head. Her father looks straight ahead; he seems solemn and serious, but she can discern a touch of emotion, which shows itself now in his eyes, in the way that they crinkle at the edges, a look she remembers so well.

Miriam turns her face towards the front of the court again, and closes her eyes for a short while. She floats away. She sees ducks by the pond now, her father handing her pieces of bread and *roti* from a brown paper bag, she sees her red shoes with their shiny square buckles, scuffed at the front where her little toes fit, she sees the necklace threaded with pastel coloured sweets that dangles down in front of her as she feeds the ducks, a treat her dad bought her from the corner shop on the way to the park, and they made a pact not to tell mum, she sees her already raggedy doll hanging from her free hand, a gift bought only recently by her parents for her sixth birthday, she sees her dad pick her up and spin her around, she is wrapped up warm in his all-encompassing hug, she feels his sweet kiss on the top of her little head.

Right now, Miriam acutely feels the absence of her mother. Never more since her mother's death when she was just sixteen has Miriam wished for her mother's hug, ached for her soothing words. And yet, Miriam knows that she would struggle to explain why she is in this courtroom, facing these allegations.

The hum of the courtroom has increased significantly. The courtroom is heaving with an air of unusual excitement.

The tall, thin Clerk stands up and announces the arrival of the robed and wigged Judge. Everyone stands as the Judge enters, and he does so with much less ceremony than one might expect given his fancy robes and important position. He takes his seat on his raised section of the courtroom, and everyone else sits back down.

The stage is set; the actors are poised for their performance, and the audience is waiting in anticipation for the drama to unfold.

The Judge, dressed in a rich red gown, as opposed to a black one which Miriam was expecting, appears, to Miriam at least, to have a kind face; he is a man in his sixties, who has thoughtful looking, deep-set grey eyes, and he has a gentle quality about him, despite the harshness of the wig. That said, the first impression is not always the best impression, or in any way an accurate impression, as Miriam has found out to her detriment.

A few hushed whispers soon dissipate, and the room gradually falls silent. Miriam remains standing. She breathes in the deepest breath she has inhaled for many days. The yoga classes at prison have done their job in helping her to stay as calm as she can in the circumstances. As she slowly inhales, time seems to stand still. She holds her breath for perhaps ten seconds, and in those ten seconds there comes to her the inescapable thought that there is nowhere for her to run, nowhere to hide, and no means of taking flight. But if she was truly honest with herself, then she had to admit that for those two years, there never had been anywhere to run to, to hide in, or to take flight to. She breathes out slowly, much more slowly than her inhalation; she feels her chest sinking and her stomach contracting, as she empties out every last bit of the deep breath from her lungs. Even though she knows full well how she has ended up in this courtroom, she still cannot quite take in the enormity of being in this space, in front of all these people, in front of all these eyes. She knows she has to accept that she has no power over what will unfurl before her. Now the time has come when Miriam has to face the truth, whatever that turns out to be. For the 'truth', whether that is *the truth* or some other version of it, or indeed a complete falsehood, will determine whether she walks free from this courtroom, or spends the rest of her life behind bars, and worse than that, perhaps, is the fact that this 'truth' will be decided by twelve complete strangers.

Further to a few moments of fussing around with some of the papers in front of him, the clerk turns towards Miriam. After obtaining confirmation of her name and address from her, he continues.

'You are accused that on Sunday 31st March 2019, you did murder Mr Zafar Hassan'.

Miriam feels the dozens of pairs of eyes fiercely on her. She knows the courtroom is not packed because of her, even if she is being tried for murder. No, people are here because of *who* she is suspected of killing. She stands accused of the murder of Mr Zaf Hassan. He was a very well-known figure; a handsome man, a celebrated restaurateur, a multi-millionaire with a successful business empire, a loyal army of diners, and a devoted social media following. A colourful, charismatic character who, in the eyes of many, was full of life and who lived life to the full. He also happened to be her husband. Miriam now stands accused of cold-bloodedly killing him after two years of marriage. She is not only his widow; she is also the sole beneficiary of his considerable fortune if she walks free.

'How do you plead, guilty or not guilty?' asks the clerk.

'Not guilty.'

2

'Guilty as charged,' said Zaf, as he and Miriam finished off their desserts of steamed lemon and raspberry ripple sponge puddings topped with a helping of sharp lemon curd, and a scoop of raspberry and white chocolate ice cream. They were coming towards the end of their meal in a newly opened, fashionable London restaurant; the top floor seating area had very advantageous views of the City, including over the River Thames. Zaf had been very insistent on treating her to a meal at the capital's trendiest new eatery which, with its almost 360-degree floor to ceiling glass encasing, allowed a panoramic view of the city in all its glittery glory. Zaf was a proud and successful restaurateur in his own right, but he was also always keen to sample good food elsewhere, and of course it didn't hurt to keep an eye on the competition. Added to that was the fact that he was always welcomed very warmly at any establishment that he occasionally chose to dine at, as having Zaf over to eat was very much a compliment to the proprietors of other restaurants.

Miriam gazed out of the window; the sky hung peacefully

above the capital, like a burnt orange shroud which glowed intensely along the skyline, but it dissolved to a peachier covering as she gazed up away from the buildings. As she lifted her head and looked high above into the vastness of the night sky stealing in, she could discern strands of sooty grey and dark indigo blue.

They had been seeing each other for three months now, and Miriam could sometimes barely believe how quickly their relationship had progressed. What she felt, and what she knew, was that she was loved and valued, and she hadn't felt like this in a long time, or maybe she had never felt like this before at all. As she looked on at the intense, smouldering golden flickers of the city lights, she felt the same glow radiate from somewhere within her. After all the strife of the past few years, she had not expected happiness to come to her anytime soon. She had resigned herself to a life of disappointments, a life of loneliness even, and yet, meeting Zaf had changed all that. Things were different. Everything was different. It was as though her *kismet* had changed, and she had a reason to smile again. When she woke up in the mornings, she wanted to cherish life, instead of cursing it, as each moment had now taken on a new meaning. Since growing closer to Zaf, she was beginning to see something that she had not seen in a very long time; when she looked in the mirror, she saw herself smile.

'If you're accusing me of rushing into marrying you because I love you and can't bear to be apart from you for any longer than I absolutely have to, then like I said, I am guilty as charged,' he said, as he stroked her left hand that bore the large solitaire diamond ring he had gifted to her as a token of his commitment.

Miriam had been swept up in a whirlwind since the day they had met, quite by chance, at his Manchester restaurant, an act of fate in the truest sense. Zaf rarely went up to the northern restaurants, as for some years now the company had employed a

Northern Area Manager who handled things very competently, so it really had been fortuitous that Miriam should be there on one of the very rare days that Zaf made an appearance. There had been a mix-up with the booking of the table for herself and her friends. Nina had suggested they leave and go somewhere else. 'After all, there are no shortages of restaurants on Wilmslow Road – we can be there in ten minutes!' she had remarked, as they sat on the leather couches in the large airy reception.

Zaf had been walking through the reception area when he had caught a snippet of the conversation. He'd approached the manager and after a few minutes of discussion he came over to the ladies.

'Good evening, allow me to introduce myself. My name is Zaf, and I would like to apologise for the confusion, clearly the mistake is on our part. The manager is fixing this right now. I have been assured that the table will be ready in about ten minutes. I hope that's okay?' He had calmly and assuredly sorted it all out, although Nina had commented that he was a bit "too smooth" for her liking. To the contrary, Miriam had thought he embodied an effortless charm which was very alluring. He had topped it all by offering to send an e-voucher for a complimentary meal for the inconvenience and delay that had been caused for them. He took Miriam's number. And it had all gone on from there.

Zaf was always kind and generous, and attentive whenever they were together; present and available in that moment, the way he would put his phone away whenever they were together. He loved all her quirks that made her unique; the way she *always* ordered chips when they dined out, regardless of how fancy the restaurant was, the fervour with which she sang along to the songs in the car which he said was quite charming, and he even indulged in her love of sweet and salty popcorn which he had previously considered to be weird. And he was the same when they were apart; accommodating, thoughtful, mindful. Nothing was ever too much trouble. When she mentioned in passing one day that she'd left her favourite umbrella on the train, he found the exact same umbrella online and had it delivered to her.

After five extremely lonely years devoid of the company of any family, it now felt so good to Miriam to be loved, to be needed and appreciated in this way; he already made her feel like she was his family. The void didn't gnaw at her like it used to. Miriam felt, once again, as though she belonged, and that the gaping hole that she had felt since being estranged from her family was now beginning to disappear.

They moved onto the subject of setting a date for the wedding. Zaf made no bones about the fact that he didn't want a long engagement. He didn't see the point. He was a true businessman at heart; if there was a deal to be done, then there was no point in hanging around - cut to the chase, agree terms, and get it finished. And much like his business deals, he wanted to seal this deal as quickly as possible.

'But getting married in four weeks' time. That's so soon! And Nina can't make it, she'll still be working abroad at the time, she can't get time off,' Miriam said, and then turned her thoughts towards Nina. They had shared so much of their lives together since that first day at university when they had stood in the registration queue next to each other, and got chatting. Another act of fate. Their friendship grew into an almost sisterly closeness which meant they were there for each other no matter what. They had supported each other through all the bad bits, and together they had shared all the good bits. They had been a sort of Thelma and Louise to each other, fiercely loyal and unconditionally caring. She couldn't imagine getting married without her at the wedding. When she had mentioned the proposed date to Nina on the telephone the day before, Nina had urged Miriam not to rush into things. 'You've always been such a wise owl', Miriam had said to her in return, and told her there was nothing for her to worry about. 'If he loves you. he will wait' is what Nina had said to her, again, urging Miriam to employ caution. But Miriam assured her that he did love her, and perhaps marrying within four months after meeting might seem a bit rushed to those looking in from the outside, but she knew how deeply they both felt for each other. Marriage after four months wasn't that unusual, she had said, trying hard to allay any misgivings that Nina had. It felt right to Miriam. She couldn't explain it as well as she felt it. Zaf made her *feel* that everything was just as it should be. Just perfect.

'I hear you,' said Zaf, bringing Miriam's attention back to the present, 'but my work commitments mean that if we don't do it next month, I won't be free for four or five months after that, perhaps longer, as we'll be working towards opening the second London restaurant, and refurbing the one in Manchester. I say we, because everything I have and do is now yours too.' He smiled as he gave Miriam's hand a gentle squeeze. 'I know it's a shame about Nina - a couple of my mates can't make it either for one reason or another, but they get it. I'll tell you what, we'll do something special with the absent friends in a few months' time whenever they can all make it. A party to celebrate, just for them, in their honour, if you like. How does that sound?'

Miriam smiled back at him, but said nothing. She had a sip of her dark Columbian coffee and took a few moments to think about Zaf's question.

'I just want us to be together, and to get on with our lives,' he continued, bringing her away from her thoughts, and towards what he was now saying. His fingertips touched to form a steeple as he rested his elbows on the table. 'Why delay happiness? If our friends are true friends, then they will understand; they'll just want us to be happy.'

Miriam tilted her head to one side and gave him a wide smile. He always had a solution to any problem; that made her feel better, made her feel protected. It wasn't that she needed a saviour, but she loved the feeling of security that he offered her. That knowledge that there is that someone who will make everything *feel* alright, even if it wasn't alright or couldn't be alright. They would be there for you. Just like she used to feel when she was younger. Before things went wrong. And with that thought, her attention veered towards the issue that could scarcely be avoided.

'And are you sure you're okay with my family not being there? You know how things are for me on that score. Are your parents alright with that?'

He lowered his hands in order to take hold of both of hers, and leant over a bit more, bringing his face closer. 'Stop worrying,' he said softly. My parents are just glad that their 36-year-old son is finally getting wed. My wealth and success mean nothing if I don't have anyone to share it with. My parents are barely over here these days, they're living it large in Lahore, enjoying their twilight years together, and they desperately want me to have someone to share my life with too. Believe me, they are ecstatic about the fact that I have finally decided to take a wife. With my sister abroad, married and settled, this is their last obligation in life, their *aakhri farz*, as they call it. And as far as the problem with your family goes, it's not an ideal situation, but, it's also not a deal breaker. I want to marry you. End of. My parents accept your position with your family, as do I. Now it's time to get on with everything.'

3

Birmingham Crown Court
4 November 2019

Everything is now in position; people are sitting in their places, everyone is silent. As the court proceedings commence, Miriam swallows hard as the enormity of it all creeps up on her; like a car that seems faraway one second but almost knocks you over the next. You have no idea how it has crept up on you so quickly, but you are acutely aware of what might happen next. She sits quietly, waiting for the proceedings to commence.

After preliminary legal issues are dealt with, most of which goes above everybody's heads, other than the legal bods who are discussing those issues, it is time for the jury to be sworn in. Miriam looks on in silence, her face calm for now, as the twelve citizens pile into court, one by one, and take their seats. Seven women and five men. *Is that good or bad?* she asks herself. At the prison, she had heard conflicting advice; some inmates had said that more men were better, as men were more sympathetic towards female defendants, and added that women were harsher. How could that be? Miriam had asked herself. Why would women be so unfair on their own sex? What happened to girl power? Sisterhood? Female solidarity? Others had said that it didn't matter what the ratio of men to women was; women accused of crimes were always dealt with more harshly than men, as society didn't expect women to be criminals. It didn't fit with society's perception or stereotypes of what women should be; mothers, homemakers, nurturers, providers - kind, gentle, soft. And yet others had said to her that if you were attractive, which they told her she was, then that would improve your chances of success. *Can freedom really be based on something as fickle as your looks?* Miriam wonders.

Miriam observes the different members of the jury intently. She can't focus on all of them immediately, not in any detail; but a few stand out to her right from the get go. There is a smart, suited Asian man, in his thirties; he has a neatly cut and styled short beard and moustache, and his black hair is gelled rigidly in place. She can't tell if he is of an Indian or Pakistani background. But aside from the fact that Zaf was clean shaven, this man could be Zaf; he looks like he is of a very similar age, height, colour, even the hair is styled in the same way. If she were to guess, she would presume that he is a businessman of some kind. Will he give her a fair hearing? She has her doubts. Then there is an almost hippy looking woman, perhaps in her early fifties, who wears large hooped earrings and a broad flowery headband which keeps her wavy hair out of her button eyes. There is a large, elderly man, dressed in a turtle neck jumper that is a pale shade of blue, and the collars of his checked shirt are popping out at the top. Next to him there is a young *hijabi* woman, of Middle Eastern or Arab origin perhaps, her head wrapped in an expensive looking navy silk scarf, and there is a white woman with a fake tan, bleach blond curly hair and bright red nails which look like gel extensions.

Miriam looks towards her barrister, Mr De Beaux QC, who is busy reading something in front of him.

The prosecution starts to deliver its opening speech, and Miriam now turns her attention towards Ms Godfrey QC, the prosecution barrister. She is a tall woman in her late fifties. She is an imposing figure when she stands up tall in the courtroom with her antiquated wig and long black robe on. She certainly has presence; she is difficult to ignore.

Miriam hardly recognises herself when she hears the cruel narrative that emerges from prosecuting counsel. Ms Godfrey opens the case for the prosecution by claiming that on Sunday the 31 of March 2019, Miriam Hassan had murdered her husband Zafar Hassan in cold blood, by ruthlessly plunging a letter opener into the deceased's abdomen and rupturing his spleen, causing the deceased to bleed out.

Miriam turns around, and she catches sight of Zaf's parents. She turns her head back around swiftly, not wishing to lock eyes with either of them. They had booked the first flight back to the UK as soon as they had heard the news about their only son. Zaf's father now suddenly finds himself back out of retirement to take care of the business, at least until the court case is over. Miriam wonders how they must feel on hearing these grisly details about their son. The loss of your child; can there be anything more devastating than this? Although her experience was not quite the same, Miriam can relate; she holds back her tears.

Ms Godfrey continues with her narrative. She further adds that whilst there were no direct witnesses to the murder, the prosecution has evidence that places the Defendant at the scene of the crime at the estimated time of the attack and subsequent death of the victim. In addition, there is forensic evidence which links her to the weapon used, and there are testimonies of witnesses which will shed light on the circumstances leading up to the murder. All the evidence will prove the Defendant's guilt. This act of brutality, claims Ms Godfrey, was motivated by greed on the part of the defendant, who stands to benefit enormously from the estate of the deceased.

And so, it begins, thinks Miriam, sitting alone in the dock, aside from the prison guards who flank her on either side. This is it.

4

26 February 2017

It was a Sunday afternoon, and Miriam noticed from the kitchen window that the late February sunshine had decided to make an appearance. It was a reassuring, welcome presence. She had turned the heating back on though, as the air was cool and crisp, despite the fact that sun deceptively beamed outside. Zaf, she had discovered, didn't usually go to work on Sundays. It was his only day off. It was two weeks today exactly since the day they had got married.

The wedding had been a lavish affair. Miriam had expected that to some degree; Zaf was extremely well-known both within his own community and outside of it too. His parents had flown over and ensured no detail was overlooked, from the luxury gift bags that the guests received, to the expensive cars that they all rode in to reach the country manor where vibrant Asian colours and the intense sounds of the dhols and shehnais took over what could properly be described as an ivy clad grand former stately home which stood proudly on the outskirts of a small sleepy English village. Much was expected of the Hassan family on the marriage of their only son, and the Hassans did not disappoint. Zaf's parents sat through the day with an air of great satisfaction; their son was now a married man, and they had hinted, more than once, even though Miriam and Zaf were barely married, that they looked forward in great anticipation to the arrival of a baby. Their lives would then feel complete.

Miriam now finished frying off the last three slightly crinkly edged *chappali* kebabs and drained them on the kitchen roll. Little speckles of freshly chopped green coriander poked though their deep golden-brown surface, as she placed the round discs of fried minced meat patties on the serving plate, and then on to the tray, which was now ready to serve to the guests who were sat in the lounge with Zaf. Three men had arrived a little while ago. Zaf had taken them straight through to the lounge, and although she didn't actually know who they were, she presumed that they were business acquaintances.

The large rectangular silver tea tray was topped with hot aromatic desi tea, and alongside the just made *chappali* kebabs, there was fresh green chutney that she had whizzed up quickly by putting mint and coriander leaves, green chillies, a touch of yogurt, and seasoning in the mini chopper. She had also placed some *badam nan khatai* on one of the blue rimmed white china plates; these almond Pakistani biscuits were Zaf's particular favourite. As she carried the heavy tray from the kitchen, Miriam noticed that what had been the bright orangey red henna patterns, so deftly woven together by the skilled *mehndi* artist into charming little flower buds and leaves on the hands which then spread to a bracelet design on the wrists, had all but faded away, leaving a barely discernible outline. What a shame, she thought, that the *mehndi* should have disappeared so quickly. She was sure she had heard her mum say in the past, although it was probably just an old wives' tale, that the longer the henna lasts, the happier the bride will be, but if it fades away quickly, it is a sign that the woman will have an unhappy marriage. Or was it that her mother-in-law would be mean to her? She couldn't quite recollect, but she suspected, and very much hoped, that it was a load of old nonsense.

Miriam smiled as she carefully entered the room with the heavy tray. The men all stopped talking as soon as she walked in. She greeted the guests with *salaams,* and they all returned the greeting. She placed the tea tray in the middle of the large mahogany coffee table. Zaf looked at her in silence. She looked back at him, and hesitated for a second or two. She didn't really know why, but there was a moment of awkwardness between them; it was quite inexplicable. The silence ensued, so she turned and left the room, and once she was out of the room, she heard Zaf restart the conversation.

She had some chores to catch up with in the kitchen, so she headed in there and turned the radio on, tuning into the eighties' hits station; she immediately started to sing along, albeit quietly, to 'walking on sunshine', keeping the volume of the radio, and her voice, low, mindful of the guests in the house. She had inherited her love for eighties' music from her late mother, who had frequently listened to both western and *desi* tunes from that era. In that sense, she really was her mother's daughter. Her mum had loved listening to everything from Abba and Wham to Nazia Hassan and Lata Mangeshkar.

Miriam started on the task of cleaning the enormous American fridge, whilst she sang along quietly under her breath. She had always sung around the house as long as she could remember, even as a little girl. Despite the problems she would encounter later in her teens, her parents had never minded her singing her heart out, and in fact it became a running joke that she couldn't possibly do the dishes or knead the chapatti dough without singing, whether it was singing along to the music on the radio, or going solo. She had been a proud member of the school choir, and her parents had never missed a single concert, although her brother on the other hand had always thought it a complete waste of time, as only an annoying sibling could.

She was singing along to 'take my breath away' and nearing the end of cleaning the fridge when Zaf walked into the kitchen with the tray. He placed it down on the worktop with a clang, which startled her for a second.

'Have they gone?' she asked him as she replaced the milk and juice cartons back in the door of the fridge.

'Yes,' he replied quietly, and walked out of the kitchen abruptly, although she didn't clock the abruptness, nor the fact that he had walked out of the kitchen, so absorbed was she in finishing the housework. When she did realise that he had gone, she just assumed he had things to do in his study, and she carried on in order that she could tick off another job off the many that had to be seen to in the large, expensively fitted kitchen. Once she was happy with the state of the fridge, she started to gather together her ingredients so she could make a start on cooking the dinner.

Just as Miriam had thought, Zaf went straight into his study; this was where he liked to spend most of his time when he was at home, and if he wasn't there, Miriam would find him in the lounge watching either the news or a documentary.

As they sat together and ate dinner a couple of hours later, she realised he hadn't spoken at all since the guys had left.

'Is everything okay?' she enquired, as she scooped up some chicken and rice onto her fork.

'What do you mean?' he asked, speaking coldly, almost angrily, whilst avoiding eye contact with her.

She put her fork down. She didn't understand why he seemed so irritated. He had a certain look on his face. Serious.

Sullen. This was probably the first time that she had seen or perhaps really clocked that 'look'. A very particular look, one that she would come to see time and time again, and one that would fill her with dread each time. His lips were pursed, and the very corners of his lips were turned down. His eyebrows were raised high. It was though his lips and his eyebrows were working against each other; the lips dragging downwards, the eyebrows pulling upwards. Never the twain would meet. She would come to know it in her mind only as *the look of doom*.

'You've hardly spoken a word in the last few hours. You've been really quiet, and I just wondered if something was up.'

'Like you don't know.'

Miriam was well and truly confused now, and thought about his statement for a little while before responding.

'I *don't* know, that's why I'm asking you.'

There followed more silence, apart from the soft sound of the tumble dryer drifting out from the utility room. Another chore she had managed to squeeze in earlier in the day. Zaf had made things perfectly clear to her just two days into their marriage; washing and ironing, and in fact all domestic chores, were her responsibility and hers alone. Cooking, cleaning, doing the dishes, hoovering, cleaning the bathrooms, the kitchen, dusting, polishing, all of it. Every Monday morning, he expected his shirts to have been washed, ironed, hung in the wardrobe, ready for the entire week. And his shoes polished if necessary, which they usually were. He would instruct her as to his dry cleaning as and when. It was her job to take his suits to the dry cleaners and have them back for whenever he needed them.

'Is it me? Have I done something to upset you?' She was sure she hadn't done anything, but she couldn't work out what was bothering him. Perhaps it wasn't her, she thought, maybe the meeting with the men who came to see him hadn't gone so well. That must be it, it can't be anything else, she convinced herself.

'Shouldn't you know if you've done something wrong?' he said.

His response surprised her. No. That's not quite accurate. The fact was that his response *alarmed* her. For it signalled that he clearly felt that she *had* done something wrong, but she herself was completely clueless as to what that could be. She shifted around in her chair a little, and then sat up straight. An uncomfortable feeling gathered in her stomach. Her heartbeat quickened, and her palms felt sticky. She tried her best to ignore how she was feeling. Anxious, perhaps. Annoyed, maybe. How she was feeling was not important right now; she knew she needed to get to the bottom of whatever it was that was bothering her husband enough to speak to her in riddles.

'But I *don't* know. That's the point. Are you saying I *have* done something to upset you?'

Zaf looked dead straight into her eyes, with an intensity she hadn't witnessed before; a sharp gaze, frozen and focused, as though his dark eyes might suddenly fly out of their sockets and physically penetrate hers.

'What? What have I done wrong?' she asked, and hated the fact that her voice now sounded grating, as though she was pleading. Like a child. She felt pathetic.

He put his hands down on the table on either side of his plate, and continued with the piercing stare.

'What do you think you were doing, parading yourself like that in front of those men?'

Miriam's mouth started to fall open, and her breath started to quicken. Did she hear him right? Did she? Surely not.

'What?' she asked slowly.

'You heard me!'

His voice rose, again something she had not experienced before, and again, she was taken aback. His tone was coarse, unfeeling. This wasn't the Zaf she knew. She now felt queasy as her nerves began to tangle.

'I honestly don't know what you mean,' she said, truthfully.

'I told you I would come to the kitchen for the tea tray myself.'

'Yes, I know you did, but you *didn't* come,' she replied, raising both her hands with a slight shrug of the shoulders, 'so I thought I would save you a job and bring it through, otherwise the food would have gone cold. What am I supposed to have done wrong?'

'It's not your job to go in there with tight clothes on and make eyes at men I have invited around to discuss business with. Moreover, one of those guys is a relative of mine. An old-fashioned, traditional type of a man, with traditional values, values that I also happen to hold dear. And in you walk with those tight leggings and that that short fitted trashy dress you've got on. You didn't even have a scarf around your neck, never mind on your head!'

'But, I did---'

'But nothing, your conduct was not appropriate. Not appropriate at all.'

Miriam stopped trying to talk for a little while. She tried to absorb what she had just heard, but the words felt like water trickling through her hands. She couldn't catch it. Not any of it. Not one drop. It was as though he was suddenly a stranger to her, as if she didn't know him at all. He had transformed into a completely different man right before her eyes. This was not the man that she had fallen in love with. She didn't recognise this person. And that started to scare her. She took a long breath before she spoke again.

'I'm sorry,' she said. She thought that this would be the best approach given how angry this man sat before her appeared to be. 'I honestly didn't know you would be offended or upset. All I did was bring the tea in and say hello,' she added. 'I was fully clothed, there was no cleavage or skin showing.' Miriam could hear her own voice crackling. She couldn't believe she was apologising to him, justifying her choice of clothes, trying to convince him it was respectable. She was dumbfounded and perplexed, and alongside those feelings of bewilderment, her sense of fear increased.

'And another thing,' he said, in a very matter of fact way.

'Yes?' she asked him; her eyes were downcast, as she stared at her uneaten dinner.

'I better not catch you singing around this house again, or anywhere at all, ever.'

Her anxiety levels now shot up to a new high; her mind catapulted frantically when she tried to envisage life without singing. Miriam had never before thought about life without singing. Her heart plummeted.

'It's not becoming,' he continued, 'especially when there are guests around, but even if there are no visitors, you are not to sing. You're my wife now, and you need to realise how to behave properly. You're 24 years old, for goodness' sake. I expect you to be able to conduct yourself in a fitting manner.'

Miriam batted her eyelashes a few times, in an effort not to cry. She was never really told off as a child, or least if it did happen, she had no memory of it, but she now knew this is what it must feel like. Here she was, a grown woman, having to endure being chastised like a little girl. She fought back the tears; she may have been reduced to feeling like an ill-mannered child, but she certainly didn't want to cry like one.

'Also,' he carried on, and she wondered when this tortuous interrogation like conversation was going to end, 'I was thinking that there is not really any point you going out to look for a teaching job in some hell hole of a dingy inner-city school, when I have a perfectly good job going at the office.'

She looked up at him now, with wide eyes, disturbed eyes, naked with agitation, no longer able to hide the angst that was building up behind them.

'What do you mean?' she asked him. They had talked about this, at length, before they wed. They had agreed that Miriam would have a bit of time off work after the wedding, and then start looking for a post down in Birmingham, having left the job she was in half way through the academic year. A job she had loved, but one she had nevertheless abandoned so she could move down to be with him.

'It makes more sense for you to work in our own family business,' he said. He rested back in his chair, with his arms folded. 'And just think, we would be able to spend a lot more time together.'

She wanted to say something, but the words seemed to be stuck like a heap of sugar lumps at the top of her throat, unable to emerge.

'It would be a good indication of where your loyalties lie,' he added, drawing his words out slowly, his eyes fixed on hers.

'It's not about loyalties,' she finally said, feeling the need to put her tuppence worth in on a matter that was so important to her. 'It's about the fact that I am a newly qualified teacher. It's my career. The profession I chose to go into. I would be far more useful in a school. It's what I've been trained for, and where I can actually make a difference. What on earth would I do at your office? I would be use nor ornament.'

'I disagree. I think you should come and work with Rachel for a few days a week. You can help with the admin. There is plenty to do in that office, believe me. The best bit is that you can do so part time; you can work three days, and that way you will have the remaining days to allow you to keep on top of the house and garden.'

Miriam remained silent, and although it may have seemed

that she was looking at him, she in fact stared past him, into the distance somewhere, seeing nothing. She didn't want to look at his face, at those downturned lips and those raised eyebrows.

'You are my wife, and you need to learn to act like it.'

Miriam was still trying to process what had now become instruction after instruction, coming thick and fast, putting her head in a spin.

Zaf leant over the table towards her face, his gaze penetrating hers with pinpoint precision, like a red dot from a sniper's gun that is nailed on its target.

'There is one thing you have to understand right now, Miriam.'

She held her breath as she waited for what was coming next from those droopy, angry lips of his. He shifted back for a second, pushed his dinner plate to one side, then rested his arms back on the table, taking up space. He carefully, slowly, leant in, as far forward as he could go. His eyeballs bulged out away from the sockets, and she knew in that instant that whatever this next instruction was, it was going to be one that he expected her to follow to the letter.

'I expect you to do as I say – to do as you are told – by me - always - without question.'

What have you done, Miriam? What on earth have you done? What have you married?

'Do you understand?' he asked, looking into her vacant eyes. Eyes which on the surface appeared expressionless, but which behind the blank expression cried and lamented with internal tears of regret. It was as though in this very moment, something precious had died.

'Well?'

Miriam swallowed as hard as she could, even though her mouth was as dry as a desert and her throat felt coarse like fresh sandpaper. With this last command of his, in that instant,

Miriam felt as though she now knew what her life was going to be like from hereon in, almost as though she could see the roadmap. This statement was to be the overarching, central decree by which her life would be lived in this marriage. She just didn't realise to what extent.

'Yes. I understand,' she replied, her voice barely audible.

'Good, because if I have to tell you again, I swear...'

5

Birmingham Crown Court
5 November 2019

'I swear by Almighty God, that the evidence I shall give shall be the truth, the whole truth and nothing but the truth.' Rachel Wiles is the first prosecution witness. She stands upright, her blue eyes are focused and alert, and she waits calmly for Ms Godfrey to begin.

Mrs Wiles is in her early thirties, smartly but stylishly dressed in a navy-blue single-breasted business suit with a creamy coloured V-neck blouse. Her smooth dark blond hair is styled into a neat bob cut; the use of what must have been excellent straighteners ensures that there is not a hair out of place. Her hair is complimented by her other attractive features; sapphire blue eyes, high cheekbones, although she has thin lips which have been overlined, and filled with a coating of a dusky pink coloured lipstick. How polished Rachels looks standing there, thinks Miriam, as she stares across at her; when the bigger picture looks so appealing, muses Miriam, most people tend not to look at the finer details.

'Mrs Wiles, please can you tell the court how you know the defendant and how you knew the deceased,' requests Ms Godfrey, who speaks loudly and crisply, rolling her r's and enunciating her t's.

'Yes. I am the Managing Director of Zaf's, based at the Birmingham restaurant. I have worked at Zaf's, which is the name of the restaurant group as well as the name of the deceased, for around six years now, and that is how long I have known, or rather knew, Zaf Hassan. I have known Miriam since they married back in, I think it was February 2017.'

Rachel steals a glance at Miriam. It is so fleeting that it is unlikely anyone would even have noticed. Rachel turns her gaze back towards prosecuting counsel.

'How was the relationship between the defendant and the deceased, as far as you could tell?'

'Well, I don't know the defendant as well as I knew the deceased, but in the main I think things were okay, or at least that was what I had believed until the day of Zaf's death.'

'We will come to the date of his death shortly, but in the meantime, can you tell me what you mean by "okay"?' asks Ms Godfrey, with her right hand now placed behind her, curled into a tight ball and nestled into the small of her back.

'Just that. They seemed alright, but then again, all couples have their ups and downs, don't they?'

'Hold that thought for now, we will come back to that later as well,' says Ms Godfrey, taking a short pause. She now grabs her cloak at the top on either side and with both hands and pulls at it sharply, before moving on. 'I believe that the defendant worked with you.'

'Yes, she did.'

'Did that surprise you, that she was working as a part time administrator, given that she was a newly qualified teacher?'

'Yes, it did, but that was what she wanted.'

Miriam feels herself wince; her eyes wrinkle at the edges, almost as though someone has just jabbed her in the guts, causing her physical pain. She takes a deep breath, and as she breathes out, her eyes uncrumple, and a sense of calm is restored to her face.

Rachel continues. 'After they got married, Zaf told me that despite her initially saying to him that she would get a teaching job when she moved down from Manchester to Birmingham, Miriam had asked him if she could work in the business instead. As you say, she is a qualified school teacher, and from what I know he thought she would continue with her career once she had settled into her new home and city. However, he told me that she had decided not to continue with the teaching and to keep her happy he agreed that she could work part time in the office with me, which was not a problem of course.'

'Did he say why the accused no longer wanted to teach?'

'Yes. Something along the lines of Miriam saying it was too many hours and too much stress, and not enough pay, and now she was married to him, she didn't need to worry about money. She said she would prefer to do something part-time.'

Miriam now bites her bottom lip as she listens to Rachel talk. She looks down at the floor, and closes her eyes for a few moments. She senses a metallic, slightly salty taste on her tongue, and realises her bottom lip is bleeding, and she refrains from biting it any further.

'So, you all worked together. Tell me, what an average day in the office was like?' Ms Godfrey asks.

'Birmingham is the head administrative office for all the restaurants, so it is always busy; replying to emails and letters, chasing suppliers, arranging appointments, updating social media, HR, troubleshooting, that sort of thing. On an average day, I would get in, check the emails and post, sort out what needed doing for the day and delegate as appropriate, to Miriam and other members of the admin team, as well as assist Zaf with appointments, preparation for meetings and the like. Zaf would always be in and out of our office, as his office was right next door to ours.'

'And how was the working relationship between the defendant and the rest of the office team?'

'It was alright, I guess.'

'What do you mean by that?'

Rachel shifts her weight from one leg to the other.

'I suppose I always noticed that Miriam was never really part of the gang, or the banter in the office, so to speak. She tended to be a bit quiet, and withdrawn, sullen even.'

'And what about her relationship with Zaf?'

'Much the same, to be honest. Zaf tried really hard, but...' Rachel's voice trails off.

'He tried hard, as in how?'

'Well, he would often buy her flowers and gifts, but she never seemed all that happy, or grateful, to be honest. It's like she didn't realise how lucky she was.'

'And how was she lucky exactly?' asks Ms Godfrey, after which she pops on her reading glasses to quickly check some notes.

'Everyone could see that he treated her so well, he was always so attentive and patient. Always buying her presents and treats. But like I said, she never seemed very happy, not with him at any rate, despite all his efforts. She was a bit better with the rest of us, and I couldn't fault her work. She was always diligent and professional with everyone in the office, and with customers and suppliers.'

Ms Godfrey looks down and strikes a red line through some of her notes in a rather dramatic fashion, and then she looks back at Rachel, offering her a faint smile.

'A little while ago, you said that you thought that their relationship had been okay until the day that Zaf died. Can you explain to the court what happened on that day?'

'Yes. I needed to speak to Zaf, so I called him in the morning.'

'What time was this?'

'It was around 11am.'

'And where were you at the time?'

'I was at home.'

'And can you tell the court what transpired in that telephone conversation?'

'Zaf was on his hands free, driving at the time, and I noticed from his voice that he seemed agitated. So, I asked him what was wrong. He told me that he and his wife had argued.'

'Did he say what the argument was about?'

'Yes, he did,' replies Rachel, but doesn't expand on this.

'And what did he say?' asks Counsel after a few seconds silence, upon realising the Rachel is waiting for her to prompt her further.

'He said that she had wanted him to take her shopping, but he had some urgent business to attend to, so he told her that he was sorry that he couldn't go out with her as promised, and either she could go alone, or they would go together another day. It all sounds a bit trivial really. But then, he said, things got ugly as she went ballistic.'

'Ballistic? Is that the exact word he used?'

'Yes. He said that she practically attacked him. She shouted abuse at him, pushed him and threatened him.'

'Did he mention exactly what words she used?'

'He didn't go into any detail about what she said, he told me more about how aggressive and abusive she was towards him. He said it had really unnerved him, and he was wasn't looking forward to going back home later.'

'He told you he had urgent business to attend to. Did he disclose to you what this urgent business was?'

'No. He didn't.'

'Thank you, Mrs Wiles,' says Ms Godfrey, 'that will be all for now.'

Mr De Beaux senses Rachel restraining a smile that is dying to make its way out; she seems satisfied that she has done well in her responses to prosecuting counsel, and he senses that prosecuting counsel herself feels much the same. Rachel chose her words carefully, and gave what seemed to be considered and thoughtful answers, conveying an assured air of balance and integrity. Mr De Beaux observed the jury carefully during prosecuting counsel's examination in chief. They seemed to appear content with what Rachel had to say, and the many hints of negativity in relation to Miriam sent the members of the jury looking towards his client with questioning eyes, and if not questioning, then at the very least searching.

Mr De Beaux is not pleased. Not pleased at all. He has come to know Miriam fairly well, and whilst a couple of the parts of Miriam's version of events don't completely add up, he does not recognise this description of her that has been painted by Rachel Wiles; a surly, ungrateful, selfish, manipulative, argumentative person. That certainly hasn't been his assessment of her. That said, although he has come to know Miriam reasonably well, he acknowledges that as a lawyer you can never know everything about your client. And you certainly never want to know *everything* about you client; that can backfire splendidly at times. Ideally, you just want to know those judiciously selected bits that will help you build the case and do your job; the job of securing an acquittal, as in this case, or a prosecution on another day. It is much like seeing a movie. Movies are always edited. You don't want or need to know what parts of the film are missing. Mr De

Beaux is not interested in what he doesn't know about Miriam, unless of course this information can help him to do a better job.

The Court adjourns for lunch. As the courtroom starts to empty, Miriam's solicitor, Sara Aziz, walks over to the dock for a brief word with Miriam.

'Are you okay?' she asks. Miriam looks flushed, much more so than normal.

'I need to speak to you and Mr De Beaux,' says Miriam; her words hurtle out from her mouth in a hurry.

'We will pop down after a bit of lunch,' Sara tells her.

'No. This can't wait. I have to see you right now. It's important.' Miriam is now stepping nervously and repeatedly from one foot to the other, as she waits for a response.

'Okay, we'll be down straight away in that case,' Sara assures her.

'What's the matter?' Mr De Beaux asks Sara when she approaches him, as Miriam is being taken down by the guards.

'We need to go down to the cell and speak to Miriam.'

Mr De Beaux raises his eyebrows.

'She says it's important,' adds Sara.

'We don't normally hear a peep out of her unless she has something significant to say. Okay, let's go,' he says, and they set about making their way down to the cells.

When they walk in, they find Miriam sitting in the far right the corner of the cell, on the shabby bench, with her knees tucked under her chin, and her arms hugging her legs tight. Mr De Beaux and Sara often find her sitting in this position. No doubt a body language expert would have some elaborate explanation of how this signifies Miriam's state of mind; perhaps defensive, or may be protective? Or does it signify some sort or retreat, or on the other hand, a feeling of shame?

'Now then, Miriam. What's all this about?' asks Mr De

Beaux. Miriam raises her head to look at this man who has been a supportive presence in her life for many months now.

He is a handsome man, most would say. Not the Hollywood type tall dark and handsome sort of a man; he is in fact not terribly tall, nor is he at all dark, but he has a good physique and charming good looks considering his age of nearly sixty years. His hair is mostly grey, but he does have a full head of it. His face displays fine, wispy lines around his eyes and mouth, and deeper grooves on his forehead, all of which make him look distinguished, as opposed to old. He speaks much more softly than one might expect him to. He stands now with his back leaning against the wall, his papers clutched in his right hand, resting by his side, his other hand tucked in his trouser pocket. And he waits for Miriam to start talking. Both he and Sara know full well that it can take a long time for Miriam to open up, but today, she doesn't keep them waiting for very long.

'It's about Rachel.'

'What about her?' asks Mr De Beaux.

Miriam hesitates for a couple of moments, before she says, 'I haven't been completely honest with you.' She hugs her arms around her legs even tighter.

'How so?' asks Sara.

Miriam looks down, and she sighs heavily, as though she is carrying an onerous burden the weight of which is now paining her, crushing her.

'I haven't lied to you,' she reassures them, as she looks at them one by one with her dark brown eyes that are now moist around the edges, 'but I haven't told you the whole truth. I thought I'd revealed enough of my humiliation to you. More than I should have had to, far more than I could bear to. But there is one further humiliation that I now think you should know about.'

Sara sits down next to Miriam on the bench, ready with her notepad and pen.

Miriam looks at the ground pensively, as her chin rests on the top of her knees. Her eyes are weary. They are coated with a veneer of a very specific kind of acute sadness that Mr De Beaux comes across only now and again, and even after all these years in the job, and even though he does not see it often, he still finds it difficult to stand by and see someone in that sort of agony. Miriam's pain is painful to watch.

'It's okay,' he says gently; just loud enough so she can hear him, and just softly enough so that she will hopefully relax and open up. 'Take your time.'

6

19 May 2017

'Take your time,' said Zaf, as he stopped momentarily in the doorway on his way out. Miriam stood in the hallway to see him off. 'As long as you are there by tomorrow afternoon, say around 5 or 6 o'clock, that will be perfect,' he added, and then he closed the front door behind him.

Miriam heard his car engine turn, and within seconds, the sound of the car disappeared down the road. She looked at her watch and realised it was only 7.30am, much earlier than she had realised, and much earlier than Zaf usually left the house. He and a few members of staff from the Birmingham team were going on ahead today, to prepare for the opening of the second London restaurant tomorrow; it had been a long time in the planning, and now, it was finally happening. Zaf had mentioned that he was giving a lift to someone or other, she couldn't remember who, and he was leaving so early as he had to drive to the other side of the city for the pick-up.

They had now been married for fifteen months, and some-times, Miriam did not honestly remember where those last fifteen months of her life had evaporated to, and yet, at other times, it felt as though she had been his wife for fifteen years rather than fifteen months.

She had spent most of those fifteen months trying to navigate and mitigate her way through a succession of mishaps, and, as she saw them, a string of failures. She almost always felt on edge, waiting for the next thing to go wrong. It was like being in a car crash that never seemed to end. She could not seem to do anything right, and no matter how hard she tried to dispel such thoughts, thinking of herself as an abject disappointment in the eyes of her husband always lingered at the forefront of her mind.

She wandered into their magazine worthy glossy oyster and jade granite kitchen and made herself a big mug of tea. It was always a big mug of tea to start the day, made with two tea bags, not one, brewed for at least two minutes, and finished off with a generous splash of milk. She perched herself on one of the swish chrome legged and leather backed stools at the breakfast bar and sipped her tea. It was now a good ten minutes since Zaf had left, and she drifted away with her thoughts.

She began to tell herself, convince herself even, that everything was going to change. From tomorrow. Because tomorrow, she told herself, tomorrow she would get it right. She would get *everything* right; how she dressed, how she talked, the way she walked, how she mingled with others as she moved around the room, saying all the right things to all the right people at all the right moments. She was sure of it. She would turn a corner. Tomorrow. And he would notice. Yes, *he* would notice, and *he* would be proud of her, and *he* would say so. Tomorrow.

The ever-festering fears about getting things wrong were not without foundation. She cringed painfully when she thought about some of the moments from the past, and she told herself that she had to do better than that. Much better.

She was deep in thought when the doorbell rang unexpect-
edly. She dragged herself away from her musing, and went to see
who it was, expecting it to be a parcel, or a sign for delivery,
although they never usually received anything this early, but
when she opened the door, to her surprise, she saw Nina
standing on the doorstep. She was wearing a crazy pair of oversized mirror aviator sunglasses, which she whipped off, and
then, with her long arms splayed wide from side to side, she
shouted 'ta-da!'

'Oh my God!' shrieked Miriam.

Few people lit up her soul like her best friend Nina Delaney.
They gave each other the biggest hug, and Nina's curly wild red
hair smothered Miriam's face, as they embraced tightly. They
had been like two peas in a pod all the way through university.
To the onlooker, they were perfectly mismatched, but they
ended up being perfectly best friends. They hardly got to see
each other nowadays, since Miriam married and moved away
from Manchester, and Nina now worked overseas. But when
Nina had recently mentioned that she would be over for a little
while, Miriam had asked her to come down to London for the
grand opening party for the latest restaurant. She knew Zaf
would prefer that rather than to have her come over to the
house to stay.

When Miriam and Zaf had originally talked about setting a
wedding date, and Miriam was disappointed that her best friend
would not be able to come, Zaf had nevertheless pushed to
marry as soon as possible, and one of the reasons he had given
was that he would be busy in the months that followed, mainly
because of the proposed opening of the second London restaurant. However, as it turned out, he was only opening it now, over
a year after the date he had originally told her about. She did
not know if he had out and out lied at the time, or if there
genuinely had been an unavoidable delay. Sometimes, when she

thought back to that time in her life, just sometimes, she secretly acknowledged that he coaxed her into agreeing to a wedding date that she hadn't been entirely happy with, and perhaps he *had* deceived her about the date for the opening of the second London restaurant. However, straight after such audacious thoughts, Miriam would chastise herself for thinking such things about her husband; over time, since they married, she had become plagued by a seemingly irrational fear that Zaf might actually guess what she was thinking, that he might somehow know that she was entertaining such treacherous, unfair, undignified thoughts about him. She never voiced these feelings to anyone, and she felt guilty as soon as they had entered her head, so she banished them with as much speed as possible. Yet the irrational fear of him having the ability to penetrate her thoughts was a constant, for it felt very real to her.

'This is a surprise! What brings you here?' Miriam said, pulling herself back to the present moment.

'Aha! Well, I thought it was high time we had a bit of fun together. Come on, pack your bag, we're off to London!' screamed Nina. She beamed her broadest smile; her teeth pearly white against the pouty red lips which had been so expertly lined and painted in.

'What? But we're scheduled to go tomorrow, you were supposed to meet me in London at the restaurant, remember? Tomorrow, that's what Zaf said, to go down tomorrow...'

'Sack that for a game of soldiers. Come on, let's turn up early and have a laugh, and surprise your husband in the process!' Nina was like an overly excited child talking about a long and eagerly awaited school trip, one where she would be sitting on the coach and hanging out with her best friend, sharing sweets and giggling out loud.

'Really? I'm not sure that's a good idea. He's going to be really busy. Anyway, Zaf said specifically to go down tomorrow.'

'Shut up! Since when do you have to do everything he says to the exact letter?' she asked, standing upright, hands on hips, eyebrows raised, demanding an answer.

Miriam accidentally swallowed a large gulp of air, which now sat uncomfortably in her chest. *If only you knew, my friend*, she said to herself, *if only you knew*.

Nina loosened her stance, and placed her hands on Miriam's arms, one either side, tugging at her slightly, willing her along. 'Come on, why the hesitation? The old, unmarried Miriam would have been ready and out that door way faster than me! Where's the old get-up-and-go girl? Where's that sense of adventure gone?'

Miriam paused for a few seconds before asking Nina, in the hope that she might get her to agree to the alternative, 'are you sure? We can chill here tonight if you want. Watch a movie, get a take away? Or go to the cinema, or to a restaurant.'

'Of course I'm sure, you silly moo. Anyway, I've already booked a room for myself in a hotel nearby, and obviously you can stay with lover boy in the apartment if you want, or if you can tear yourself away from him then come stay with me and we can catch up and yap all night! Here's the plan,' continued Nina as they both walked down the hallway towards the kitchen, 'if you want, we'll show our gorgeous faces at the new restaurant later on today and say hello, but otherwise we will let Zaf and his workers get on with whatever it is they need to do, and we'll go out tonight and have a fab time, paint the town red, just the two of us. Maybe catch a show down the West End or something? Or dinner up The Shard? Now there's a thought. Neither of us have done that yet. Whatever you like. And then we can join in properly with the grand opening stuff tomorrow, all dressed up, ready to meet and greet the Mayor and all the politicians and whichever celebs he's got coming, Bollywood, Lollywood divas and heroes and all that jazz. If you pack quickly and we leave now we'll be in London for lunchtime!'

'It does sound great!' replied Miriam, now also enthused with the prospect of letting her hair down with her bestie. Miriam thought about their university days, and how different life was back then, and, despite her personal problems, how much she and Nina used to laugh together. Wherever they had gone, whatever they had done, they had always managed to end up in fits of laughter about the silliest of things. Some of that old sense of excitement started to stir inside of Miriam. She started to feel alive. Giddy, even.

'Alright then. Let's do it!' screamed Miriam, in return for which she received a massive hug and an even louder scream from Nina. 'What time is your check-in at the hotel Nina?'

'I'm not entirely sure, I'll have to check the email on my phone, but if I'm not mistaken then I'm pretty sure it's either three or four o'clock.'

'Okay, well there is a spare key for the apartment somewhere, we can drop off both our bags their first, instead of carrying them all around London, and then head out. I think the key is up in the bedroom somewhere. Let me go find it,' said Miriam excitedly, as she started to gallop up the stairs.

'Go on then – grab that key and let's go. London, here we come!'

The London traffic was just its usual rammed, jammed, London traffic; bumper to bumper red buses, black taxis, and an array of motor vehicles from commercial vans that barely chugged along to Porsches and Bugattis that had zero chance of showing off their 0-70mph speed capabilities. The black cab driver seemed to know a multitude of short cuts, as they so often did, which eventually led to him getting them to their destination quicker than Miriam and Nina had thought. The taxi parked up outside the apartment, and Miriam turned towards Nina.

'You can wait in the taxi if you like; I'll go up and quickly dump the bags inside. We can stop back off here later on, and you can take your bag to your hotel this evening.'

'Are you sure you don't need a hand to carry the bags up? Wait, I'll help you.' Just as Nina started to undo her seatbelt, her mobile phone rang. She fished it out of her jacket pocket.

'No, don't be daft, it's not as though there is much to carry, is there? Just two little bags. You take that call, and I will be right back,' said Miriam with a reassuring smile.

The one-bedroom luxury apartment was purchased by Zaf over three years ago. To say it was situated in a prime spot would probably be an understatement; adjacent to the Palace of Westminster, a stone's throw away from the London Eye, and with remarkable and uninterrupted views of the River Thames, this was as good as it got. Unlike his northern restaurants which he rarely visited, Zaf came down to London often, and when he was down in the capital, this was his base. Miriam had only accompanied him and stayed over in the flat a few times; Zaf usually came alone.

As Miriam walked into the apartment block, she thought back to the first time she had come here, and how bedazzled she had been. It wasn't the sheer luxury of the place that had blown her away; not the grandeur of the building, not the stylish décor throughout, not the expensive fitments in every part of the apartment block as well as the flat itself, not the large space that the apartment occupied. No. All of those were of course impressive. But what had taken her breath away had been the view from the balcony; the panoramic sight of the city of London, the glimpse of the River Thames gliding past, the iconic bronze glow of the Palace of Westminster. It was the sort of first sight that stayed with you, stored safely at the back of your memory bank, a sight you would never forget.

Miriam came out of the lift, and wandered down the pristine corridor, lined with beautifully framed drawings and paintings of various illustrations of nature; autumnal scenes of forests covered in a thick covering of red, yellow, and copper coloured leaves, trickles of glittering streams snaking down a rugged mountainside, the meeting of a dark blue sea and a golden caramel sky at sunset. The pieces were fairly modern in style, but each told its own distinct and timeless story.

She took the key out of her coat pocket when she arrived at the door to the apartment. She unlocked it and then opened the door gently. She was going to leave the bags just inside the door, in the hallway, and head straight back out, until she realised that she really needed the bathroom, and thought she may as well make a quick trip now she was here.

The apartment had a distinctively modern day, and yet, indulgent, feel to it; there was a large, open plan living space, with the kitchen, dining area, and lounge areas all transitioning and blending together seamlessly. The décor was modern chic, with natural undertones; the use of pale wooden fitments, soft ceiling spot lighting, a light marble floor and exposed brickwork all seemed to work well together, leading to a sense of quiet peacefulness here on the inside, in sharp contrast to the noisy hubbub that was ever present on the outside.

Miriam walked towards the bedroom in which the ensuite bathroom was located, on her right, a few yards from the lobby into which she had entered. As she approached the bedroom door, she realised there was someone in the flat. She could hear a voice coming from within the room. It was definitely Zaf. She assumed he had popped over for a shower or something. On his phone as usual, she thought to herself. As she was about to push the door, which was already slightly ajar, she heard a woman's voice. It was a voice that sounded very familiar. Miriam pushed the door a smidgen, and as soon as she did, she wished she had stuck to her original plan of leaving the bags just inside the entrance and heading back to the cab. There are some things in life which, once seen, can never be unseen.

Miriam felt repulsion, and yet, however repulsed she was by what she was witnessing, she couldn't tear her eyes away. She was sickened by it, but she couldn't stop looking. As a child, she had once fallen off the see-saw at the park, and she had grazed her head. She remembered her head hurting a little, but she didn't cry. 'You are such a brave girl' her dad had said to her. When they got back home, her mum had told her not to look in the mirror. 'There is nothing to see' she had reassured her. But Miriam couldn't help herself. She *had* to look in the mirror. And when she saw the huge bump on her forehead, she couldn't stop looking at it, and suddenly, her head hurt so much more than before, and in fact, the pain became unbearable, and no amount of consoling by her parents could stop her from crying profusely.

Miriam stood frozen in the same spot by the bedroom door, dumbfounded, her feet stuck to the ground whilst the world around her spun; the stark image of these two people she knew so well but who now looked like total strangers seemed to move closer and closer, and yet, despite all of this, her legs wouldn't shift. It felt as though she must be in a dream, or this must be a scene from a film. It couldn't be real.

She looked on with her eyes fixed upon the reflection of the two of them in the mirror which was directly opposite the bed, and Miriam knew that what she was seeing was neither a bad dream nor a movie scene. This was real. She, her work colleague, he, her husband, together, in the same bed that he had shared with Miriam on at least three occasions.

Zaf and Rachel were both slouched in bed next to one

another. their heads propped up by plump pillows, their bodies semi-naked, not quite fully covered by the satin sheets. They were comfortable and at ease with each other. They were both completely oblivious as to her presence. Miriam remained in her uneasy position, glued to the spot in which she stood, looking through the slit of a door that she had pushed ever so casually, not realising that it would slip open to just the right place, to the millimetre, to enable her to witness this hideous sight.

'Are you sure even after over a year of marriage, she doesn't suspect anything?' Rachel asked Zaf, as she rested her head on his shoulder

'No, don't be silly. She hasn't got a clue. Even if she does, so what, you still have nothing to worry about. Everything is under control,' replied Zaf, and then he picked up his mobile phone to check his messages.

'Apart from the fact that I have a husband and two kids.'

'Honestly, you need to stop stressing, otherwise this all stops being fun. That's the best bit about it, isn't it? The secrecy, the excitement. Anyway, even if she did find out, what would she do?'

Rachel didn't respond.

'I tell you what she'd do,' he added.

'What? What would she do?' asked Rachel, sitting up straighter against the crushed velvet headboard, pulling the bedsheets up with her.

'Nothing. Absolutely nothing,' he replied, now looking at her, instead of his phone.

'What makes you so sure?'

Zaf let out a short, cold laugh. Rachel stared at him, her eyebrows wrinkled, her eyes strained, and she waited for him to explain.

'Listen to me. She's my wife, and I know her better than

anyone. Yes, she's moody, yes, she's always complaining about something or other, and yes, she loves to pick an argument with me, but when it comes down to it, I don't think she has enough of a backbone to try and challenge me in any way, and whilst I'm being honest, I may as well add that she doesn't have much of a brain either.'

Hearing these comments from her husband hit hard, but from that place of hurt, Miriam's mind drifted briefly back to a time when she recalled that she perhaps had too much backbone for some. She didn't know where that old defiant spirit had gone, much less did she know if it might ever return.

Miriam could see that Rachel's response was to raise her eyebrows, but she said nothing.

'I know I shouldn't be so critical,' continued Zaf, 'but only I know what I've had to put up with, having her for a wife. She's such a sap. She relies on me for everything, and she's got used to having a cushy life as well, thanks to yours truly. Believe me, she won't jeopardise that for anything. In any event, it would be her word against ours, against mine, and I think I know whose version most would believe; everyone already thinks she's a bit neurotic, and dare I say it, a tad strange. And, most importantly, we have been really careful. Why on earth would she, or anyone else for that matter, suspect anything?'

He planted a brief but passionate kiss on Rachel's lips, as though that should be reassurance in itself. Then he drew her close to him; she placed her head on his chest, he wrapped his arms around her, and squeezed her, tight. There was a display of warmth coming from Zaf; it wasn't necessarily love, but there was definitely a level of affection in that exchange, and yet, seeing Zaf in this way was something very alien to Miriam. He was not, nor had he ever been, so benevolent with her, at least not since their courtship and honeymoon period.

'If only we'd met sooner,' said Rachel, half whining, half

wishing. She lifted her head up to gaze at his face, her eyes almost starstruck, like a teenage girl who has just met her pop idol.

'Hmmm,' was his only response. He leant over and picked his mobile phone back up again. Rachel snatched the mobile phone out of Zaf's hands now and threw it to the bottom of the bed.

Zaf didn't respond. Instead, he swung his arm behind his head to and leant back to rest his head into the outspread palm of his hand.

'Why *did* you marry her?' she asked, gently pulling his face towards hers.

He placed one hand to her cheek, and stroked it lightly. 'You know why.'

Rachel didn't respond. Zaf took both her hands into his, as he continued.

'My parents were on and on at me to find a wife. It's the way it is in our community, whether you're rich or poor. You reach a certain age, you find a girl, you tie the knot, you have kids. They were putting so much pressure on me, and around the same time, I met Miriam. She ticked most of the boxes in a theoretical sense, apart from her situation with her family, although if I'm honest, not having to deal with in-laws has proved to be a bonus. Same religion, right age, just pretty enough, just educated enough, and just domesticated enough. I knew that if I married her, that would be one headache gone; my parents would stop harassing me, and spend more time in Pakistan, and probably return whenever the first baby came along. But she couldn't even get that right.'

Miriam felt sick after she heard the last sentence which came from Zaf's mouth. *How could he say such a thing?* She closed her eyes as she felt them fill up. She thought about that awful day. The worst day of her life, hands down.

'You can't blame her for that,' said Rachel, as she locked her eyes with his.

'Maybe. Maybe not. I guess at least it meant one less visit from my parents. I prefer it when they're over there. They came over a couple of times in the early part of our marriage, but now they seemed to have backed off. When they're here, my dad only tries to interfere with how I run the business. I know he started it all, and he still sees it as his empire, even though he's retired, but it was me who developed and grew the business, me who took it to new heights, me who made it the success that it is today, and it's also me who continues expanding it, and ensuring that it keeps on growing, winning awards, creating more jobs, increasing profits.'

Rachel let out a short, sharp sigh. 'Still, I wish things could have been different.'

'How? It's not as though you were available at the time, was it? You were busy playing happy families with that good for nothing husband of yours. And you know what, that's fine. You were already married, and now I am too. But it doesn't change anything. We still have our arrangement. This way, it's better. This way, we get the best of both worlds. It's called having your cake and eating it. Although that doesn't really make sense, does it?'

Rachel frowned, and donned a more serious look. 'But we're *not* together though, are we? They're just stolen moments here and there.'

'So?'

'So, what if I said I was fed up with our arrangement?'

'What do you mean?'

'What if....'

'What if, what?' asked Zaf, as he reached for a cigarette.

'What if...what if I left my husband...would you do the same? Would you leave Miriam?'

Zaf took the as yet unlit cigarette out of his mouth and gave her a sideways stare, his mouth open, his eyes strained, his whole face as tense and as stretched out as an elastic band.

Miriam's legs finally unfroze. They went from something akin to two solidly rooted ancient tree trunks to something resembling two long slender reeds trembling in the wind. The tears could no longer be restrained, and they began to run free, out from her traumatised eyes, and down her cheeks. She had seen enough, and she had heard enough. She didn't want to hear the rest. She didn't want to know his answer, she didn't want to hear whether he would leave her or not.

Miriam uprooted her legs and started to leave. She walked away from the bedroom, quietly. Her quivering legs carried her away slowly, away from what had felt like being trapped in a confined space near a pit of snakes.

She stopped by the bags. She picked them up and placed them inside the floor to ceiling cupboard that was in the lobby. She knew he would never look in there. She would come back later when she was sure he wasn't around, take both bags and stay with Nina for the night. He need never know that she came down a day early.

She made her way back down, and stopped in the foyer downstairs for a few moments; she sat in one of the plush purple leather chairs, and took her small make up kit out of her handbag. She looked into the compact mirror, and using a face wipe, she carefully cleared away the remnants of the last few tears, and dabbed a little bit of concealer followed by powder over the top. She had become an expert at this. No one could ever tell that salty tears had sat on her cheeks just a few moments ago. Her broken face was plastered over one more time. The cracks hidden yet again. The canvass now retouched. A dusting of peachy pink blusher and a lick of china rose lipstick added a much needed lift of colour, and it was job done.

She smiled at Nina as she got back into the cab, and apologised for taking so long. She explained to Nina that she'd needed the bathroom and that was why she was gone a little longer than she had intended. Nina retorted with a 'TMI', accompanied by a contorted face and the raising of one hand which she fanned back and forth in front of her nose. Miriam let out a little laugh in response, as though nothing had happened, as though everything was normal and well in her world. Miriam's mask was firmly on, and fixed in place, and her friend was none the wiser. Miriam never mentioned it to Nina, and nor did she ever mention to anyone else what she had just seen and heard. She never told a soul. She never could.

7

Birmingham Crown Court
5 November 2019

'Could you, please, tell me about your relationship with the deceased, Mrs Wiles?' is Mr De Beaux's first, rather probing question at the commencement of the cross-examination.

Rachel shifts her weight from the left foot to the right, and thinks about the question for a little longer than one might have expected her to. She looks towards her husband who is sitting in the public gallery. He has taken the day off work to come and support her. He gives her a humble smile of encouragement when they exchange glances, his doting eyes fixed on hers. Rachel looks back at Mr De Beaux.

'My...my relationship. How do you mean?' she almost mumbles the words.

'It's a straightforward question,' explains Mr De Beaux with a poker face. 'What was your relationship with the deceased?' Mr De Beaux steeples his fingers together whilst he waits for an answer.

Rachel stands up straighter. She rests her weight equally on both feet, and decides to answer with a renewed sense of focus, chin up, eyes wide.

'We had an employer employee relationship. I worked for him, and he paid my salary.' She now sounds very matter of fact. The previous chink in her armour seems to have vanished.

'Was it normal for you to call your employer on his, and your, day off?'

'Very occasionally, if something cropped up, then I would phone him. But it wasn't a regular thing, no. Although I did need to speak to him on this particular day.'

'What about?'

'It was something to do with work.'

'What was that then?'

Rachel presses her lips together momentarily. 'I can't recall exactly.'

'Astonishing!' says Mr De Beaux, with a wave of his right hand in the air, his fingers curled upwards as though he is holding an imaginary grapefruit in his palm. Then he takes a pause, and everyone around the courtroom waits eagerly to hear what he will say next. The youngest male member of the jury has now perked up, and sits with a back as straight as a plank of wood. Up until now, he has been slouching, as though he is sitting on his comfy sofa at home with the television on as background noise.

Mr De Beaux now smiles at Rachel. He pauses for a few seconds longer, holding Rachel's gaze. 'Astonishing that you can remember a great deal from that conversation that puts my client in a very bad light indeed, as the scornful, threatening, malicious wife, but you don't have any recollection as to why you phoned in the first place, on the weekend, something that, by your own admission, you did not normally do.'

'I obviously called him about something to do with work, but I can't recall it now, because we never really got around to discussing it as he started talking about his problems with Miriam.'

She is good, Mr De Beaux silently thinks to himself. Yes. She is good, but not *that* good. 'Very well then. Can you tell me, given he was quite comfortable to talk about his marital problems with you, would you say that you considered him to be a friend, as well as your employer?' asks Mr De Beaux

'I suppose so.'

'Meaning what?'

'Meaning that he was not a close friend, but given the length of time I had worked there, you could say we had become friends, in the same way as he was friends with many other members of staff.'

'Just how *friendly* exactly were you with each other?'

Ms Godfrey jumps to her feet in an overdramatic fashion. 'Objection, My Lord, my learned friend's question is vague and unnecessary.'

The judge peers over his gold rimmed glasses towards Mr De Beaux. 'She does have a point; if you are going somewhere with this, then just get to it, man,' orders the Judge in his matter of fact, straight talking style.

'Very well, My Lord.' Mr De Beaux shifts his gaze from the Judge back towards Rachel, his lively eyes giving away his fervour to pursue this witness which the rest of his body does not. 'Let me get straight to the point, or rather, straight to my question, which is simply this: were you having a sexual relationship with the deceased?'

There are some audible gasps from the public gallery, and a couple of the members of the jury who looked like they may nod off any time soon are now sitting upright and alert upon hearing this question from Mr De Beaux. The blonde woman in the jury, perhaps in her forties, who looks and dresses like a wannabe Marilyn Monroe, looks towards Rachel and raises her eyebrows; the look of disapproval on her face is difficult to ignore.

Meanwhile, the rest of Rachel's face turns a shade of peachy pink to match her blusher, and though she opens her mouth to speak, she does not emit any sound. The fragile hesitation has returned. Her lips remain pursed.

'Mrs Wiles, please answer the question,' requests the Judge, 'and remember that you are under oath.'

Rachel bends forward, her almost military stance now wilts like that of a solitary limp rose, or perhaps the drooping flower in Monet's Purple Poppies would describe her better. She grips the front of the witness box hard, her shiny white knuckles piercing her pinkish white skin. She sighs almost as hard, as she moulds her hands firmly around the wood whilst she contemplates her answer, with her head dropped down, and her eyes focused on the ground. Yet still, she hesitates.

'I will repeat the question—'

'Yes. I was!' she cuts in, loudly and quickly.

The huffs and puffs from the courtroom are much louder this time around. Many members of staff from Zaf's are in the public gallery and this revelation has come as an utter shock to all of them. They are sitting together in a huddle, almost like a small delegation, here as a physical presence to lend their support to their fellow worker, and to hopefully discover what really happened to their boss. Has this colleague of theirs really killed her husband? That is what they are waiting to learn, but Rachel's confession has taken them all by surprise; they look like a little family of rabbits caught in headlights. Rachel and Zaf had certainly hidden their relationship extremely well judging by their reactions; that is what they are all now thinking, surmises Mr De Beaux. It would seem from their reactions that none of them ever suspected a thing.

Mr De Beaux observes that Miriam, on the other, appears to

feel nothing; her face displays no reaction, and it all washes over her like yesterday's news. Old hat. No sweat. For this is no big deal for her; no shock horror, no big expose. He knows that this was and still is a private humiliation that she would have preferred to have kept private. The gasps from her co-workers do not move her, but he knows that they also do not escape her attention. As she now looks around, no doubt her mind shoots towards thinking about another casualty. Mr De Beaux is in no doubt that Miriam feels bad for having disclosed this affair to her legal team, and for it then to have been put out on public display like this, in front of all to see (the gorier details yet to come), because amongst the audience of onlookers, co-workers, gossip-mongers, press people, and the like, is Rachel's husband. An innocent by-stander in this car crash of a mess who has now also become another victim. Another life ruined. And if you add in their children...there is no question that this situation is most uncomfortable for her. Mr De Beaux turns his focus back onto his witness.

'And you had been in this relationship for some years?' he asks.

'Yes,' Rachel now almost whispers her reply, chin lowered, eyes downcast.

'Speak up Mrs Wiles please,' chips in the Judge.

'Yes,' she repeats, a little louder, through gritted teeth.

'And is it true that you had wanted to leave your husband for him?'

Rachel does not reply. She lifts her head and looks at her husband. His supportive smile has faded away. His face is a pale shade of grey, his eyes are glassy, he looks like he may pass out at any moment. It proves too much for him. He cannot bring himself to continue to look back towards his wife, or hear what else she has to say. This is the woman he married over ten years ago, the woman who gave birth to their two children, the woman he has shared his innermost thoughts and feelings with. The relationship in which he invested his time love and energy, blown apart in front of him, so openly, so humiliatingly. He is crushed. He stands up and quietly walks out of the courtroom. Everyone notices him leave, and it is difficult not to feel a pang of sorrow for the man. Miriam's face appears strained, as though somewhere inside she is sincerely but quietly weeping for him.

Rachel's face has now turned from the bright peachy pink that it was at the start to being almost devoid of colour, soaked in a pale shade of bone off-white.

Mr De Beaux decides to now jump in at just the right point in this tense period of silence that has gripped the court, marred so far only by the sound of Rachel's husband exiting the room, an act which has only served to further heighten the sense of drama.

'Now then, here's my theory, and it's only a theory mind,' he says, as he tucks his left hand behind his back, and lightly strokes his clean-shaven chin with his other hand. 'I put it to you that when you told the deceased that you wished to leave your husband for him, he told you that he had no intention of recip-rocating. He was not interested in any of kind of commitment or permanent relationship with you. He was quite happy with the arrangement that you had. You were nothing more than his bit on the side. That is so, isn't it?'

'No, that's not true!' protests Rachel. She clasps her hands behind her back, where she intertwines her fingers nervously. She looks over at Miriam and their eyes lock. Rachel does not appear to be fazed by Miriam. The damage has already been done. She seems determined now to speak the truth; her truth, as she probably sees it. 'I meant more to him than that,' she adds, with her head now raised high again, portraying an air of defiance, a hint of pride even.

Marilyn, who is sitting in the middle of the front row of the jurors, shakes her blonde head of curls in disbelief, and rolls her eyes for good measure.

Mr De Beaux presses on. 'You *thought* you meant more to him than that, but it was all in your head, wasn't it? You were madly in love with him, I am sure, but when it came to the crunch, you found out how one sided the relationship really was. For a man like him it boiled down to this; you were available, and it was easy, but there was nothing more to it than that.'

'No!'

'And perhaps in a fit of rage at this terrible rejection, *you* were the one who decided to go around to his house that fateful day and...'

'Objection, My Lord,' shouts Ms Godfrey once again, with some force, 'this is pure speculation. Mrs Wiles is not and never has been a suspect!' She dishes out a mean stare in Mr De Beaux's direction to boot.

Mr De Beaux slips in before the Judge has an opportunity to comment. 'It is true that she was not seen as a suspect by the police, but then I would contend that Mrs Wiles withheld important information from the police.'

'I will ask the Jury to ignore your last but one comment,' says the Judge, as he looks towards the jurors briefly. 'Mrs Wiles is not on trial for murder here. You may continue Mr De Beaux but keep from straying too much.'

'I'm obliged My Lord,' says Mr De Beaux, with a sideways glance dished back at his adversary who is now sitting down again. 'Members of the jury, I would simply say that Mrs Wiles failed to disclose the nature of her relationship outside of work with the deceased, and that is very much relevant. Mrs Wiles, a married woman and a mother of two children, had been lying about her relationship with the late Mr Hassan to both her husband and her work colleagues for a considerable amount of time. She worked in the same office day in day out with the woman whose husband she was sleeping with. This level of duplicity, coupled with the fact that she didn't disclose critical information to the police, casts doubt on both the credibility of this prosecution witness and, I would add, the investigation into this murder which was fundamentally flawed and without possession of all the pertinent facts.'

Mr De Beaux looks back at Miriam, and gives her a small nod of reassurance, as though he is throwing her a flicker of hope.

Later on, that same evening, back in her prison cell, unable to sleep, Miriam thinks about the day's events. An assortment of thoughts jumps into her mind, as happens so often when she sits alone in her cell at night. She struggles to find any peace within this bubble which she has now found herself in. This is a new kind of bubble that has taken some getting used to. She lived in a bubble before Zaf's death too, but that was of a different kind. The old one was similar to the kind of bubble she blew as a child, the sort which, after much puffing and blowing, appeared wondrously through the end of what the child in her deemed to be a magical wand. That translucent round globule, its exterior streaked with the colours of the rainbow, would appear irresistibly beautiful to the onlooker; it was sparkly, radiant, enticing. It was perfectly formed. It floated gracefully, effortlessly, and no strife touched it. This had been the outward appearance of Miriam's bubble during her marriage to Zaf. This is what people on the outside of the glossy bubble saw. Inside the bubble, however, Miriam's life had been so very different. Inside the bubble, she had been trapped; constantly fighting a series of painful ordeals from which there seemed to be no means of escape. The shell encasing the bubble was so very delicate, and yet, for her, it was impenetrable. Those on the outside of the bubble could neither see nor comprehend what it was like to be on the inside, looking out. They only saw the shiny, colourful exterior.

Her new bubble, however, is in stark contrast to the old one. It has lost its outward sheen; the pretty protective layer has gone. This bubble is transparent in every sense, and it shamelessly exposes her inner troubles for all and sundry to see. For the public to scrutinise. For the newspapers to run sensational stories on. For all to judge. For the jury to decide her fate on.

She sits and thinks about what tomorrow will bring at court. She wonders what on earth will be said about her next; will she be portrayed in an even worse light? She thinks about how she will have to listen in silence, powerless to change the narrative, unable to shout out the truth, and yet, equally, she is scared to her core at the thought of ever having to be made to speak the truth.

She closes her eyes amidst her thoughts, and takes in her yoga breaths; she breathes in and counts in her mind slowly to five, breathes out even slower, and counts to ten. Closing her eyes and concentrating on her breathing allows her brief moments of escape. *Find the ease*, she tells herself. *Find the breath, find the sukha*, something she learnt from her yoga instructor. *Find the good place through your breath; let it linger, let it fill the chambers of your heart and lungs, let it permeate you not only physically, but let it sink into your mind, into that fortress from where you dare not let escape those memories of the past. They say the truth will set you free, but sometimes, the truth is that which may destroy you.*

As her breathing now settles into its own rhythm, she adds her daily *thasbeeh* prayers; she rolls the pale lilac coloured prayer beads between her right index finger and thumb, saying a special short recitation with each. This daily ritual of the prayer beads, as well as five times a day *salah* prayers, are something she has taken up since being remanded in custody. She is not being radicalised, as quite a few have assumed. Some of her inmates and a couple of the prison guards have let her know that her increasing worship has not gone unnoticed. There have been overt remarks, sometimes she can hear surreptitious whispers, other times it is out and out abuse, and a bit of pushing and shoving added for good measure. *Here, she is, the wannabe terrorist! Watch out, here comes the jihadi! Here she is! Mad Mullah Miriam!* But they are all wrong. They know nothing about her. And yet, they judge her. She is so tired of being judged. She has always had a connection with her Islamic faith, but she has not married that with regular worship before. Now, stuck inside, she has all the time in the world to practise it as she wishes. Daily prayers, recitation of the Qu'ran, the 'Hail Mary' like mutterings with the prayer beads, she does it all, and she takes the flak for it. This daily reverence towards her faith is in fact novel to her. Yet she perseveres, and takes the hostility from the others because she feels it is worth it. It is worth it to her because she knows that it gives her some peace, and somehow, and she knows not how, but somehow, it imbues her with a small degree of patience and courage.

She closes her eyes, and she recites *Alhamdullilah,* praise to God, with each twirl of the cool smooth prayer beads, and as she does so, she allows herself to imagine that she is somewhere else; she is sitting on the top of a rugged clifftop, way up high, watching the white tips of the waves rolling along in a clear turquoise sea, and then the image has gone. Now, she is lying in a vibrant red poppy field looking up at the cottony clouds floating by in a clear blue sky that is blemished only by the wispy trails left behind by the planes. She now moves on to another scene in her mind; she tries to imagine a walk to freedom, carrying her small bag of belongings, walking out of the prison gates...but she struggles. The image lasts for a couple of seconds and then it is gone. She tries to recover it, but it will not reveal itself clearly. She does have faith, but perhaps the walk to freedom dream is too painful to imagine right now. In her experience, dreams *don't* come true.

Miriam's head now feels heavy, her eyelids start to droop, and somewhere between awake and asleep an incident comes to her mind, as they often do at this time of the night. Memories she would love to shed like dead skin simply refuse to shift; they cling to her stubbornly, drifting back to cruelly taunt her, as though her present troubles are not enough.

8

---

20 June 2017

Enough time wasting already, Miriam told herself, as she deliberated over what to wear. Zaf had told her that they would be having dinner in the evening with Raza and his wife Sheree. Raza was an old schoolfriend of Zaf's as well as a business connection. Their respective families had been friends for years. Miriam wanted to make a real effort, as whilst she had come across Raza briefly in the work sphere, she had never met his wife, and this was their first social engagement as couples.

Zaf had told her to dress 'properly', and impressed upon her to make sure that she did not disappoint him. 'Properly' was the exact word he used, and there lay the problem for Miriam. Within the very word that formed the command, there were a myriad of possibilities, and she never knew which version of that word would be acceptable today. The word 'properly' could mean two entirely different things on two different days. Sometimes his instructions were vague, like today, and other times he would give her very specific instructions; Miriam preferred the latter, because then there was not as much umming and aahing on her part, and she had a fighting chance of getting it right. When he was not clear, she always struggled; procrastinated, and worried, about whether she was making the right call. Sometimes 'properly' equated to being dressed in traditional *salwar kameez*, at other times this may extend to a floor length, all covering *abaya,* depending on the company that day, or the place they were visiting, as in the case of a mosque, sometimes he would order her to wear no makeup at all, other times he would say 'wear some make up' (but not say how much), and she knew she would be told to 'take that muck' off her face if she got it wrong. And yet at other times, he would tell her to 'doll up' and expect her to look good enough to be a worthy attachment on his arm, fabulously glamorous, a pretty but otherwise useless ornament. Miriam had fretted all day as to how she should dress 'properly' so as not to 'disappoint' him, having tried on at least half a dozen outfits in an effort to get her look right this time.

Raza, Miriam soon discovered that evening, was a very pleasant man, as was his wife, Sheree. They both had a very easy way about them; there were no airs and graces, they were very affable and chatty, and Miriam felt at ease very soon after meeting them.

The guests enjoyed all the trappings of a meal served in the restaurant where the boss of the place was doing the entertaining. Zaf's restaurants had won many accolades for the revolutionary fusion cuisine that it was now famous for, and dining at Zaf's was not seen as just going out for a meal, but rather, it was regarded as an 'experience', from the stylish and opulent décor right through to the highly original and imaginative dishes, all of which were completely mouth-watering and very Instagramable. Zaf's restaurants were not like other restaurants. At Zaf's, every diner that walked through the door was treated like royalty and always left with the memory of a superb experience. People often travelled for miles, from different parts of the U.K.

and even further afield, to get to one of the restaurants that were dotted around the Kingdom, as far up as Edinburgh and as far south as Brighton. Customers happily queued outside in the rain just to eventually be able to take a seat and savour the ambience and sample the food at one of these coveted eateries.

This particular evening's serving of food was a typically innovative selection; moist chicken *boti* kebab glazed with a ginger and Turkish pomegranate molasses sauce, beetroot and in-house produced *paneer* samosas made with a crispy mustard seed spiced pastry, tender *karahi* lamb shanks slowly stewed in Nihari style spices, and finished with baby leeks, fenugreek leaves and wild garlic, flaky buttery *parathas* stuffed with finely sliced spring onions and creamy Italian buffalo mozzarella cheese, hot tandoori naan brushed with a thin coating of herby olive oil, and a decadent saffron infused French brioche and Spanish almond bread and butter pudding served with Cornish clotted cream that had been delicately imbued with fragrant ground cardamom.

The chatter was on the whole very relaxed, and easy for Miriam to join in with; Raza talked about his work running an IT company which was a family business, although he had before that worked for a few years as a secondary school teacher. He was keen to get Miriam's thoughts on teaching generally as soon as she mentioned that she had trained as a teacher. Sheree worked in hotel management, and there followed much conversation about the hospitality industry, particularly between Zaf and Sheree.

'Where are you teaching now?' asked Raza, just before he devoured another bit of the lamb scooped up in a piece of meltingly buttery paratha.

Miriam froze for a few seconds; she had one of those brief moments of panic, where she was not sure what Zaf would expect her to say. Raza looked towards her, expecting a simple answer to a simple question. Simple was never that easy to come by for Miriam. 'I'm not teaching at the moment...'

'She's taking a break from it.' intervened Zaf. He looked at Miriam, his eyes conveying a silent instruction, and Miriam immediately understood what she had to do next.

'Yes, that's right,' said Miriam, 'I'm having a bit of time out, especially as I moved down mid-way through the academic year, so it wasn't the ideal time to apply for new posts.'

'The kids at her last school had run her ragged, so I figured my darling wife needed a breather,' said Zaf, as he reached over and clasped Miriam's hand on the table. His hand felt cold and sweaty; inside, she flinched when she felt his clammy touch, but outwardly, she turned her head towards him and smiled at him, and although her insides now churned, she let him rest his hand on hers for as long as he liked.

'Teaching is definitely not for the faint hearted!' said Raza, and Miriam nodded her head in agreement. 'Hence I decided to take over the family IT business.'

Raza and Sheree had been a delight to dine with. They didn't make Miriam feel anywhere near as inadequate as she normally felt when Zaf took her to other events, like the high-powered dinners and drinks receptions they were often invited to, mingling with well-known politicians and influential business people, often in grand hotels and the like.

Miriam dared to conclude that the evening had gone splendidly. She felt as though she had nailed her look; a black dress with a stylish maroon shrug cardigan accessorised with small drop pearl earrings and a matching bracelet, finished off with a black clutch bag that she had picked out carefully due to its pearl detailing at the front which co-ordinated well with the rest of her look. These were all items that Zaf had bought for her in the past. Her makeup was fairly neutral; a light base, brown eyeshadow, black eyeliner and mascara, peachy pink blush, and

a pink nude lip. She certainly hadn't received any criticism from
Zaf about the way she looked. She didn't feel as though she had
said or done anything wrong. She had been attentive towards
the guests, she had smiled throughout the evening, she had
spoken only at appropriate and timely intervals, and added to
that, she did not think she had done anything that Zaf could
construe as being disrespectful towards him. When the meal
was over, and after they had seen off their guests, she had left
the restaurant with a slight smile on her face as, though she
could barely believe it, she was pleased with herself, pleased
that she may have finally got it right, that she may not have
disappointed him in any way.

When they arrived home, she went straight upstairs to get
changed, and was followed swiftly into the bedroom by her
husband.

He was very quiet. He had been quiet in the car all the way
home, and now he was still not speaking. She was never sure
whether she should leave him be, and run the risk of being
accused of not caring about how he was feeling, and of
neglecting him, or whether she should ask him what was wrong,
and then run the risk of inviting his wrath. Eggshells always
came to her mind when she felt like this. She could almost see
them scattered all around her; sharp, jagged, fragmented pieces,
large and small, littered under her wherever her legs moved as
gingerly as she could manage, paining the soles of her feet with
each step she took, the slightest crackle waking the sleeping dog,
tempting his fury.

Miriam had suffered from occasional nightmares since her
mother had passed away, but these had heightened and become
much more frequent since she had married Zaf. There was one
recurring dream that she had been plagued by since the first few
weeks after her wedding. In this dream she would see herself
outdoors in some faraway place, running frantically, barefoot,

and as she did so, she would look behind and see a trail of bloody footprints. Trickles of blood would seep from her feet, from what, she didn't know, for there were no cracked egg shells in the dream, in fact there was nothing on the ground but soft pale green grass. She would run until she reached the edge of a cliff, and she didn't stop there. She would start to fall off the edge, and as she was still falling, gliding down through the air as lightly and as softly as a feather, anticipating that moment when her body would strike the ground and smash to a million smithereens, various thoughts and accompanying images would flash though her mind; would she land on her head, or would it be on her back. But she never saw the outcome. She would suddenly wake up, mid-air, still falling, never landing. She wondered if she would ever see herself hit the ground, if she would ever see herself dead, so that this nightmare could end. She often thought death would be better than the nightmare she woke up to almost every day.

Why are you thinking about this blasted nightmare whilst you are awake? She asked herself. She twisted around and looked over towards him, but remained seated at the dressing table. She stared at him, but she said nothing, and he continued to give her the silent treatment. She turned back around to look at the mirror and started to take her jewellery off. After he got changed into his nightclothes, he went downstairs and switched the television on. She could hear the news. When he watched television, he almost always watched the news. He would sometimes watch a current affairs documentary about something exceedingly depressing; terrorism, or drugs, or world conflict. But it was usually the news, often for hours. The same stories, the same intro music, the same headlines, over and over again.

Make up removed and pyjamas now on, Miriam was in two minds as she sat on the bottom edge of their super king size bed; go down and speak to him, or just brush her teeth and go straight to bed. She locked her fingers together and rubbed her palms profusely, something she often did when the eggshells came to mind, when her anxiety levels started to ramp up.

She smoothed one of her hands over the soft and very expensive caramel coloured silk bedspread. Zaf's choice of colour, of course. Miriam found the brown shades of coffee, taupe, and tan that occupied the entire bedroom a little dark at times, but she knew she didn't really have a say in the choice of décor or furnishings. She had tried once to suggest purchasing what she considered to be an elegant looking side table that she had seen, only to be told by him that she could not be trusted with making decisions about matters such as furniture and décor because her taste was 'cheap and tasteless.'

Miriam turned her head around and looked back at the huge bed, and thought, what a waste of space. She always slept on her left side facing outwards, on the very edge of her side of the bed. The very edge. The very edge felt safe. Much safer than the middle.

She weighed up the options in her mind. If she went down to talk to him, it could end up in an argument, as no doubt he would tell her that his current mood was her fault, as it was as a result of something which she had done wrong, or had omitted to do. It didn't matter that she had no idea what she had or hadn't done. That was never a defence. He would have his tantrum, and she would end up grovelling for forgiveness, for what, she didn't know. On the other hand, if she went straight to sleep, it was highly likely that he would come and wake her up in any event. She knew that if he did that, she wouldn't have a choice. Being his wife meant being available for sex whenever and however he demanded it. She had long hated the mechanical and unfeeling way in which he would just mount himself and expect to be satisfied. There was no tenderness, no affection, no emotion in any of it. He dictated the process, cold and vulgar as it was, because he could, and he did. She didn't feel like she had an option. In fact, she knew she didn't have an option. Just like she knew that she would just endure it, again and again. It was her lot. She had to deal with it. She chose to marry him. She chose this life for herself. There was no turning back. Who would she turn back to? What *was* there to turn back to? Answers; no one, and nothing. Whatever had happened or was yet to happen, this was it for her now, for better or for worse, she had to find a way to be content. At least, that's what she told herself. Over and over again.

She finally made her mind up and grudgingly got up from the bed. She went downstairs and into the kitchen, and made two mugs of cocoa. He often liked to have hot chocolate in the evenings. Not the instant type, but the proper cocoa, made by boiling full fat milk and then whisking in the pure fair-trade cocoa powder with a good helping of sugar. She finished it off by carefully dusting the frothy top with sifted cocoa powder. He didn't like any whipped cream on top, or any sprinkling of marshmallows; he was averse to that "nonsense" as he called it. She put the mugs down on the coffee table and sat on the sofa next to him. For a few seconds, she quietly observed the bubbles on the foamy top of the mugs as they slowly popped, before she spoke.

'What's wrong?' she asked him as softly as she could manage.

He grunted something, but she couldn't discern what it was. She could see the look on his face though. *That look.* Oh, how she detested *that look.* The downturned lips and the raised eyebrows. The contorted pulling away in opposite directions. The look of doom. It was back. She joined her fingers again and gripped them tightly, and then she persisted, gently.

'What is it? What's the matter?'

'What the hell do you think you were doing tonight? he

lambasted her. Right out of nowhere. No build up, no inkling, no joining of any dots, no clue dropped, no hint given. Straight in, rapid fire accusation. That was his style. No enemy warning. Pure shock and awe.

'I have no idea what you are talking about,' she said, warily.

His eyes penetrated hers callously, and the look of doom worsened.

'Flirting with Raza like that all evening!'

If she had been standing when she heard this accusation she would surely have fallen over in a heap. The expression of horror on Miriam's face could not have escaped him, and yet the look of doom remained secure on his face, plastered on like a tight-fitting mask, unwavering in its efforts to unnerve her, as much today as it always did.

'What?' It was all she could muster. Her eyebrows rose in the middle, and little wavy lines swam across her forehead.

'And in front of his wife, too. That poor woman, the epitome of class, so elegant and dignified, she didn't know where to hide her face. Have you no shame at all?' He was absolutely relentless tonight. He tried to outstare her, and succeeded very quickly. The look of doom always sent a chill right to the core of every single cell in her body.

Flashbacks from the evening ricocheted through her mind; Raza and his wife smiling, laughing, chatting, nodding, eating, drinking, relaxing.

'I don't know why you're saying all this. I wasn't flirting. I was just being polite and sociable, not just with Raza, with both of them. His wife seemed perfectly fine to me; in fact, they both did.'

'Are you actually for real? Do you think I'm blind? That I can't see what's going on right in front of my face?'

'What? I didn't do any—'

'Don't give me that rubbish. Do you know what? I don't get it.'

Miriam didn't respond. If she spoke, it bothered him. if she didn't speak, it bothered him. She pushed her lips together resolutely, and literally held her tongue between her teeth.

'Ask me.'

Miriam brusquely wiped away the rapidly escaping tears from her cheeks with the back of each hand. But her lips remained pursed, determined not to unlock.

'Ask me!' he leant over and shouted right into her ear. Her insides jumped up with fright, and her ear began to ache, as though he had physically put his hand through and punched right through her eardrum. On the outside, her body froze. The only movement that came was from the blasted tears that continued to roll their way out. She knew she couldn't maintain the reticence.

'What? What don't you get?' she whimpered, praying that there would not be any further noise thrust down her ear.

He leant over towards her; he was almost in her face when he now spoke. He didn't shout, he spoke calmly, almost wickedly, and a sinister tone rung out from each word. 'I don't get why you act so trashy? Huh? What's the point of me buying you designer gear, sophisticated clothes like the ones you wore this evening, if you are going to behave in such a cheap, tarty manner.'

Miriam's belligerent tears continued to trundle out of her eyes and down her burning cheeks, no words escaped her mouth though.

'It's no wonder your family disowned you, the way you behave. You make me sick! Get away from me. I hate looking at you!' he now shouted again, paining her ears once more.

Miriam ran back upstairs and jumped into her bed. She knew that she ought to be used to it by now, but once again, his harsh words punctured her like a stab in the heart. She felt, in that moment, the same way as she always felt, after each and every such episode. Every time he did this to her, every time he reduced her to a place where she felt even more worthless than the last time, every time he skewed her perception of reality, every time he polluted her mind with ideas of her supposed ineptitude and stupidity, every time he slammed her for the way she looked, every time he knocked her for the way she dressed, every time he mocked what she did or said, every time he tried to destroy a little bit more of her, he succeeded, as every time he did this, she felt as though another little piece of her died.

Miriam's eyes closed involuntarily, and she nestled the left side of her tired head into the softness of her pillow. Her thoughts slowly melted into a deep sleep where she hoped she could escape the distresses of the day, unless of course her nightmares were waiting for her.

9

Birmingham Crown Court
6 November 2019

Her nerves are getting the better of her today; Miriam sits in her cell and wonders why proceedings have been delayed. She knots her fingers together tightly, and rubs the palms of her hands against each other, gently at first, building up the speed and ferocity. When she realises the intensity with which she is now rubbing her palms, she unclasps her hands quickly.

She closes her eyes and takes a few deep breaths as she sits back in the corner of the small cell below court. The pitch-dark silence is disturbed when she hears the door to the cell being unlocked; she opens her eyes and in walk Mr De Beaux and Sara.

'How are you feeling?' asks Sara. Her question is met with a shrug of Miriam's shoulders.

'How do you think it's going?' asks Mr De Beaux. Miriam thinks it should be him answering that question, but she doesn't say so. She knows he is only trying to help, in his own way. But she honestly has nothing to say. Nothing valuable, at any rate.

'Have you thought any more about giving evidence?' he asks her, and now she realises why they're both here. At least he's got pretty much straight to the point; she prefers that to the long-winded version.

'We've been through this,' Miriam finally speaks, sooner than her legal team expected her to, for this question about giving evidence normally pushes Miriam into a prolonged silence.

'And we need to go through it again,' says Sara; harsh words dressed up in a kind tone of voice.

'I can't!' says Miriam. Her heartbeat quickens as she acknowledges that like a bitter pill that she may resist swallowing, the inevitable can't be put to one side indefinitely. She really does have to talk about this, but she desperately, vehemently does not want to. 'I can't do it!' she tells them again.

'You *can* do it,' says Mr De Beaux.

She looks at him with her signature fraught eyebrows, the look of anguish which he has become so accustomed to.

'Okay then, in that case, I don't *want* to!' says Miriam, like a petulant child who just won't listen, who just won't do as she is told. Perhaps a small part of her is using this opportunity as an act of rebellion; after over two years of only listening to Zaf, of only doing as she was told by him, and nothing more, all the resentment that has built up over time is now coming out. However, that is not the overriding reason. Nowhere near it. There is more to it than that, but she can't open up. She just cannot go there. It would be too awful to go there.

'Of course, we can't make you do this, and we wouldn't, but,' and here Sara hesitates, so Mr De Beaux finishes the sentence off for her. 'But you need to know that not giving evidence will seriously hurt your chances.'

Miriam closes her eyes and takes a few deep breaths in and out. 'Alright,' she finally relents, 'I will *think* about it, but I'm not making any promises. Can we leave it for now, and talk again when I finally have to make the decision?'

Mr De Beaux nods his head, and gives her a warm smile. Sara gives her a little pat on the arm, and they both leave the cell.

It is a late start to the proceedings, and on this occasion, it is the Judge's fault, but he doesn't feel the need to explain to anyone why he is so late to arrive at court. Two hours after court should have commenced, everyone is finally seated and silent.

Mr Nigel Dodds takes the oath and stands up tall in the witness box, as he is in fact a tall man. He is meticulously dressed in a black suit and red and grey striped tie. He is a retired businessman, and he has lived at 8 Parkfield Close with his wife for many years now.

'Mr Dodds, I believe you are a neighbour of the accused and the deceased?' asks Ms Godfrey.

'Yes, that's right. I live at number 8 with my wife, immediately to the left of their house as you look straight ahead at the houses from the road.'

'Have you been neighbours for long?'

'For the past seven years, since Zaf's family purchased the house. Zaf's parents also lived at the house, until they retired and moved to Pakistan a few years ago now. They left a couple of years before Miriam moved down from Manchester when she married Zaf.'

10

Zaf. What will Zaf say? That was her first thought as soon as she ended the call. Miriam speculated about how best to approach Zaf with this. She had just promised to go up to Manchester for a weekend get together with all her old university friends; Nina was going to be over from Dubai too, an added bonus. Miriam was six months into her marriage now, and so far, she hadn't seen any of her Manchester friends since her wedding day.

She had got her inbox at work down to just five emails that needed responding to, which she couldn't deal with just yet, as she was waiting on others to supply her with bits and pieces of information.

Adam popped his head around the door. Adam was the in-house accountant who was one of the few people that Zaf showed any respect to, or saw as almost an equal. Perhaps because he was a polished, professional individual, perhaps because he dealt with all the company's finances and knew a bit too much. But what was sure was that Adam was a sound, dependable person and he had made Miriam feel welcome from day one.

'You fancy a cuppa?' he asked.

'Oh, go on then. But give me five minutes, and I will come and join you. I just need to go have a word with Zaf.'

'Okey dokey. Rachel not in?' he observed.

'No, she's out for a couple of hours,' replied Miriam.

Adam walked off and Miriam slipped into Zaf's office next door in order to broach the subject that was weighing on her mind. The office was unusually quiet today, which was not the norm, and if she didn't make a conscious effort to step away from her desk, she could quite easily end up glued to it all day, only veering away for a bathroom break, or when she desperately needed a cup of tea. Sometimes she ate lunch, but often she didn't, and when she did, it was at her desk whilst she continued to work.

Miriam walked into his room and sat in one of the chairs opposite him. He didn't look away from his computer screen. It was as if she wasn't there. She didn't need a cloak of invisibility; she was almost always invisible as far as he was concerned, unless of course she had done something wrong. In that case, there was never anywhere to hide.

'Zaf.'

'Yeah, what is it?' he replied, still focusing on the monitor.

'I was wondering. Would you mind if I went up to Manchester next weekend?' she asked, tentatively. It was enough notice, she thought to herself, surely.

He now looked away from the screen and towards her for the first time since she had walked in. 'What for?'

'The uni girls are having a get together and they've asked me to come too. Nina's going to be over as well. Everyone's going to be there.'

Zaf sat back in his dark brown leather chair; he placed his

right index finger on his pursed lips. and thought about it for a minute. 'Hmmm. Next weekend you say. That's going to be tricky. I need you to be at home,' he told her, and then started typing again.

Miriam waited for an explanation, but he didn't offer it.

'Why? What's happening next weekend?' she asked him.

'Don't tell me you've forgotten? That guy is coming to the house. Remember? It was you, a while back, who said the carpet on the landing upstairs was looking tatty,' he said. This forget-fulness was becoming a theme now. Recently she had mislaid both her passport and driving licence, although she had managed to find them eventually after almost a week of searching. She decided, on Zaf's suggestion, to give them to him for safekeeping rather than risk misplacing them again.

Bewilderment washed over her right now. Had she said that about the carpet? She couldn't remember saying that. She thought he had mentioned it. But she must have said it, right? But what guy was he talking about?

'I've managed to find someone to come over to remove it. He'll put the solid oakwood flooring down, just like you wanted. He's coming on the Saturday. In all probability it will run into Sunday, as he is going to do the downstairs hallway as well.'

'Oh. I see.' Miriam searched around in her head, but she didn't recall anything. She sighed quietly.

Zaf folded his arms as he rested his head back. 'He comes highly recommended. It was a job and a half to get hold of him, he's so busy. He was good enough to move other work around for us. So, you need to be home; I'm going be at work. Obviously.'

Miriam's eyebrows creased, and her confounded look did not escape him.

'I did tell you about this.'

'Did you?'

'Yes, a few days ago, over dinner.'

Zaf turned back to his screen now, and started typing a new email.

Why could she never remember anything these days? She had gone from having a brilliant memory, to one that retained nothing whatsoever. Nothing seemed to stick in that tiny brain of hers nowadays. She could see the disappointment on Zaf's face; disappointed that she had once again forgotten what he had told her.

'Oh. Okay,' she replied, with a tone of despondency daubed through the two words.

He stopped typing, and looked away from his screen once again; he turned to face her properly, resting his hands on the desk.

'Listen; if going to see your friends is more important to you than getting the house fixed, then so be it. This work at the house, it does need doing, and you were the one who wanted it done, but it will have to wait if you aren't going to be home. I can try and rearrange it but I have to say it is pretty damn hard to get hold of good workmen like him. Do you want me to cancel him?'

'No.' Her response was instantaneous. 'No. It's alright. I can meet up with them another time.'

'Are you sure? I don't want you to feel like I'm stopping you from going to see your friends,' he said. His voice did not seem to carry any genuineness, even though, on the face of it, he was saying all the right things.

'Yeah, of course I'm sure. I know I have responsibilities down here now; my friends will understand that.'

'And if they don't, then trust me, they're not worth having as friends.' Zaf leant over towards her a little. 'You have to be careful you know.'

Miriam looked at him quietly, and this was invitation enough for him to expand on his last statement.

'I say that, because I've noticed that there's a lot of jealousy around,' he explained. 'When other people see that you're happy in life, that you're making a success of things, that you have a good husband and a great marriage, they can feel resentful. And believe me, those envious people can even include your closest friends.'

'My friends aren't like that,' she responded, half defiantly in loyalty to her friends, half meekly so as not to offend him and his opinion.

'I'm sure they don't seem like that to you, and who knows, maybe they're not. But I have known quite a few marriages fall apart because the wife put her friends or family or sisters before her husband. I'm sure the wife doesn't intend for things to go wrong, but when these so-called friends start putting stupid ideas into the wife's head, then it's a recipe for disaster. The husband and wife will be perfectly happy, until the friend or sister or whoever it is drips little bits of poison into the wife's mind; *he doesn't help you with any of the housework, I wouldn't stand for that, you should be more important to him than his career, is that all he got you for your birthday, or he didn't remember to do such and such a thing, that's outrageous.* Before you know it, the wife starts arguing with the husband; she begins to disrespect him, refuses to listen to him, and it's a slippery slope after that...'

Miriam looked down towards the ground, still listening to his sermon-like speech, but at the same time drifting away slowly. For a short while, maybe thirty seconds or so, she didn't hear a word he said; she was secretly mourning the loss of not being able to see her friends. She could picture them all together; out for a meal, back at their favourite haunt on Wilmslow Road, their table full of life with laughter and chatter, ordering too much food, not being able to finish the jug of *lassi* because of all the colourful mocktails they ordered as well, then going on to their favourite dessert place even though they were stuffed, because they had to have the hot chocolate fudge cake with vanilla ice cream, the freshly made Belgian waffles with cookie crumble strawberries and whipped cream, and the old school jam coconut sponge cake served with piping hot custard. But then, his preachy voice seeped back into her ears.

'...down the line, these women end up divorced and bitter. You know, men will always be able to move on, to easily remarry, to start again, because that's what men do, that's what society expects of them. But it's not that easy for women, especially in our community. It's sad but it's true. No one wants damaged goods, or baggage, do they? Do you understand what I'm saying?'

'Yes. I do,' she said, now firmly back in the present, the echoes of the laughter of her friends presently fading away into oblivion. She replied with a feeling of undetectable inner frustration with the world laced through her words; *why was it like this?*

'It's great when a husband and wife understand each other, isn't it?' he asked her, his eyes secured on hers, making sure she got what he said, loud and clear.

'Yes, it is,' she replied. 'I've got loads of work waiting for me,' she added, as she stood up to leave the room, having forgotten all about promising to join Adam for a quick tea break. 'I best get on,' she said, deciding to continue with the day as best she could.

11

Birmingham Crown Court
6 November 2019

'Could you tell us what you were doing on the morning of 31st March 2019, Mr Dodds?' asks Ms Godfrey.

'Of course. Yes. I was out gardening on that particular morning.'

'Where abouts in your garden were you?'

'In the front, to the side of our house. There is about a 4ft wooden fence that divides number 6 and number 8, and on our side, we have a hawthorn hedge that goes up above the wooden fence, and next to it on the ground we have a rectangular patch of soil that runs along the length of that fence and hedge at the front of property. Like I said, I decided to do a bit of gardening, and on that morning, I was crouched down, planting some dahlias along that part that I just described. March is a good time to plant dahlias, as is April as well I suppose. Anyway, like I said, I was on my knees planting away quietly, when I heard them both come out of the house.'

'Just so that there is no misunderstanding, can you confirm

who you are referring to when you say you heard "them" come out of the house.'

Nigel Dodds looks towards Miriam for a brief moment. 'It was Miriam, and Zaf. I don't think they realised I was there, because they couldn't see me, and I too actually couldn't see them at all, but I could hear them.'

'And what did you hear?'

'I heard them arguing,' he replies, clasping his hands together in front of him.

'What was the argument about, Mr Dodds? Did you hear any of what they said to each other?'

'I couldn't tell you exactly, word for word. But I did catch some of it. I heard Miriam say something about him going out when he was supposed to be taking her somewhere or other, I don't know where. She sounded very upset and annoyed.'

'Did you often see, or hear them, arguing?'

Mr Dodds gives a small shake of the head. 'No, not at all. This was the first time ever. They're a quiet couple, I would say. We would interact with them here and there. Zaf sometimes came around if he was going to do any work to his house, as a courtesy to let us know. He was polite and considerate in that sense. Or if they were going to be away, he would ask we keep any eye out on the house, which of course we didn't mind. He always asked so respectfully.'

'And Miriam?'

'We saw her a bit more, though not so much recently. In the early days, she would sometimes bring food over. When I first met her, I mentioned that I love curries and spicy food, and Miriam would often bring her home cooked food around. And my wife does quite a bit of baking, so she would sometimes take home made cake and biscuits over to them. But that was it really, nothing much more than that.'

'How do you find Miriam?'

'In what sense?' he asks, and turns his head again to look at Miriam. She looks pale, her face devoid of any makeup. She seems weak, clearly having lost a lot of weight. She doesn't look at all like the Miriam he was used to seeing, he thinks to himself.

'In terms of her nature, her personality,' Ms Godfrey clarifies.

'I don't really know her *that* well,' says Mr Dodds, which he follows with a short sharp cough.

'Very well. You mentioned that she used to bring food over in the early days. Did she stop bringing food over?'

Mr Dodds doesn't answer the question straight away.

'Was there a problem between you?' Ms Dodds persists.

He looks upwards for a few moments, as though somewhere in the vacant space above him he is seeing scenes and hearing conversations from the past.

'For the first year or so, she used to pop around with all sorts of lovely dishes; samosas, biryani, curry, kebabs, *roti*. Home made by her, not from the restaurant. Very delicious, this food was. She is actually a very talented cook. But then...' His voice trails away.

'Then what?'

He glances towards Miriam once again, and pauses for a few seconds. Miriam averts her gaze, which now rests on probably the oldest member of the jury; she looks like a proper granny, thinks Miriam. From the curly, albeit thinning, silver hair, to the pale blue cardigan which looks hand knitted, probably by her, to the round pearly clip-on earrings. She should be sat at home in her favourite armchair watching daytime television, or pottering about in her garden, or taking her grandchildren to the park. Or maybe she is the adventurous type, thinks Miriam. Perhaps she enjoys canoeing trips, or rambling around the countryside, or paragliding from the cliff tops. Whatever she does or doesn't like to do, she shouldn't have to sit here at her age for hours and days on end. *I wonder what she makes of all of this?* Miriam thinks to herself, and then her attention turns back to the witness.

'Then it stopped,' continues Mr Dodds.

'Why?' asks Ms Godfrey.

'I don't know why to be honest. You would have to ask Miriam that. My wife and I just couldn't work it out. She was very warm and friendly towards us, and then all of a sudden, she just kind of cut us off.'

'Cut you off?'

'Yes, there is a particular day that comes to my mind. After she had heard it was our wedding anniversary coming up on this day, she told my wife she would be coming around to drop off some food in the evening. She made a big song and dance about it to be honest, saying she was going to bring a very special meal over, but then, to our surprise, she never came. We hadn't cooked anything, obviously, so after waiting for quite a while, and after not receiving any replies to the messages my wife sent to Miriam, we ended up ordering a takeaway. We assumed that either something very urgent had come up, or that Miriam had simply forgotten. We saw that Zaf's car was in the drive, so we didn't want to go round and disturb them.'

'What happened next?'

'My wife went around the next day, just to check if she was okay, as it wasn't like her not to come if she said she was going to. We thought maybe she was ill or something. And my wife took round some flapjacks she had made in the morning. But for some unknown reason, Miriam was very stand offish. She didn't let my wife past the front door, and refused to accept the flapjacks. She was a bit curt, to be honest. My wife was quite upset because she thought she and her were more like friends than mere neighbours. After that day she never came around, and my wife stopped going over as well, and subsequent to that we never really saw much of Miriam.'

12

2 February 2018

Miriam fried the crescent moon shaped thin slivers of red onions until they turned a deep bronzy brown, and then she scattered them all over the chicken *haleem* that she had placed in the pristine white serving dish, choosing not to use a Tupperware box on this very special occasion. She also sprinkled over some finely sliced green chillies, a few thin slices of lemons, freshly chopped coriander leaves, and juliennes of peeled fresh root ginger. She packed some lemon wedges and extra fried onions in a separate container. She had already wrapped the freshly made *rotis* in foil. And she had placed the *hara masala* lamb chops accompanied with turmeric and mustard potatoes in a pretty white platter, and covered it with foil, and the *channa* pilau rice had also been packed.

She enjoyed making extra food and sending it next door, but today was a bit different; today was their thirty fifth wedding anniversary. The traditional symbol for thirty-five years of marriage was coral, or so she had discovered when she had googled it, and the modern symbol was the gemstone jade, which she assumed was far easier to give as a gift. She wondered, whilst preparing the food, if she and Zaf would make it to their thirty fifth anniversary, but the thought didn't linger for very long, as she had much to do. The Dodds' were not going out to celebrate their anniversary until the weekend, when their children and grandchildren would all be over. So, Miriam had told them that she would bring a special meal around later and they could have a mini celebration tonight. For Miriam, evenings at home on her own in a huge house were a lonely existence, and these little activities kept her mind from drifting towards a place that was not only lonesome but emotionally damaging. For her, the whole process of cooking and creating, especially for others who appreciated it, was more like therapy than a chore, and it gave her a pleasurable purpose.

She assembled all the dishes and the bits of food into a sturdy cardboard box, picked it up carefully and headed towards the front door. However, before she even got to the door, it opened, and she was startled to see Zaf walk through it. He was always at the restaurant until late, and she was taken aback to see him at home so early in the evening; it was only half past seven.

He closed the door and then stopped in his tracks when he saw her with the box.

'What's in that box you're carrying?'

'It's just some food I made,' she answered in a tiny voice.

'Where on earth are you going with it?'

Miriam started to quickly weigh up in her mind what to say next. He was staring at her with hawkish precision, so she had to be quick.

'I made a bit too much food, so I thought I would pop some of it around to next doors.'

'Next door?' Why?'

This time, she didn't respond. She told herself that right now silence was probably her best friend.

'This is something you do all the time, is it? When I'm out, working my backside off, this is what you get up to?'

She still said nothing. The silence remained in situ for now.

'Well?' he demanded.

The point had now been reached where silence was no longer an option. 'No, no I don't. But today, it's the Dodds' wedding anniversary, they just happen to mention it in passing, and so I thought that as I have made so much food, it might be a nice thing to do, just to take some over to them. They bring cakes over quite often. It's just a neighbourly gesture, that's all.'

'Put it back in the kitchen.'

'What?' She thought she might have misheard him. He couldn't be serious.

Zaf came up close, and hovered over Miriam. Suddenly the food started to feel much heavier; it felt more like a box full of bricks than a few pots of food, and it now threatened to slip right through her hands. She clung onto it tightly, almost lovingly. She wouldn't let it drop. She would hold on to it tight. She cradled it firmly.

'Listen. I hate to break it to you. But those neighbours don't really like your food, you know. They're just very polite old people, and they don't want to hurt your feelings.'

Miriam couldn't believe her ears. Surely not. They always raved to her about how they loved her food, and what a great cook she was, and how it never tasted this good in the restaurants. No. She refused to believe this.

Zaf clocked the dubious, confused look on Miriam's face. 'The old fella,' he continued, 'he told me as much, a couple of weeks ago when I popped round to give them that letter that had come to ours by mistake.'

'Really? He said that?'

'Pretty much, yeah. You didn't have to be a genius to read between the lines.'

Miriam's eyelids grew heavy, as she stared into space and thought about what she had just heard. Perhaps it *was* true. Perhaps they were a bit fed up of her, perhaps she had been making a nuisance of herself and she just hadn't realised it, so wrapped up she was in her own world. Maybe they thought she was a bit needy. Maybe they *did* wish she would stop foisting food on them all the time. She had been sending food around quite often lately, even though she dared not tell Zaf that. Perhaps, she thought, perhaps Zaf was right. She wondered how she always got things so wrong. Time after time.

'Anyway, I know what you're trying to do. I can see right through you,' he now claimed. He started to undo the top button of his shirt, and then walked off towards the kitchen, without finishing what he had started saying. She followed right behind him.

'I'm not trying to do anything, except to take some food next door,' she said, trying to reassure him.

'Oh sure,' he snorted. 'You love acting liking a saint in front of other people. You just can't help yourself, can you?'

'No. That's not what I'm doing.' *I'm just taking some food round, that's it. No agenda, no pretence, no subterfuge.*

'You can stop all this goody too shoos stuff; it's getting tiring, and quite frankly, it's getting boring. Seeing as though they don't much appreciate your cooking efforts anyway, and who can blame them, and they're pretty fed up you turning up there all the time, I suggest you don't have anything more to do with them.'

This was hard to take. *No, no, no. Don't take this away from me! Please.*

'But I don't understand. I haven't done anything wrong. I'm

just trying to do something nice for our neighbours. They're good people. And I'm just being a good neighbour, that's all.'

'What the...you need to take a good hard look at your priorities. You can't even be bothered to give my mum a call once in a while, to see if she's okay; your own mother-in-law, but you can stand around for hours cooking fancy meals for strangers.' He yanked his tie off, then walked across the kitchen to the fridge to grab a drink.

'They're not strangers, they are our neighbours. And anyway, I call your mum regularly.'

'Oh, okay, so I'm wrong now, am I?'

Silence.

'You calling me a liar?' he shouted across the kitchen at her.

More silence.

'Are you?' he probed, with a look that informed her in an instant that remaining silent was no longer a choice she could make.

'No, of course not. I'm not saying that at all. But I do speak to your mum, in fact, to both of your parents.' She should stop here, she thought to herself, but she couldn't. 'And I probably speak to them more often that you do because you hardly ever answer when they phone you on your mobile or leave messages, and then when they text me, or when they leave a message on the landline, it's me who calls them back, to ask them how they're doing, to reassure them you're okay and you probably didn't call them back because you've been so busy, but that you will call them back soon, which you only do once in a blue moon.'

Now she wished to God that she had kept quiet. *Why, oh why, do I never learn?*

'You think you're clever, do you? You think that you're smarter than me, huh?'

She didn't answer him.

'Well?' he demanded.

'No.' She could feel her insides doing somersaults. She suddenly realised that she was still holding onto the box, and she quickly placed it onto a worktop just in time, for the bottom of the box was ready to fall through any second.

'Why are you stood there gawping at me?' he asked, before he hurriedly downed half a glass of mango juice.

Miriam stared at him in a daze, her mind foggy, uncertain as to what she should now do. He hadn't actually instructed her yet. *Don't do anything. Just wait. The orders will come very shortly.* And it wasn't long.

'Put that food away, all of it. And from now on, I don't want to hear that you've taken food over again to next door, or to anyone else for that matter. I run a chain of restaurants. There's no need for my wife to cook and deliver meals to every Tom Dick and Harry. It's bloody embarrassing!'

She stood and stared but didn't utter a word. Her renewed silence persisted.

'Do you understand?'

'Y-yes.'

She started to empty the cardboard box with a heavy heart. Tears clouded her vision as she delicately took out the dishes and containers, one by one. For a split second, she thought about throwing the contents of the dishes and containers away; the hours spent cooking over a hot stove, crying whilst she had sliced the onions, washing the four different *daals* in numerous changes of water creating a symphony of colours as the red orange green and black lentils were mixed together, getting the delicate balance of the fresh herbs and the dried whole and ground spices just right, all straight into the bin. But she couldn't do it. She never could waste food, and so she placed the boxes and dishes carefully into the fridge, with love, and regret, accompanied by pointless tears that she could not hold back.

13

Birmingham Crown Court
6 November 2019

'Back to the morning of 31 March, Mr Dodds, can you tell us what else you heard in the argument between the defendant and the deceased?' asks Ms Godfrey.

'As I mentioned before, they were arguing about some promise Zaf had made to take Miriam out, but he said he needed to go somewhere else, and so he had to cancel, and she should let whoever it was know that they couldn't make it. Her brother, I think, yes, let her brother know. That was it.'

'Did you hear him say where he had to go in such a hurry?'

'I didn't, no.'

'And the defendant? What did you hear her say?'

'She implied that he was going out to see another woman.'

'Another woman?'

'Yes, she said something like "you're going to see *her*."'

'And what was his response?'

'He was very dismissive, if I'm honest.'

'And did you hear anything after that?'

'Yes.'

'What was that?'

'Erm...'

Nigel Dodds hesitates, and shifts around awkwardly on the spot.

'Mr Dodds?'

He looks over at Miriam's sallow face. She is looking towards the jury, and doesn't notice or acknowledge his gaze. He clears his throat a couple of times before answering.

'Miriam said...'

He hesitates yet again.

'Yes, Mr Dodds, what did she say?' Ms Godfrey persists, speaking slowly, trying to hide the irritation she is now feeling at her witness's apprehension, but she is still met with a wall of silence.

'Please, you must tell the court what you heard,' adds the Judge. He takes his glasses off to give Mr Dodds a good solid stare.

Almost everyone in the courtroom is on the edge of their seats; no one moves a muscle, or utters a sound. There is pin drop silence.

'She said, *after today you're dead to me!*'

'That will be all,' says Ms Godfrey. She reveals the tiniest of grins as she looks towards Mr De Beaux.

Eruptions of chatter ensue around the courtroom. Miriam doesn't take any of the noise in; the sounds that are coming from all the different directions seem distant and vague to her. Nondescript. But a few seconds before the bubbles and squeaks of sound, she did hear what Nigel said; listening to those words has sent the room around her into a little lopsided spin, and now she feels quite faint. *Breathe*, she tells herself. *Breathe. Slow even breath in, longer even breath out.* Miriam's sense of centre begins to return. She now looks around her, taking the atmosphere in, and immediately she detects the thick cloud of tension that now hangs heavily in the court room. Most of the jurors are looking towards her, even though some of them are trying not to make it obvious. The Asian businessman doesn't even try; he is blatantly staring straight at her, with a toffee-nosed look of disdain. It is as though the contempt that he so obviously feels is permanently etched into his eyes, for when-ever she looks at him, that disparaging look is always present. Sometimes the rest of his face joins in too; his lips grimace a little, or his nostrils flare a tad, but his penetrating, disapproving eyes don't change. The man in his forties sat two away from the Asian man, who Miriam feels must work at a bank, for he looks like someone who would work at a bank, is the polar opposite to the Asian guy. He doesn't even look at her. He is leaning back in his chair, and letting out a long yawn.

The courtroom settles down after the little bit of excitement that set everyone talking, and now Mr De Beaux rises to his feet. He looks at Nigel Dodds thoughtfully for a few seconds before he commences his cross-examination.

'Mr Dodds, would you say that, when you refer to the occa-sion when the defendant did not come around with the food as promised, that was out of character for her, from what you knew of her up to that point?'

'Yes, I would say so, especially as she knew it was our wedding anniversary that day and she was the one who had insisted that she wanted to bring the food over.'

'And when your wife went around the next day to check on her, and the defendant was, as you said, quite curt with your wife, would you say that this was also out of character?'

'Most definitely.'

'Can you expand on that? Can you tell us how this was out of character?'

'Previously, she would have invited my wife in, and gladly

accepted the flapjacks, in fact they would have eaten them together with a cuppa which she would have made for both of them. Prior to this, she had never been rude in the slightest, not to either of us.'

'Now then, coming to the argument which you heard on the morning of the 31 March. In your opinion, was this also out of character for the defendant, for her to stand on the doorstep and say the sort of things that you heard, to argue in such a flagrant manner?'

'Yes. I had certainly never heard anything like this from her before.'

'And when you heard her say "*after today you're dead to me*", what do *you* think she meant?'

Nigel Dodds stroked his chin for a few seconds whilst he deliberated. 'I suppose she said it to let him know how annoyed she was with him, and it was just blurted out amongst other things that were said as part of the argument between them.'

'Were you in any way concerned about the safety of the deceased, concerned about what the defendant may do to him?'

'No, I wasn't, like I said, I just thought that it was something she said in the context of a marital disagreement, in the heat of the moment, so to speak. I didn't think that later that day he would actually end up dead.'

14

19 February 2018

Dead, your baby is dead.

These words would forever haunt Miriam, until she breathed her last on her dying day.

The miscarriage, just after the first year of her marriage, was the most traumatic event of her life, and one that she would probably not get over for the rest of her life. She had once heard a saying, from one of the elders, that if you look into the soul of most women, you will find a baby story in there somewhere. But this wasn't just a story, it was her tragedy.

She was 13 weeks pregnant. She'd had her scan at 11 weeks, and baby was fine, she was told. But as she started her 13th week, she began to feel small twinges, which she was told was quite normal, followed by period like back and abdominal pain, which again she was told was normal for some women. However, this was then followed by blood, which she knew was not normal, and was a cause for concern.

On the day in question, she woke up at around 1 a.m. to go to the bathroom, something she was doing with more frequency in the night. Through her sleep glazed eyes she noticed the large red stain; it didn't seem real at first. She hastily rubbed her eyes and saw it more clearly now. Blood. She darted back into the bedroom and tried to wake Zaf up.

'Zaf, wake up,' she said, trying not to shout, but raising her voice enough that he would detect the panic she was feeling inside, He didn't stir, so she shook his arm a little. 'Zaf, please wake up. I'm bleeding.' He opened his eyes slowly.

'What? What did you say?'

'I'm bleeding!'

He shot out of bed, got dressed and drove her for the twenty minute journey to the hospital. As it was the middle of the night, the staff at the hospital couldn't perform a scan. They carried out some basic tests, but beyond that they could not say any more. 'Come back at 12.30pm and we will get you in for a scan, after which point, we will know more,' said the doctor. She was a gentle woman in her early forties, who dealt with Miriam in a caring, attentive manner. 'In the meantime, take plenty of rest, and if you suddenly get worse before your appointment, then don't delay, come straight back in. I don't want to alarm you, but I do have to tell you that you may be in the early stages of a miscarriage, in fact, it is probably likely that you are, although I can't say that for certain until we have performed the scan. It may be not be as bad as all that, I hope, anyway. But, if it is the onset of a miscarriage, it may take a little while, or, things may deteriorate very quickly, and if that does happen, then I would urge you to come back in straight away. Okay? Make sure you look after her now,' the doctor told Zaf. He nodded before adding, 'of course I will, and don't worry, I will bring her straight back at the first sign of anything like that happening, rest assured.' The doctor nodded in response, they said goodbye and headed home.

On the way home, there was only a little conversation between them, mostly Zaf talked and Miriam listened.

'I told you so many times to rest, didn't I?' said Zaf, the rebuke emphasised forcefully in each word, like a boom, boom, boom.

Miriam looked at him, lost for words at present, as she tried to recall such a conversation, but she did not have any such recollection. She turned her head away from him and looked out of the window. As they drove over the curved flyover and the car took the long winding bend way up high up, she could see the city lights glitter in the near distance. The night was still and peaceful, there was no movement, and the only brightness came from the twinkle of those lights, for it was an overcast night and there were no stars in the sky. How the city glowed from afar, she thought. How alluring and beautiful it looked. Go a little nearer, look a little closer, and suddenly it wouldn't be so appealing. Not when you saw the countless homeless men and women sat along the pavements outside, a steady stream of them all the way from the charming century old Moor Street Station to the newly rebuilt shiny New Street Station, sleeping with soggy blankets so sodden with the rain that they provide no protection from the unforgiving elements in the slightest. Not so alluring when you come across the beggars at traffic lights who knock on your window and plead for loose change, but you're too scared to wind down your window in case they throw acid in your face. Not so appealing when you walk past the drug addicts huddled away in dark corners, or the prostitutes walking the streets dreading the next abusive man that might come along, or the violence of the gangs, the shootings, the knife attacks, the hate crimes. People and places seem pleasant from afar, polished on the surface, glowing attractively from a distance. Get closer, look deeper, and you discover that they turn out to be very different. All that glitters is not gold. A cliché. But true.

Did he say that? She asked herself, when the car had descended the flyover and she no longer had the panoramic view. Perhaps he did, and her pregnancy brain just hadn't registered it. But then again...her confused thoughts were like jumbled up pic n mix. They tossed around in her head. Presently, she neither had the clarity of thought nor any surplus energy required for her to say anything meaningful. She turned her head, and in silence, she looked at him again.

'What? What are you staring at? I did say it to you, don't you remember?' he asked, his tone accusatory, his voice severe, his eyes seeking, no, demanding the correct answer from her.

'Yes.' Miriam replied softly. It was the best answer right now, and although it would probably keep on niggling her, she would keep that to herself.

A part of her always wanted to give him the benefit of the doubt, maybe because that was the easier option, or perhaps he might be right; on this occasion, like many others, she honestly couldn't remember the conversation. However, another part of her was doubtful; if she were to be frank with herself, she would have to admit that she doubted *him* more than she doubted her own memory. At this precise moment, there was one thing she was absolutely in no doubt about; she was definitely not going to argue with him. Not here in the car. Not when they got back home. Not today. Not at all. He was clever with his words, not just clever, he was quick, quicker than the speed of a cheetah chasing a gazelle. Zaf had a readymade answer for everything which he seemed to pluck out of thin air, and even if she *was* right, even if he had never said such a thoughtful thing, even if he had never expressed any such concern, by the end of it all, he would outwit her to such an extent that she would be ready to believe that she was wrong, and he was right. So, she would save herself the trouble and stay silent.

Whether he did or did not, at some point in the last three

months, maybe even fleetingly tell her to rest, whether she did or didn't remember him saying this, she definitely *did* remember the events from two days before; here there was no uncertainty in her mind whatsoever. The memory of what happened two days ago was as clear as water.

Two days previously, when Zaf had arrived back home from work, Miriam was lying on the sofa; she had been watching television, but at this point her eyes were closed, unable to resist the lure of sleep any longer. The television was still on, and even the latest nail biting episode of Line of Duty could not prevent her from drifting off. She was exhausted. She had been feeling this way for almost a week now. Totally, utterly shattered. Tiredness like she had never known before in her life. Even little jobs that she would never have previously considered taxing appeared before her like steep rocky mountains that seemed impossible to climb; getting up to answer the front door, or walking to the kitchen to make a cup of tea, or standing and photocopying a few sheets at the office all seemed to wear her out. She had heard that the first few months could be draining, but she had never imagined it would be this bad. And so, she would quite often drift off to sleep whilst watching the television, or whilst reading a book.

Zaf walked into the living room and stood in the middle of it, staring at her. Miriam sat up when she eventually realised he was there, her eyelids trying to resist the need to open, her head heavy with a longing to just sleep. He let out a little grunt, although she didn't know why. He then walked over to the television and put his hand on it.

'This thing is piping hot. How long has it been on for?' he asked.

'I'm not sure, an hour or two maybe.' She grabbed the remote control from the coffee table and switched it off.

'The heat from this television would say otherwise. It's red hot. How long have you been slobbering on that sofa for?'

She didn't dare answer him. Whatever answer she gave it would be the wrong one.

Zaf then walked over to the mantel piece and ran his right index finger along the surface, winding his finger around the ornaments and photo frames. This was something he did every now and again, and usually it would be spotless, however, today, Miriam knew he would have cause to complain. She hadn't dusted for the past few days, the daily nausea, heartburn and fatigue having got the better of her. He walked over to her and almost shoved the dusty finger in her face.

'What the fuck is this?'

Silence. Her best friend for now.

'You're a part-timer at the office as it is, the least you can do is tidy this place instead of lolling around on the sofa all day! It's no wonder you've put so much weight on. Look at the state of you. You're only three months pregnant but you look like you've put on three stones! God alone knows how bad you're going to look by nine months.'

Miriam's ears let the insults stream in, unobstructed, unfiltered, uninterrupted. It was true. She had put weight on. Definitely not three stones, but still quite a lot of weight in a short period of time. She knew that. She had to do better. She knew that too. But right now, the fatigue was such that she did not care about her weight, not one bit. Of course, she didn't tell him that.

He walked away from her and he hovered about in the middle of the room, like a nasty odour that you can't shift. She remained seated, and looked up at him. He stood still, crossed his arms, and took a wide stance. She wondered what was coming next.

'You're not at work tomorrow, are you?'

'No.'

'Then tomorrow you had better get this place sorted. And it's not just this room. The whole house is a tip.'

'I will.' Miriam assured him, and stifled a sigh with the back of her hand. *Please don't say any more, Zaf, I'm so tired. Please.*

'I'll be checking,' he threatened, but after that he said nothing further, to Miriam's utter relief.

The next day, Miriam set about cleaning the house from top to bottom; bedrooms, bathrooms, kitchen, stairs, the lot. She vacuumed and mopped, scrubbed and polished every nook and cranny, every trinket, every surface, until everything she touched gleamed back at her. When she was a couple of hours into the cleaning, she had started to feel a few aches and pains, but she had ignored them. She had to get the whole place done before the inspection in the evening.

As she now sat in the car on this awkward journey back home from the hospital, she couldn't help but speculate if any of this frantic, heavy duty cleaning, the physical exertion for hours on end, had any bearing on what was happening with the baby.

When they arrived back home, Miriam went straight to bed. She was knocked out as soon as her head touched the pillow, and for a while, she slept surprisingly well. At 8 a.m. she was awoken by the sound of Zaf answering a call. She looked over and could see him with his mobile phone in one hand talking to whoever it was, with his other hand stuck in the wardrobe, searching for a suitable tie. He already had his dark blue suit on. This was very early for Zaf to be up and dressed. He finished his call and slipped his mobile phone into his trouser pocket.

'You're not going to work, are you?' she asked him, as she rubbed her eyes.

'Yep. I have meetings all morning.'

'But...'

'But what?' he asked, as he pulled out a red tie.

'But I thought you would stay at home with me today, after

what the doctor said. And we have to go to the hospital, remember?'

'That's why I'm going in so early so I can be back in time to take you for the scan. Like they said, there's nothing that can be done right now. Just go back to sleep.'

His dismissiveness didn't deter her, at least not yet, for she desperately didn't want to be alone today, and so she persevered. 'Please, stay home with me. You can work in the study, I won't disturb you, I promise. What if something happens. I'm really scared.'

He had his back to her, but she could see him in the reflection in the wardrobe mirror as soon as he closed the wardrobe door and started to do up his tie. He didn't turn to look back at her, nor did he look at her reflection in the mirror. He only focused on his tie. He was, evidently, pretty unmoved. It seemed to be an ordinary day to him. He behaved as though there was nothing wrong, and yet, to Miriam, everything felt wrong.

'I will be back soon, I told you,' he said, and finally turned around. 'I know you're not well, but just for once, try not to be so melodramatic eh? Nothing is happening right now, is it?'

She didn't answer, instead, she merely looked at him with sad eyes.

'Is there anything wrong with you right now? As in, are you having a medical emergency this minute?'

'No, not an emergency as such,' she replied, in a timid voice, and not at all convincingly.

'There you are then,' he said, with a nonchalant wave of his right hand. 'Just relax, go back to sleep, and I will be back before you know it.'

He showed no emotion, no affection, no concern. There was no kiss, no hug, no reassurances. He simply, quietly, and coldly, left her.

Miriam yawned, as she stretched her arms to the side, and

realised that she was no less tired despite having managed to catch some sleep. Maybe he was right, she thought, perhaps she was being over the top. Maybe.

She lay back down and fell sleep again for about an hour and a half. She then woke up around 10 a.m. doubled up in pain. She could see from the stains on the bedsheet that blood had now seeped through her sanitary towel and clothes, and was coming heavier and thicker. Her body, now burdened with pains that started to violently pierce her insides, began to shake; she had never known such an agonising feeling before in all her life, as the one currently taking over her body. She got up from the bed with the intention of going to the bathroom, but couldn't even take one step. She felt light-headed, and she also felt sick, so she sat on the floor, leaning against the side of the bed. She grabbed her phone from the bedside table, and she called Zaf. He didn't answer, and it went to voicemail. She didn't leave a message. She phoned again. And again. And again. He still didn't pick up. She phoned yet again, and this time she left a voicemail, her flustered but clear message told him she needed him to come home straight away.

She had now advanced to panic mode; fear presently accompanied the physical agony, and it washed all over her, continuing to grow, like the waves of the ocean that build to a crescendo. She was finding it difficult to breathe, and the pain was taking on new shapes; it felt like there was an enormous weight sitting at the bottom of her abdomen, involuntarily thrusting downwards, piling on intolerable pressure, like a huge weight had bedded down there. She now knew that she no longer had any control over her body in the slightest. The crueller side of Mother Nature was taking over and there was nothing she could do about it.

Miriam now dialled the office landline, but the receptionist didn't answer. She pressed Rachel's extension, but it went to her voicemail. She phoned again, and this time she pressed Adam's extension. Adam was usually in his office which was right next door to Zaf's, and as she had hoped, he picked up. Finally, someone answered her call.

'Hello, Adam Anis speaking, how can I help?'

'Adam. It's me. Miriam.'

'Hi Miriam. How's it going?'

'Is Zaf there?'

'No, he left the office a little while ago. He and Rachel have gone to meet a new supplier in town, I believe. Can I help at all?'

'I've tried phoning him but he's not answering. I need to get hold of him. It's really urgent.'

'Are you okay? You don't sound very well.'

Miriam just winced, and was grateful that he couldn't see her right now.

'I can try calling him for you, if you want,' said Adam.

'Don't hang up on me. Phone him from your mobile, I want to stay on this line.'

'Okay.'

Adam put the landline receiver on his desk, and dialled Zaf's number from his mobile, on speakerphone. Miriam waited anxiously as she heard the rings of the call.

'Hi Adam. What's up? Is everything okay?' asked Zaf.

'It's all good over here, don't worry. It's Miriam, she's been trying to get hold of you. She says can you please call her.'

'Yeah, sure, I'll give her a call in a bit.'

'No, can you call her now, it sounds pretty urgent.'

'It's alright, Adam, calm down, she may be claiming it's an emergency, and you might not know this but she has a tendency to get all hyped up about stuff which usually turns out to be nothing, just a storm in a teacup, that's Miriam for you. I'll phone her in a bit. Listen, I'm just about to go into this meeting, so my mobile phone will be switched off for the next hour or so, but I will phone her straight after that. Okay.'

'But—' Before Adam could finish his sentence, Zaf had hung up.

Adam felt his face turning red, realising what a dumb thing he'd done by making the call on speakerphone, knowing Miriam will have heard everything. He picked up the landline receiver.

'Hi. Miriam—'

Miriam was now bent over, clasping her tummy with her free hand, crying uncontrollably from the cramps that were sucking the life out of her.

'Miriam. What is it? What's wrong?'

'I'm miscarrying Adam,' she cried, 'I'm losing my baby!'

This revelation came as a complete shock to Adam. No one at the office had known that she was pregnant. Miriam hadn't mentioned anything because Zaf had insisted on not telling anyone until she was showing. She had wondered why. He didn't like mixing his personal and professional life, but she had always suspected there may be something more to it.

'I can't move, Adam. I'm dizzy, and it hurts like hell, and there's blood everywhere. I really, really don't feel well.'

'Where abouts in the house are you?'

'I'm in the bedroom.'

Miriam's shrieks of pain felt like compass ends being stabbed into his eardrums.

'Okay, listen to me. Listen really carefully. I'm going to hang up in a second. Then I'm going to phone for an ambulance. Okay? But you are going to have to do one thing for me, you are going to have to somehow get yourself down the stairs and open the front door to let the paramedics in.'

Miriam tried to stifle her cries as she listened to what he said.

'Can you do that for me? Miriam? Try now, and tell me if you will be okay to do that.'

Miriam tried to get to her feet; she clung to the side of the bed in an effort to help herself up, but it was no use. She collapsed back down onto the floor. It was though her legs didn't exist anymore; she could feel no power in them. They had lost all their vigour. They were like hollow tree trunks; lifeless, and of no use at all. The blood was now seeping into the carpet, rippling around her body where she sat. She clenched her teeth hard to try and negate the pain.

'I can't, Adam. I can't get up. I won't make it to the bedroom door even.'

'Alright. Erm...I can come over and break a window or something.'

'His desk,' muttered Miriam, find it increasingly difficult to breath and speak.

'What?' asked Adam, totally perplexed.

'He has spare keys in his desk for everything,' she continued, whilst at the same time, she gasped for air. 'There's a key for the front door there too. It's on a Ferrari key ring.'

'Alright, I'm hanging up now. I will be with you as soon as I can.'

As the minutes ticked away, Miriam felt progressively woozy. The pain was cutting her up in every direction. She clenched her calves in the hope this would stop her from fainting. She had read that in a magazine once. There was a burning compression in her core, in her very centre; a sensation of heaviness that was difficult to explain. An eternity seemed to have passed before she heard the door open, followed by quick footsteps up the stairs.

'Miriam!' Adam stood still in the one spot in the doorway for a few moments, as he wasn't at all prepared for the shock of seeing Miriam like this. Doubled over in pain, screaming in agony, struggling for breath, and the blood. So much blood. Never before had he seen this much blood. He ran over and knelt down beside her for a few seconds. She looked at him briefly from the corner of her eye. He then dashed to the bathroom to grab some towels, which he carefully placed around her, and then he knelt down on the champagne-coloured towels, his trousers and the towels now both awash with crimson stains, although they were more visible on the towels than his trousers, as he had his black suit on today. Miriam's eyelids were closing. She started to fall to one side, and Adam grabbed hold of her very gently but firmly. 'Stay with me, Miriam, please,' he pleaded with her, his eyes strained at the outside corners, his forehead already damp with nervous sweat. 'Come on, stay with me.'

'Hello? Paramedics,' came a voice from downstairs a few minutes later.

'Upstairs!' shouted Adam.

'It's okay,' he reassured her, in a voice that sounded faraway to Miriam, but a voice which was nevertheless gently audible, calming and soothing, 'you will be okay,' he softly whispered into her ear.

She partly opened her eyes and looked into his. 'Look at me,' she muttered achingly slowly. 'How is any of this okay?' she said, straining to get her words out, her breathing laboured and erratic.

Two paramedics came up behind Adam.

'Excuse me, sir,' said one of them, as they took over and he stepped back.

They got to work immediately; they talked to her, quickly ascertained all the important details about her pregnancy, agreed with each other that she needed oxygen, told her what would happen next, comforted her in the most soothing manner. Her heart silently swelled, as she thought about how between the two paramedics and Adam, she had received more care and concern in the last five minutes than she had received from Zaf in the past 13 weeks of her pregnancy. She would never say it out aloud, but she allowed herself to think it in this moment, even the usual fear of him somehow knowing what she was thinking did not, today, stop or stifle these thoughts.

Adam locked the front door of the house, and stood at the back of the ambulance as they carried the stretcher inside. The male paramedic walked out of the back, and went round to the front of the ambulance to drive, and the woman who remained in the back with Miriam shouted to Adam, 'well, come on then, hop in, we need to get her to hospital pronto.'

Adam quickly jumped in and sat next to Miriam without much hesitation. Adam looked at Miriam, who now had the oxygen mask on. Her eyes were closed. She appeared so vulnerable, so helpless. He didn't know if it was the right thing to do, or the wrong thing to do, but he held her hand ever so lightly. Her hand was warm, and soft to the touch, like the feel of a smooth, silky handkerchief in your palm. In contrast to his gentle touch, she gripped his hand as tightly as she could manage; it lacked the physical force of an energetic squeeze, but the action spoke for itself. He placed his other hand over the top, enclosing her hand in the middle. He encased her delicate, limp hand tightly, for he sensed that this was what she wanted. This was the only sort of protection and support he could give her right now. A human touch, a touch that implies he cares, and is there for her. She turned her head towards him, and opened her eyes a little. Her dark honey brown eyes were heavy with pain. He saw a lonely teardrop seep out of the side of her left eye. He could not in all honesty remember the last time in his life when he had felt this sad.

A couple of hours later, Zaf marched down the corridor in the hospital with some gusto, and found Adam by the drinks machine. He was grabbing his third coffee. He wasn't sure why, because the coffee was truly awful; a beige concoction of instant coffee granules and instant milk powder mixed with tepid hot water which all combined to taste of nothing much and looked like dirty dishwater. But he figured it gave him something to do, other than to look at his mobile phone, or read the same magazine for the fifth time, whilst he waited for an update from the doctor.

'I came as quickly as I could. What's happening? Where's Miriam?' asked Zaf, sounding all concerned, but not really convincing Adam, who hesitated before replying. He stared into Zaf's eyes for a few moments, and he felt nothing but anger and hostility towards him. But then he had to remind himself that whatever else had happened today, this guy was still his boss, and Miriam's husband. He tried his best to keep a civil tone in his voice.

'She's lost the baby. I'm sorry.'

'Oh. I see,' replied Zaf. *That's it?* thought Adam. *That's all you've got to say?*

Adam filled him in with more details about exactly what had happened.

Zaf still showed no emotion of any kind, and Adam wondered if this was going to be the extent of his reaction, or rather lack of reaction, at having just heard that his wife had suffered the most painful experience probably of her entire life, having lost their unborn child. He gave him a little bit of time for any further response of any kind, and none being forthcoming, Adam continued.

'She lost a lot of blood, they have had to give her a transfusion, and now they've taken her to theatre for some surgical procedure. I'm not sure exactly what that is. To remove all the tissue from the uterus, I think the doctor said. He told me the name of the operation, but I can't remember it. They've put her under general anaesthetic, and they did say the operation won't take too long. And she will have to stay in overnight at least.'

'Okay, well thanks for everything you've done, I can take it from here.'

'I don't mind staying, really.'

Adam couldn't explain it to himself in any kind of a logical way, but he really didn't want to leave her here with him. He didn't want Zaf's to be the first face she saw when she woke up, didn't want her to be alone with Zaf when she came around from the general anaesthetic. He always had a niggling suspicion that perhaps things between them weren't quite as hunky dory as most people thought. The wall between his and Zaf's office was pretty thin, and he had probably heard more of the conversations between them than he should have. He doubted anyone else in the office had heard what he had. They hadn't been loud arguments, and there was no shouting by either of them, not even raised voices really, but the tone of their respective voices had always struck him when they had engaged with each other in the privacy of Zaf's office. She was quiet and submissive, giving short or one-word answers. He on the other hand sounded authoritative, demanding even. He never saw or heard this very same interaction between them outside of that environment. And he never really gave it much thought at the time. He put it down to their personalities; she always struck him as quite a subdued woman, and a dutiful wife, whereas he knew Zaf to be a businessman right to his core, and Adam supposed that he conducted his marital relationship in the same way as he did his business; giving out orders and instructions, and expecting them to be followed. Adam knew that Zaf could be taxing, he would even go so far as to say he was very bossy towards Miriam, but what happened today was different. Today Adam had witnessed a level of wilful neglect on Zaf's part that he just couldn't ignore. The medical staff had told him that, when Miriam and Zaf had been in hospital previously, they had specifically informed Zaf that although they had booked Miriam in for the scan, she may miscarry suddenly at any time before that, and if that happened then they should get back to hospital without delay. If Zaf knew that, why hadn't he stayed at home with her, why hadn't he looked after her? What was so urgent about that mystery meeting which Rachel couldn't handle by herself? What sort of a man would leave his wife all alone at a time like that? He had so many questions that he knew would not be answered.

'No. You go back to work. She's my wife. I've got this,' Zaf said coolly.

Both men stared at each other, as though it were a competition to see who would blink first. Adam would have preferred to stick around to see if she was okay, but gave up on this thought given Zaf's insistence. He was her husband after all. Adam, in contrast, was just an employee, albeit an important employee that Zaf relied on heavily, more than anyone else who worked with him, but right now he was just an employee who had stepped in to help out in an emergency, and now that was over, so was his involvement.

'Alright; give her my best when she comes around.'

'Of course,' said Zaf.

'Right, I will be off then,' replied Adam.

15

Birmingham Crown Court
7 November 2019

Adam Anis walks into court and towards the witness box in readiness for Mr De Beaux to begin his questioning. The Prosecution's examination in chief is done; it was, by and large, uneventful, and was over with quite quickly. There were no huge bombshells, no hidden secrets unearthed. It went as expected, in keeping with the statement he had provided to the police. The statement which had, quite inadvertently, turned out to be favourable to the prosecution case, when that really had not been his intention.

Miriam looks at Adam as he walks through the court room. He is dressed in what is probably his favourite black suit; tailored flatteringly to fit his lean body. He has worn with it a geometric patterned royal blue tie that sits on top of a white shirt. His pitch black, often unruly, and naturally curly mass of hair is tamed by a good helping of hair gel to keep it away from his forehead, and out of his eyes. His best feature, thinks

Miriam, is his smile; when he does smile, it is almost always a wide, warm, open-hearted sort of a smile. She hasn't seen that smile from him so far, and she very much doubts that she will.

Adam enters the witness box, and immediately looks over towards Miriam with a renewed sense of disbelief. He can never, and will never believe that Miriam could do such a thing. Despite the awful way in which Zaf had treated her at times, he doesn't think her capable of murdering him. Not Miriam. No. And yet, sadly, he thinks, he hasn't really helped her case much. His remark in his statement to the police, perhaps naively, that he believed Zaf had not treated Miriam well at times, and added to this, his recollection of an argument he heard between them on the phone at the office on the morning of Zaf's death, meant he ended up being summonsed as a Prosecution witness. That had not been his objective in the slightest. Yet that is exactly what has happened. He told the bare truth in a straightforward manner, and has ended up as one of the puppets for the Prosecution. He sees now what he hadn't seen when he had initially been questioned; he sees that the police and the prosecution are only interested in him as a means to helping them to prove their assertions; that Zaf's seemingly 'unfair' treatment of Miriam, coupled with the argument Adam heard on the day that Zaf died, prove that Miriam had all the motive she needed for murdering him, as well as the very appealing prospect of her inheriting his fortune. The latter is another thing he refuses to believe about Miriam.

As it is the turn of the Defence to have a go, in his heart Adam desperately hopes that he can now somehow redeem himself, in some way undo some of the damage, as he sees it, that he has quite unintentionally caused to Miriam's case. He isn't at all sure how he is going to do this, but he is certainly going to try. Mr De Beaux has his own ideas about how this can be turned around.

'If I can turn first to the argument between the defendant and the deceased on the morning of his death. You were at the office. Do you normally go in on a Sunday morning?' asks Mr De Beaux.

'No, I don't, and neither did Zaf usually. I was there because I had booked the coming week off work, but I wanted to leave a tidy desk, so I went in to finish off a few bits and pieces, as I didn't want to come back to a mountain of work the week after,' says Adam.

'It is my understanding that on this day, when you nipped into Zaf's office to speak to him, you heard an argument in full flow, on the telephone, between Zaf and Miriam.'

'Yes.'

'And you heard Zaf say *"Miriam, stop threatening me"*, is that correct?'

'Yes. That is correct.'

'Did you hear the actual words of any threat or threats that the defendant allegedly made?'

'No. I didn't. I could hear her voice, but I couldn't make out what she was saying. I could only hear what Zaf said.'

Mr De Beaux scratches his chin lightly with the top of his Mont Blanc pen for a few seconds.

'Therefore, you only had Zaf's word that Miriam was saying things that were threatening, because you yourself did not hear anything that she actually said?'

'That's right,' confirms Adam.

Mr De Beaux crosses his left ankle with his right foot and leans back a little. He looks at Adam with a slight smile on his face. A reassuring smile.

'What sort of a man was the deceased, in your opinion?'

'In what way do you mean? Personally, or business-wise?'

'Generally speaking, as in how would you describe him? In a few words, say.'

'Very successful. And very ruthless,' replies Adam.

'Very...ruthless,' repeats Mr De Beaux, slowly, as he looks towards the jury, pausing between the two words.

The granny of the jury raises an eyebrow, and folds her arms tightly, waiting for Mr De Beaux to ask, and for Adam to divulge, about this hard-nosed aspect of Zaf's character.

'Can you give us any examples of this ruthless streak Mr Anis, apart from any incidents concerning the accused. Examples of how he dealt with other people.'

'There have been quite a few over the years that I have worked there. Just recently he'd had a number of...disagreements, shall we say, with some of his business friends and acquaintances.'

'Disagreements?'

'Yes, fallings out with people, but quite unfairly in my opinion.'

'As in the deceased had acted unfairly?'

'Yes, I believe so.'

'Can you elaborate please? Who and what are you referring to?'

Adam thinks about Mr De Beaux's questions for a few moments, trying to get the thoughts clear and ordered inside his head before he starts answering the question.

'Sure. There are three fairly recent incidents that come to my mind. The first one concerns Mr Raj Patel.'

'What happened with this Mr Patel?'

'After agreeing to go into partnership with Mr Patel, after giving his word, Zaf later reneged on the deal. Did the dirty on him, you could say.'

'Objection My Lord, this is pure speculation and not particularly relevant,' Ms Godfrey interjects.

'My Lord, Mr Anis is a trusted employee of the business with intimate knowledge of the same. He is a key witness. He therefore must be allowed to continue if we are to receive a balanced and accurate picture of the deceased,' argues Mr De Beaux.

'Objection overruled,' replies the Judge. 'Continue Mr De Beaux, but try to keep it relevant,' He peers over his half-moon reading glasses for added effect.

'I'm obliged, My Lord,' says Mr De Beaux, and he turns back towards Adam Anis. 'You were telling us about Mr Patel.'

'Yes, Zaf and Raj had known each other for quite a long time. Raj is from a family of very successful, specialist wedding caterers, with years of experience in the field. His father and Zaf's father had been good friends in the old days from what I know, but sadly, Raj's father passed away about five or six years ago. Raj wanted to diversify his business, and he mentioned this to Zaf at one of the Chamber of Commerce dinners. Zaf in response suggested the possibility of them doing something together. I was there too, on the same table, when they had this initial chat. They had quite a few meetings after that, and Zaf agreed to go into a new venture with him.'

'And what did this new venture involve?'

'It involved the setting up a chain of café style outlets, serving the same sort of fusion cuisine but in a more casual setting and vibe, and with a more stripped-down menu; street-food style fusion food, you could call it. I sat in on some of those meetings, to advise on the financial side of things. On the say so of Zaf, Raj went ahead and spent a lot of money on securing some initial sites. He paid for valuations, structural surveys, arranged finance, paid brokers fees, legal fees, he put down non-refundable deposits and the like, only for Zaf to turn around at the last minute and say he was no longer interested in going into partnership with him.'

'Do you know why?'

'No. And he never gave an explanation, or at least not one that I know of. When Raj came to the office to tackle him on it, there was quite a heated argument. There were raised voices and I had to go in to Zaf's office at one point and check if everything was okay.'

'And you can't think of any reason why Zaf did this U-turn on the project?'

'I couldn't tell you for certain. As there was no legal agreement between them, Zaf could do whatever he wanted. The whole thing had come about on the basis of mutual trust and understanding. If I am completely honest, I fear that Zaf may have simply used Raj.'

Granny's other eyebrow has joined the first one and is arching even higher. This look of disapproval on granny's face is shared by a few of the others in the jury, including the hippy looking woman, who makes no secret of it; she noticeably shakes her head, and her long dangly feather tipped earrings shake along for the ride.

'In what way do you think Zaf had used Mr Patel?'

'Most of the good ideas for the new venture had come from Raj, especially in terms of marketing the new brand, and also with regards to much of the proposed menu, as he had far more experience with street-style food, whereas Zaf only had in-depth knowledge of high end, à la carte dining with a fusion menu. Raj had some really innovative, impressive plans. I don't know if it had been his intention from the very beginning, or if it developed somewhere along the way, but Zaf intended to pinch Raj's ideas so he could go it alone in the near future.'

The banker man in the jury nods his head ever so slightly, as if to say *why the sly dog!*

'That is quite an allegation, Mr Anis. What evidence do you have of this?' asks Mr De Beaux.

'He told me so himself. He said that he was probably going to pursue it on his own.'

'I see. Going back to that rather heated meeting between the two of them, how did that conclude in the end?'

'Raj left Zaf's office in a fit of anger that day, swearing revenge and the like.'

'Swearing revenge, you say. Can you remember exactly what he said?'

'Something like he would get him back, destroy him, words to that effect.'

Miriam thinks back to that incident. She was at work that day. She was in her office at her computer when she heard the commotion. When she walked out of her office and looked down the corridor, she saw Raj Patel waving his arms around and shouting, and she recalls that Adam was trying to calm him down. Eventually, Adam, the diplomat that he was, did succeed in placating him, and then he disappeared off with him, she assumed to accompany him to the exit. Zaf had never told her what it had all been about, and she was not so brazen as to ask.

'And who else had the deceased had a run in with in the period leading up to his death, that you can personally recall,' asked Mr De Beaux.

'There was Raza Latif.'

'And what was the story with this Mr Latif?'

'Very much like the relationship with the Patel family, Zaf's family and the Latif family went back a long way. Raza's late father used to be head chef with the business many years ago, and had also been a good friend of Zaf's father. He had given many years' services to the business before retiring. The sons didn't follow suit; they set up various businesses, including an IT security firm which Raza now runs. Zaf's as a business has always outsourced all aspects of IT security, and for the past nine years or so the contract had gone to Raza's firm. This contract covered all aspects of IT security and equipment for all the restaurants. After agreeing to renew the contract, which was up for renewal just before he died, before anything was actually signed, Zaf changed his mind, and he signed the contract over to someone else.'

'And do you have any idea why he did this?'

'I have no clue at all, as we had never had any problems with them. Their work was good.'

'And how did Mr Latif feel about all this?'

'Raza was pretty upset, he told me that when I saw him a few weeks later at a social gathering. I think he was especially disappointed given the long connection he and his father had had with the company, and what he saw as his own friendship with Zaf, or at least he had thought them to be friends. He was angry about the treatment he had received, that's for sure, and said he had a good mind to come over to the office and give Zaf a piece of his mind, but in all honesty, he is not hot-headed like Raj. He is quite a pragmatic guy, and he thought it best just to try and move on. As it happens, his company recently merged with another outfit, and he has moved abroad now, and by all accounts is doing very well.'

From the limited number of times she had met Raza Latif, he had come across as a polite, calm sort of a man. She couldn't understand why Zaf would ditch him like that, but then neither could she comprehend why he had tormented her the way he had, or why he had done the dirty on Raj Patel. Goodness knew how many more disgruntled people there were out there, having been lied to or cheated by Zaf.

'Were there any arguments between the deceased and Mr Latif, as there was with Mr Patel?'

'Not that I heard. They had a few telephone conversations, I believe, but no arguments as such as far as I am aware.'

'I see. And you said that there were three recent disagreements from the period of time close to his death which sprung to your mind. What was the third one?'

'Ah, yes, there was Fraser Hunt.'

'Who is?'

'He's a surveyor and a planning consultant.'

Miriam has heard this name before, but she has never met Fraser Hunt, nor is she aware of what had transpired between him and Zaf. Miriam sits perfectly still, waiting to hear, once again, new details that are about to emerge about her late husband that she is wholly ignorant of.

'And what happened with him?' Mr De Beaux asks.

'This is going back a little while now. The second London site had a lot of issues, but the one that was causing Zaf the biggest headache was the planning. He couldn't secure the permission exactly as he wanted it. Planning permission had been issued but subject to certain pretty onerous conditions that Zaf wanted rid of. Everyone told him it couldn't be done. Fraser Hunt agreed to help him with what was thought to be an impossible situation. He worked damned hard for Zaf, and somehow, whether it was through his connections or because of his sheer determination, he managed to get the conditions dropped, so that Zaf ended up with the planning permission exactly as he'd wanted it. Initially, before Fraser started the work, I was in a meeting with both of them, when they discussed the matter at length, and I gave my input in my role to advise on the financial aspects of the project. Zaf promised Fraser many things in that meeting, should Fraser be successful. This was in addition to his fees, which Fraser kept to a reasonable sum in any event because of these other incentives.'

'What were these incentives?'

'Things like personal introductions and endorsements in relation to certain influential and well-connected people that would secure Fraser lucrative work in the future, a promise to help him get onto the Chambers of Commerce Board, and a few other things which I can't recall. But as soon as Zaf had the permission for the second London restaurant just as he wanted it, he cut Fraser off. He never said why. He stopped taking his calls. He refused to see Fraser when he turned up at the office one time. Zaf sent me to reception with instructions to calm him down, and then to get rid of him. Fraser was obviously unhappy, but in the end, he didn't feel there was much he could do about it, apart from, as he told me, to tell anyone and everyone who would listen about what a snake Zaf had been.'

'Would you say, therefore, that the deceased had a good few enemies?'

'Yes, that would be a reasonable comment.'

'All of them holding some sort of a grudge?' asks Mr De Beaux.

'Yes.'

Mr De Beaux feels satisfied, and a little lucky that the Judge has given him a good run. 'Thank you. No further questions,' he says, and sits down. He looks towards Ms Godfrey but she is preoccupied with some notes. She's scribbling away frantically with a red pen.

'Do you wish to re-examine Ms Godfrey?' asks the Judge.

Ms Godfrey finishes the last red scrawl, and then jumps to her feet. 'Just a few questions, My Lord,' she replies and turns to look at Adam.

'Mr Anis. Did you personally see the defendant physically mistreating any of these three men that you claim he had disagreements with?'

'Not personally, no. It was just--'

'Did you witness him shouting at any of them, being verbally abusive or threatening?'

'No.'

'In the incident with Mr Patel, which you had to go and intervene in, who was doing the shouting or threatening?'

Adam pauses for a few seconds, but knows he can't escape giving an answer. 'It was Mr Patel.'

'The deceased was not the one yelling?'

'No.'

16

16 July 2017

'No, you're not driving that banger anymore,' said Zaf as he walked past Miriam. She was just about to pick up the keys to her beloved old Honda Jazz from the sideboard in the hallway.

It was the first car she had ever bought, and now, five months into married life down in Brum, she found it very nippy about town in the busy Birmingham traffic. Sneaking into small spaces and switching lanes at Five Ways roundabout was a synch in this car. She had bought it second hand, but with a sense of pride, after having saved up enough money from her part time work as a student to buy it outright. She and Nina had had some fun times speeding around in that little "electric blue baby", as Nina used to refer to it. Driving out for midnight snacks in Rusholme, sometimes to eat hot and spicy *samosa chaat*, other times it would be to grab something to feed that sweet tooth they both had, and that usually meant them going into Delhi Sweet Centre and devouring freshly fried fat spirals of orangey golden *jalebi*, dripping with the cardamom and rose water infused sugar syrup in which they had been dunked. It was a shot of sticky sweet heaven, and oh so satisfying. There were also random trips to the beach, the compulsory spin out to the shopping malls, or just a drive out to hang out with friends. She recalled one summer when the two of them had hopped over the Pennines back into Miriam's home county, and visited Bolton Abbey late at night. They hadn't intended to go that late, but with one thing and another, they got there just as the night was drawing in. The darkness had made the place initially feel eerily scary, but that feeling oddly morphed into a sense of calm and serenity. It was just the two of them, in this vast expanse of land in which sat the remains of the 12th century Yorkshire monastery, bursting with the history and drama of the medieval era. It had been a memorable experience; they had laid back on the grass and looked up at a clear, crisp, silent night. They had never seen so many stars in their lives. They felt a strange sense peace which could only have come about as a result of being there at that peculiar time; such solitude was normally hard to come by at this popular spot, as in the daytime it thronged with tourists and travellers from near and far, walking the grounds, or sitting in the tea shop eating hot buttered sultana teacakes washed down with copious amounts of Yorkshire tea.

Miriam dragged herself away from her reminiscing, and decided to find out what Zaf was talking about in relation to her car. He had already settled himself in the lounge and switched on the news channel. BBC today. An episode of Hard Talk.

'What do you mean, Zaf, about the car?' she asked him as she entered the lounge, but before she could get a reply, the doorbell rang. He continued watching the interview on the television; the host was grilling some politician from some South American country. Of course, she went to see who it was at the door. This was an unsaid rule; Miriam always answered the door, unless Zaf said otherwise.

When she opened the door, she was a little taken aback to

find one of the waiters from the restaurant stood in the doorway. This was quite a surprise. Members of staff rarely came to the house. Before she could speak to the man, Zaf came up behind her. 'Miriam, go put some chai on, and fry a few pakoras,' he ordered her.

She could hear them exchanging *salaams* as she walked off. Miriam went straight to the kitchen without any hesitation, although she did secretly wish that Zaf would tell her in advance about any guests that he had invited to the house, and the need for her to prepare refreshments. He would often spring things on her without notice. But she had grown accustomed to it. She kept any grumbles that she felt to herself; they lay quietly simmering inside her.

She got to work fast. She quickly peeled and sliced the potatoes and onions, very thinly, so that the they were virtually see-through, then she added them to the *besan*, and into this chickpea flour she added chilli powder, cumin seeds, salt, dried fenugreek leaves, *amchoor*, chopped fresh coriander, and enough lukewarm water to form the batter. The addition of the *amchoor* was something she had learnt from her mother; the dried mango powder gave the pakoras a tangy hit. The same could be achieved with *anardana*, her mum had told her. If anything, the dried pomegranate powder was even tangier. She put the large wok like *karahi* of oil on to heat, placed a pan of water on the hob also, to boil up for the desi tea, and in less than half an hour she had the tea, pakoras, chutney and biscuits ready on a tray. She knocked on the door to the living room with her foot, holding onto the tray with both hands. She waited for a response; either he would come and take the tray from her, or she would be told to come in. She heard her husband tell her to enter.

Miriam placed the tray in the middle of the coffee the table. She placed Zaf's newspaper on the lower shelf of the table. She noticed that Zaf had not turned the television off, rather he had paused the programme; the guest on the interview had his mouth wide open and his right hand raised; Miriam thought he looked rather comical.

'*Assalam-u-alaykum,*' said the waiter guy.

'*Walay-kum-asalam,*' she replied, turning her head away from the frozen politician on the screen and towards their guest.

'I can't thank you enough times, Madam, really, it is most kind of you, sister,' declared the waiter guy.

Miriam tilted her head to one side as she surveyed the man; his toothy smile lit up his otherwise uninteresting face. He couldn't be that grateful for the refreshments, could he? Or could he...Miriam wondered. It was only desi tea and some pakoras. No big deal. The grin on his face seemed to say otherwise.

'You and Sir are very big hearted, I mean to say, who does helps any person these days,' the waiter guy continued in his strong South Asian accent, 'peoples, they talk very much, when they say if you need anything let us know. As soon as you say you need their help, nowhere they are to be seen. Acting like they never know you.'

Miriam listened quietly, whilst she remained standing in the middle of the room. She was unable to fathom what on earth the man was talking about.

'I mean to say you are both most kind and generous to gives your car to us.'

Miriam looked at Zaf, unsure if she had heard right.

'It is our pleasure,' declared Zaf, speaking for both of them. He sat comfortably in his oversized leather armchair, his arms splayed wide on the armrests, his demeanour like a king on his throne, whose subjects had been summoned before him. 'Like I said, I have ordered a new car for Miriam, and I know that you and your wife are in need of a small run around, so it suits everyone.'

'But are you sure we can't pay something for this, Sir?' asked the waiter.

'We wouldn't hear of such a thing, would we darling?'

Miriam's brain finally caught up with the conversation in the room.

'No,' Miriam said quickly, 'of course not,' and she promptly walked out of the lounge.

She strolled out into the back garden for some fresh air. She walked down towards the far end of the huge manicured lawn, and sat on the bespoke blue cushioned wooden garden swing (hand made by a carpenter to Zaf's specific requirements) complete with a matching blue canopy. She looked at the perfect green stripes; lines of deep emerald green going one way, and a paler green, like the shade of a conference pear, going the other way. This was not her handiwork; the gardener came regularly to mow the lawn, and attend to the hedges. Still, that left her much to do in terms of planting, weeding, trimming and the like.

This was her place to escape to, whenever it was possible, and necessary, if things inside the house got a bit too much; when she felt suffocated, as though the walls were closing in on her, or when she gasped for air because one of her panic attacks started to come on. At such times, she came out here, right to the back of the garden, to breathe. She liked to sit down here to inhale the calming scent that drifted from the flowers down in this section; the heady smelling lavenders and lilacs on the one side, and the sweet honeysuckle on the other. Not only did their fragrance calm her, but their beauty never failed to soothe her eyes. And she loved to watch her beloved birds feeding on the food that she put out for them every day, or observe them frolicking in the bird bath. She needed this whenever she felt panicky.

She thought back to her first panic attack. It was seven weeks and two days after she married Zaf. She remembered it exactly. She was out at the time, at the supermarket doing the grocery shopping, on her way back from work. That was another one of those jobs that was her responsibility, Zaf had told her. She was at the till, piling the groceries from the trolley onto the conveyor belt when he phoned her on her mobile. She quickly fumbled around in her bag for her phone, and dragged it out just to answer in time. 'Did you send the package I gave you, the one I said had to go by guaranteed next day delivery?' he asked her. 'Yes, I posted it, but I sent it by signed for delivery, because that's what you told me to do.' There was a three second delay, and then the verbal tirade began; how dare she lie, he definitely said guaranteed next day delivery, if the recipients didn't get it by tomorrow, she would be responsible and she would suffer the consequences, how many times had he told her now that she has to listen to him more carefully, show some respect, do as she was told. And so on, and so on. He continued with his outburst, and she let him, for she could find nothing else to say in return. When he got off the phone, that's when it happened; there and then, in the supermarket, at the till, she suffered her first panic attack. She violently gasped for breath, like a fish pulled out of water; it was as if her throat had been sealed up, and instead of letting any air go in, her body was trying to push out whatever air she had left in her lungs. The cashier left her till and came around, but Miriam still could not draw breath. The woman held her hand whilst a few of the other shoppers gathered around. 'Give her some space!' shouted the cashier to the spectators. 'Slow, easy breaths,' she said to Miriam, who continued to struggle for air. She could hear the other shoppers, whispering, feeling sorry for her. But her gaze was fixed on the ice cream on the conveyor belt. It will melt, she thought to herself. The Haagen-Dazs double Belgian chocolate chip ice cream, Zaf's favourite, was in her eyeline as she spluttered and fought for air. One of the shoppers suddenly jumped forward. 'It's okay, I'm a nurse,' he said to the cashier. 'I heard the commotion all the way up the bakery aisle. Now then, let's have a look at you.' As soon as he saw Miriam, he got to work. It took him a little while, but he talked her through the breathing technique, to bring her out of the attack, and eventually managed to calm Miriam down, so that she was back to a normal level of breathing.

Since that first attack, she was now slowly getting better with her breathing, and coming out to the garden whenever she felt overwhelmed certainly helped to prevent her reaching the advanced stage of a full-on attack. When she was out here, alone, she could think about stuff. Her brain felt like it could relax, and contemplate. Right now, she was annoyed with Zaf. It wasn't about not getting any money for the car, or not wanting to help this man and his family. She would just like to have been asked, and if not asked, then at least told, in advance, that a man would be coming to take her car away because Zaf had promised it to him. It was her car after all. Okay, so it wasn't worth much, but it was *hers*. By doing what he did, it felt to her as though Zaf had stripped a piece of her identity away from her; without her permission, without even simply the courtesy of a mention. Just like that. But she couldn't say any of this out aloud. Because if she did, he was sure to say she was being ungrateful. Was she? Maybe she was. Maybe she should perhaps stop being so ungrateful, right? She could hear him saying it to her *"I'm buying you a brand-new car, none of my friend's wives drive such an expensive car, and yet here you are crying over that rust pot. What exactly is your problem?"*

What *was* the problem? Miriam asked herself. She said it out as loud, almost yelled it, but only in her head, only to herself.

Generous, benevolent Zaf. Saint Zaf. Ungrateful Miriam. That was the truth, wasn't it? Or was it?

People saw what they saw, and what they saw was that which was presented to them. Like a foregone conclusion.

It was all about perception, and perception did not equal reality. What people witnessed, as opposed to what actually happened, were two entirely different matters which could not always be reconciled. There was a disconnect, and Miriam herself could not understand where the two met, if ever.

On the outside, the general consensus was that Zaf was a devoted husband. The *duniya*, the world, as Miriam saw it, (for she *was* all alone, and everyone else out there was just "the world" to her) could only see the doting husband. The world decided that it was she who had bagged a good catch in Zaf; a husband who saw to her every need, who spoilt her rotten. So, who wouldn't want to be married to Zaf? Handsome, rich, intelligent, generous to a fault. This is what everyone was meant to see, and this is what everyone *did* see. But it was all a deception. Most of the time Miriam herself could not extricate the reality from the mirage. But she knew that it was all an illusion, carefully crafted by the master of illusions.

After she had moved down to Birmingham and was told by Zaf that she was to work in the family business, she had received clear, detailed instructions from him.

'From the salary that I pay you, you will be responsible for all the household expenditure; groceries, household goods, utility bills, items for the garden, things for yourself. And you will not spend frivolously. Got that?'

'Yes,' she had replied, whilst continuing to acclimatise to the new reality of taking and following instructions. He never wrote any instructions down; there was no record. He said it and she had to remember and act upon it.

When he had ordered the brand-new Mercedes C-class

Coupe on lease purchase, the deposit had come from *her* bank account. And the monthly rental and insurance payments were debited from *her* bank account. Yet somehow in eyes of the world, *Zaf* had paid a fortune for her expensive new car. How generous of him.

Every month, Miriam watched the pennies, as her money dwindled out of her account to pay for all the bills and expenses for such a large home, and she made payments on the car that she never asked for.

When the mood took him, he himself would buy her expensive jewellery, designer shoes, clothes and handbags. There would then often follow the directives as to what to wear, where to wear it, how to wear it, which shoes went with which dress went with which bag went with which necklace went with which watch. But not always. Other times, he would give vague, ambiguous instructions; dress smartly, get glammed up, dress modestly, cover your head, wear the Armani jeans, don't wear jeans. These episodes where these indistinct, fuzzy instructions were given were hard for, and hard on, Miriam. If she got it wrong, always unintentionally, she would be told about it, and reminded of it, for a long time to come.

He himself would choose and buy all of the expensive items. Never her. Mentions of material possessions and designer brands would be carefully dropped into conversations with others by him, never her. 'Oh, I've just ordered Miriam the new C-class...Miriam loves Louis Vuitton...she can never choose what her favourite perfume is so I always order her a few...I love the new cashmere collection at Harrods, I ordered Miriam some at the weekend, three different colours...Prada sunglasses definitely look great on Miriam...'

When they went out as a couple, she would be paraded on his arm, donned in the finest gear for all to notice. People would see Burberry, Chanel, Calvin Klein, her shoes, her dress, her handbag, her jewellery, *but not her*. People would see a generous, loving husband who looked after his little wife who had been blessed enough to marry him. Between the designer labels and the adulation for Zaf, she felt invisible. She *was* invisible.

There was a dichotomy that went further; on the outside she would remain calm, she would keep smiling, be the perfectly dutiful wife, show no cracks in the veneer, but on the inside, the emotional hurt would continue to grow and fester, shielded from the rest of the world, left unchecked, furtively thriving like a cancer you cannot see, but one which has the potential to kill. The toxicity of the internal effects due to the treatment she endured at the hands of her husband would continue to flourish to such dangerous depths that even Miriam herself would not realise that, instead of fearing Zaf, she should instead be more fearful of her own self. She buried her head in oblivion; her only thoughts were how to get from one day to the next, how to survive from one mistake to the next, how to cope with one episode of feeling like a total failure to the next. The only inescapable certainty uppermost in her mind was that she had to somehow endure this sorrowful existence, lurching from moment to moment. She had never once anticipated that all the inner, unseen, mental damage caused by the behaviour of this man would land her in a crown court trial accused of his murder, and nor did she foresee that it would lead her to a point in her life when she questioned if she could ever find any reason to carry on.

17

Birmingham Crown Court
8 November 2019

On his arrival in to the witness box, the next prosecution witness, Saeed Shah, or Sid as he is more commonly referred to by those who know him well, takes a wide stance, and spends a few moments adjusting his tie.

Ever the lawyer, he is dressed in a slick dark blue Tom Ford pin striped suit, with a thin pale blue tie. The smooth look is accessorised with shiny round signature Mont Blanc cufflinks. And some of the more observant in the courtroom may have caught a glance of his gleaming Gucci black leather shoes. He lifts his head, but not for long, as for the second time he fidgets with his already dead straight tie. He makes no effort to look towards Miriam. She knows it's a very deliberate thing with Sid, avoiding catching her eye. On those occasions in the past when she had seen him, a couple of times at work, and a few times socially, he used to do the same thing; he would say the bare minimum to her, the very least that he could possibly get away with, and, generally speaking, he had no time for her. She fancied he thought himself far too superior, or he determined that she was far too inferior, or perhaps both. Whatever the reason, he has certainly never given her the time of day.

Presently, Miriam has her suspicions about how this is going to go. She knows that he and Zaf were close, very close, and Sid was the one person, perhaps the *only* person, Zaf used to turn to for advice, someone he could lean on, or go to for an ear when he needed a sounding board. Sid was also most likely the *only* person Zaf confided in, and, as far as she could tell from her two years of marriage, Sid was the one and only person that Zaf showed equal respect to.

'Mr Shah, can you explain how you knew the deceased, and for how long you had known him?' Ms Godfrey asks Sid.

'I was Zaf's lawyer, and also his friend. We had known each other for over fifteen years. We met at university.'

'As his lawyer, presumably he turned to you in relation to all his legal affairs?'

'No. I dealt with his personal legal affairs only. He had different lawyers for his company and business affairs; a large London law firm. They attended to all his non-personal matters.'

Ms Godfrey twirls her blue pen around between her fingers, as she bobs her head between reading her notes and looking at her witness. 'You met with the deceased on the day he was killed. Can you tell us about that?'

'I received a call from Zaf at around 11.00 am. He asked if we could meet up. He said that it was urgent. I asked him where he was, because I could come to him, as I wasn't busy myself. He told me he was in his office at the restaurant at the time, but he told me not to come to the office. He didn't want us to meet there. He asked me to meet him in St Paul's Square instead.'

'In the city centre?'

'Yes. In the Jewellery Quarter.'

'Why do you think he asked you to meet him there?'

Sid cocks his head to one side, and scratches his neck for a couple of seconds. He stands a little wider, taking up more space, before answering. 'I wasn't sure at the time. But I think in hindsight perhaps he just didn't want our conversation to be overheard by anyone at the office.'

'I will ask you about your conversation with him shortly. But first, can you tell us,' continues prosecuting counsel, now raising her eyebrows high for extra impact, 'how did he seem to you when you met him?'

There is a brief pause before Sid responds. 'He seemed a little...agitated.'

Ms Godfrey crosses one arm across her waist, and raises her other to rest the palm on the side of her face. She asks gently, 'why did you think that was?'

'I had assumed that he was a bit stressed with work. At the time, I didn't think anything of it beyond that.'

'What did he want to see you about? Was it a legal matter?'

'Yes. He said he wanted to make a will.'

'Was that that to replace an existing will, or did he not have a will already?'

'He didn't actually have a will, like many people I know. I had been on at him for ages about getting his will sorted, and whilst he always said that he would get around to it eventually, despite my frequent nagging, he never did. This was the first time he had sat down with me to talk about preparing his will.'

Ms Godfrey puts down her blue pen, and now rests both her hands down on the table front of her. 'What did he say to you when he talked about his proposed will? What did he want his will to contain?'

'His instructions took me by surprise if I'm honest.'

'In what sense?'

'The main provision that struck me was that...erm...'

'Go on, please.'

'...the main thing that he wanted, quite adamantly, was to exclude Miriam from his will.'

The courtroom starts to buzz with chatter for a few moments, which subsides when the Judge gives everyone a disgruntled look; he doesn't even have to say anything this time. The man in the jury who looks like a retired headteacher, wearing a beige Argyll jumper under his brown blazer, perks up, and looks intrigued by this revelation. He begins to chew the nail of the middle finger of his right hand, and like the audience and his fellow jurors, waits pensively, keen to hear what Sid has to say next after this latest disclosure. It's not long before the whole courtroom is as quiet as a feather landing on the ground. Sid still manages to avoid catching Miriam's eye.

'He wanted to exclude his wife from his will,' says Ms Godfrey, slowly, rhythmically, with little high and low notes, stretching those few words out as far as she can. 'Did he say why?'

'He told me that things had not been good between them for some time. They didn't really get on, he said. He told me that he had tried really hard to make things work, but nothing ever seemed to please her. He was also troubled by the fact that her family were now on the scene, after having nothing to do with her for years, and to be frank he distrusted their motives.'

'In what sense did he not trust their motives?'

'In the sense that: was Miriam's father really keen to reunite with his estranged daughter? Or had he, and his son, Miriam's brother, suddenly seen pound signs now they knew who she was married to.'

Miriam looks down at the ground. There is a speck of something white on her navy flats. *How did that get there?* she wonders. There was always a blemish where it ought not to be, a stain where it ought to be spotless. She always found it, or it found her.

'He suspected the latter,' adds Sid, although Miriam doesn't hear it, as she has zoned out for a few seconds. Zaf's voice is now ringing in her ears. He is managing to get to her from beyond his grave; *your dad never cared about you before, for all these years, and now he's suddenly missing his beloved daughter. Yeah, right! F-ing social climbing gold diggers!*

Miriam's body spasms abruptly, and she is back again. She lifts her head up, and tells herself she will not to let Zaf speak to her in this way. *He has gone. Remember? He can't control you anymore.* She just needs to believe it.

'I see. So, you were instructed to draft a will which would completely exclude the defendant?' asks Ms Godfrey, dragging her words once again, hammering the point home even though this point has not escaped anyone in the room. Mr De Beaux rolls his eyes at the unnecessary repetition and time-wasting.

'Yes,' says Sid.

'What were his other instructions?'

'He wanted his parents to be the beneficiaries of 75% of his estate, in equal shares, and his sister would get 25% of the residuary estate, after payment of legacies, debts etc. I did explain to him that excluding Miriam from the will could be legally challenged, but he didn't care about that. I also said we should meet with his tax advisor to look at the most tax effective ways of arranging matters before drawing up the will. However, he didn't care about that either. He did not want any delay at all, he wanted the will in place as soon as possible. I warned him against rushing things, but he was absolutely adamant. He said he would email me details of the trustees and information about legacies and other specific instructions in the evening, and he asked that I start drafting the will as soon as possible after that. I told him I'd make a start on it as soon as I received his email, and whizz it across to him by email for approval in the next day or two.'

'Obviously this proposed will of the deceased was never even drafted, let alone executed. If we put this current court case out of our minds for just one moment, can you tell the court, Mr Shah, who would benefit from the deceased's death in the absence of a will?'

'Under the laws of intestacy, the defendant would be the sole beneficiary.'

A number of mutterings flare up around the room once again, and this time the Judge has to speak up; his request for silence is eventually heeded and everyone slowly pipes down.

'Was there anything else that he discussed with you?'

'Yes. There was.'

'What else did he say to you?'

Now, finally, Sid looks at Miriam. He has never liked her. But equally, she has never liked him. She has never liked his face. You instantly warm to a face, or you don't. And she never warmed to his. His button eyes have a shade of cunning imprinted into the small dark rounds, his eyebrows are brooding and pervasive, his jaw is angular and harsh. But then again, Miriam knows it isn't solely about how his face looks, it is also more about the vibes it gives. Her mother used to say that you can often see the goodness in a person by the *noor* on their face. This has nothing to do with beauty, she had told her, it is about the purity of light that a face radiates, a positive aura that seeps out of them, an invisible glow that warms the heart of the observer. Sid looks away, but Miriam continues to look at him. There is nothing good about this man, she has always sensed this with certainty, and she knows that whatever is about to come out of the mouth of this man will not be anything good either.

'He asked me to start preparing divorce proceedings.'

Once again, whispers start fizzing around the courtroom, as this revelation really has come as a surprise to everyone.

'Silence in the court!' announces the Judge, now beginning to sound like a cracked record, and slowly, the hum evaporates back into silence.

Miriam feels her heart pounding rapidly against her chest as the revelation hits her like a punch in the gut. She takes in a few calming inhalations. She locks her fingers and rubs her palms together, and finds that the repetition begins to soothe her.

'He asked you to prepare divorce papers; based on what?' asks Ms Godfrey.

'Based on the defendant's unreasonable behaviour.'

18

31 March 2019

'Unreasonable behaviour – yes, you can go with that but I will need particulars,' said Sid.

'Hmph. I can give you a list as long as your arm,' replied Zaf.

They sat on a bench in the middle of the last complete remaining Georgian Square in Birmingham, an old haunt of Zaf's from days gone by. The bench overlooked St. Paul's Church; a stunning rectangular shaped Grade I listed building constructed in the 1700's. Whenever Zaf was down in London and he happened to drive past St Martin in the Fields, he never failed to notice how similar they were. Zaf liked this square. There was a period of time, before Zaf married Miriam, when the business had a litigious case which lasted a number of years; Zaf's sued another restaurant company for passing off, and eventually, after a three-year battle, they won. The Chambers at which Zaf's barrister was based was happily situated over-looking the square and the church. Zaf would often sit in the square to think about things, or when he needed a breather from the conference with counsel, although he hadn't been down this end for a few years now. If it had been good enough for the giants of commerce, industry and revolution such as Matthew Boulton and James Watt to frequent, then it was good enough for him.

'I thought things were okay with you two,' Sid remarked.

'Appearances can be deceptive.'

'I do recall at the time I did tell you not to rush into marriage with this girl.'

Zaf tutted loudly. 'Is this your "I told you so" moment? Go on then, now's your chance.'

'No. I'm not having a go mate, I'm just saying. You should have learnt from me if nothing else. You know full well what I think of these desperate, lower class, trashy northern girls; all doe eyed and naive looking, they flutter their eyelashes at you, and us being the suckers that we are, we fall for it. Fall for their supposedly innocent charms, and their propensity to indulge us with what seems like their unswerving devotion. But really, it's all an act, a good one mind you, but an act nevertheless; they're just out to fleece you for whatever they can.'

Zaf looked up at the dull sky. Clouds continued to gather and threaten; he zipped up his jacket and folded up the collars, encouraged to do so by the nippy breeze which he felt most acutely across his ears and neck.

'I know Sid, you're right,' replied Zaf, with a weak shake of the head. 'I admit it. I should have listened to you, but she kept pushing me to marry as quickly as possible. At the time, I was besotted, I thought she was the one; she was pretty, kind, thoughtful. But I went on to discover that not only are we two completely different people and mismatched in that sense, but she wasn't the loving, caring person she made herself out to be. She put up a good show in the beginning. But not long after we were married, I saw her true colours. But of course, by then it was too late.'

'I understand all that. But being "different people" isn't enough to get your petition through the courts. Nor are vague statements like she wasn't the woman you thought she was, or you just don't get along with each other. I need at least four or five solid incidents and details of her unreasonable behaviour.'

'Four or five? Hmm. I can give you forty or fifty, mate. Mood swings, flirting with other men, embarrassing me in public, being ungrateful for everything I give her, being unsupportive, neglecting my needs. The list goes on and on. I could write a bloody book about it!' Zaf let out a small snigger, which then diffused to a tiny pursed smile.

'Okay, I hear you. When you get back home, start putting things down in writing; I need a timeline, I need dates and I need full particulars for each act of unreasonable behaviour that you want to use. It may not feel great revisiting everything like that, re-examining all the problems in your marriage, but it has to be done. Then email it across to me together with a copy of your marriage certificate. You can give me the original next time we meet.'

'Cool. I will make a start when I get back home.'

'Is that all?' asked Sid.

'No. There's one more thing.'

'What's that then?'

'It's about my will,' said Zaf, as he turned to look straight at Sid, with a serious look on his face. 'Apart from excluding Miriam, there is something else that I need you to do.'

19

Birmingham Crown Court
8 November 2019

'Do you think, Mr Shah, that the deceased was justified in making the decisions he had made, and which he disclosed to you on the 31 March 2019?' Mr De Beaux looks alert and raring to go, his perky eyes indicating that he is relishing the idea of grilling Sid.

Sid clears his throat briefly before answering. 'It's not my job to judge. My job is to give legal advice and to carry out my client's instructions,' he replies, very self-assuredly.

'But you didn't have just a client lawyer relationship, did you? You were also very good friends I believe?'

'We were friends, yes, but that was completely separate from our professional relationship.'

'Hmmm. Seeing as though there was a social element, did *you* personally ever witness any unreasonable behaviour on the part of the defendant?' asks Mr De Beaux, whilst flicking over a page in his ring binder of papers.

'I can't say I did personally, but I am sure that if Zaf said *she* behaved unreasonably, then she probably did behave unreasonably. He had no reason to lie to me.'

'*She* has a name,' remarks Mr De Beaux, half defensively, half forcefully.

Sid doesn't respond.

Mr De Beaux leans over in Sid's direction, and places both his palms on the table. 'Mr Shah, how many times have you been divorced?'

Ms Godfrey takes to her feet quickly, like a bouncy jack-in-the-box. 'Objection, My Lord! This question has no relevance.'

'Sustained. Stay on track please Mr De Beaux,' says the Judge, letting out a slight sigh at the end of his sentence.

'I was merely wishing to explore whether after three divorces this might have impaired his opinion—'

'Enough, Mr De Beaux,' the Judge chastises him, in a slightly raised voice, and he seals the reprimand with a long, solid, unnerving stare to demonstrate his objection to Mr De Beaux cheekily sneaking that piece of information into the jury's ears, and yet, Mr De Beaux suspects that His Lordship, in his younger days, would have done exactly the same thing in his shoes.

'Very well, My Lord.'

Mr De Beaux stifles a faint grin, and flicks further through a couple of pages of highlighted notes quickly before continuing.

'Mr Shah. You have explained very briefly the provisions of the deceased's intended will. However, do you think there may be any detail that you have omitted?'

'I don't believe so.'

'A straight yes or no is what I am after.'

'As far as I can remember, no.'

Another qualified answer, thinks Mr De Beaux, expressed with a proviso that is very much a lawyerly type of get out clause – as far as I can remember, as far as I am aware, to the best of my knowledge and belief...never just an upfront yes or no. He can't put his finger on what it is about this slippery eel that is not quite sitting right with him, but Mr De Beaux has enough miles on the clock to realise when someone is hiding something. This man is not perhaps being so much dishonest as he is being selectively honest. Mr De Beaux quietly acknowledges to himself that it is time to decide, within the next few seconds, whether or not he wants to pursue this hunch of his, this feeling that he is holding back. He's done his research in case he needs to pull a few rabbits out of the hat, and now he has to decide whether to take a chance on it or move on. Decisions, decisions, thinks Mr De Beaux. *Oh, hang it,* he finally resolves, *I'm going in!*

'I wonder if I may remind you of a certain investigation by the Solicitors Disciplinary Tribunal back in 2016 where it was alleged, and found, that you had been dishonest?'

'Objection, My Lord. This has no bearing on the current matter,' says Ms Godfrey, jumping up and out of her box again.

'To the contrary, I believe, as I am sure the court does too, that the honesty and integrity of a witness is of uppermost importance,' says Mr De Beaux.

'Overruled. Continue,' orders the Judge.

'May I remind you that not only are you here as a witness and under oath, Mr Shah, which comes with its own responsibilities, but as a Solicitor of the Supreme Court, you are held to higher standards than the general public, and you are duty bound to uphold those rigorous standards set by your profession. In particular, standard 4, to act with honesty, and standard 5, to act with integrity.'

'Yes, of course, I understand all that,' he replies, with a speculatively raised eyebrow. Mr De Beaux can tell that Sid is trying to get the measure of him, but perhaps he's not quite sure yet. His right eye twitches a couple of times, and he blinks it out.

Mr De Beaux pauses for a short while, as he so often does for effect. Time to bring out another piece of information that may or may not yield anything. This guy knows everything about Zaf's personal life, and counsel is sure he will know something about this too, if it is of any importance in the first place, that is. *Blast it*, he thinks to himself, *in for a penny, in for a pound.*

'My client has informed me that a few months before her husband's death, when she was carrying out the administrative duties set by her husband, she saw a bank statement for a personal account of his that she had never seen before.' Mr De Beaux slowly places his left arm behind his back before continuing. 'She wasn't aware that he even had an account with this particular bank. She noticed a specific payment that was made by the defendant from this personal account to an unknown person or persons, the only reference on the bank statement being "SKR" followed by a series of numbers. There was no name. It was a large sum paid by standing order. The reason she remembers it well is because when she mentioned it to her husband later that day that she had come across the statement for this specific account that she wasn't aware of, and asked him where he wanted her to file it, as she couldn't find a folder for it, his reaction was a little over the top, shall we say. He was very angry with her. He told her it related to some legal matter which was of no concern to her. He accused her of being nosey, and told her she was not to enter his office again to see to his filing unless he was also present in the room, and that in any event he would file his own bank statements from thereon in.'

Sid blinks a few times, and then looks down at his Gucci shoes. His eye is twitching again.

'Do you know anything about this mystery bank account and payee?' asks Mr De Beaux.

There follows a brief pause, giving Sid a few seconds to collect his thoughts.

Mr De Beaux knows he is very much on a fishing expedition with this piece of information that Miriam has only recently revealed to him, but he thinks it worth pursuing until the Judge tells him otherwise. It may pay off, it may not, but there is certainly no harm in fishing, Mr De Beaux thinks. The up to now self-assured, overly confident Sid doesn't look quite so confident anymore, and is yet to answer the question.

'Let's put this another way; did you discuss anything else on that day when you met the deceased at St Paul's Square, apart from what you have already divulged to the court? You made mention of other legacies; what did you mean by that? Legacies to who? Did the defendant make provision for anyone else in the will?' asks Mr De Beaux. A long shot, thinks Mr De Beaux, but the further you cast your line, the more chance you will catch something.

Sid opens his mouth with some hesitation. 'Yes,' he eventually replies.

Bingo! Mr De Beaux shouts in his mind, although he knows he can't count his chickens just yet. The additional information may prove to be useless in the end. *Let's see.*

'What else did the deceased say to you?'

'He told me something, but he made me swear not to tell anyone else. He must have known that I would never disclose anything he told me to anyone anyway; I always treated whatever he said with complete confidence. But even knowing that, he still made me promise to keep it to myself.'

'Keep what to yourself, Mr Shah?'

'He asked me to...'

'Yes? Go on,' urges Mr De Beaux.

'He asked me to prepare...a secret will.'

Fishing does pay off sometimes, Mr De Beaux thinks to himself; he feels as though he might have caught a big one! Time to reel it in.

'For the benefit of the members of the jury, can you explain what a secret will is.'

'Yes. A secret will is also known as a secret trust. You can have a half secret trust or a fully secret trust, and Zaf wanted the latter. So, in basic terms, in his will he was going to make a legacy in favour of person A, and he asked me to be person A, and I would then hold the property on trust for another person, person B, known as the beneficiary, the one who would receive the legacy. Neither the existence of the trust nor the identity of the secret beneficiary, person B, would be stated in the will.'

'Who was the secret beneficiary?'

'The simple answer is, I don't know.'

'Did you not ask him?'

'Yes of course I asked him, but he said he would email all the details to me in the evening, along with everything else that I had asked for, which seemed perfectly reasonable to me at the time, so I didn't push him on it. However, he was killed that afternoon, before he had a chance to relay his full instructions to me, so I never got to discover who this secret beneficiary was. I'm not sure that we will ever know now. The thing is, this whole meeting, the impulsive behaviour, wanting to make a will and petition for divorce at break neck speed, it wasn't like him. I asked him, why the rush, why now. He said something like, you never know what's around the corner, and that he had do this now.'

'What happened after that?'

'I suggested we should go for some coffee, or grab a bite to eat. Zaf looked at his phone and realised it was 2 o'clock and he said he needed to go home. He had to talk to Miriam.'

20

9 January 2019

Miriam smiled to herself when she read the text from Nina. She was back in the country tomorrow, and she said she was going to make time and come and stay over. It had been a while since they had seen each other. *Would this weekend suit?* She had asked Miriam. She was thinking of coming down on Friday evening, and leaving on Sunday morning.

'What are you looking so pleased about?' Zaf asked Miriam, although his eyes had not moved; they were still fixed on the latest news bulletin on the television. She sneaked a sidelong glance at him. She didn't know how he did it. He saw everything, even without looking, even without trying. He heard everything, even if he wasn't there. He always *knew everything*. It was like he could see through walls. Actually. No. It was more than that. It was like he could break into her mind, penetrate her thoughts. It was as though he could peer into her soul. It made her shudder.

'It's Nina,' she replied, no longer smiling.

'What does *she* want?'

Miriam looked down at the message for a few seconds before

answering, unsure if she should tell him what the message said, or not, but she decided to just come out with it. 'Is it okay if she comes over to stay?'

Zaf picked up the remote control and flicked from BBC News to Sky News. The same headlines, just in a slightly different order, told a tiny bit differently. 'When?' he asked.

'This weekend. Friday evening through Sunday morning.'

He raised his eyebrows, but said nothing, and then turned the channel over to Al Jazeera. The main story was different to the other two channels at least.

His silence lingered, and in response to that, her heartbeat accelerated. She felt a tad nervous about pursuing it, but at the same time, she wanted an answer. 'I can say no if it's a problem, but you will be at work for most of that time, so we won't be in your way, and she will be gone by the time you're up on Sunday morning.' Miriam didn't rate her chances. The first time Nina had wanted to come and stay over, Miriam was forced to pretend that she and Zaf were going to be away at the exact same time. And the last time Nina had planned to come and see her, Miriam had to feign that she was ill with vomiting and diarrhoea, and didn't want to pass it to her, so it was best that she didn't come. When Zaf said no, it meant no. It was never up for debate.

'Okay,' said Zaf.

Miriam blinked a couple of times, but said nothing at all, and allowed Zaf to continue watching the television. He had finally settled on watching Al Jazeera News; the leading story was a report on the dire situation in Yemen, and he was quite engrossed in the story. This really was a first, though, him agreeing to Nina coming over for the weekend. She wondered why...Perhaps even *he* thought that making an excuse yet another time was a bit much. Whatever the reason for his change of heart, she was grateful.

When Nina arrived on Friday evening, Zaf was at work, so they were able to relax and have the house to themselves. However, Nina didn't seem to be her typical, chirpy self. The last time they had met up was when they had gone to London together, over 18 months ago. On that occasion, she had been the normal, bubbly Nina. Today, she was subdued. She had lost her father not so long ago, perhaps she was still grieving, thought Miriam.

'What's wrong?' asked Miriam, as she walked across the kitchen and handed Nina a mug of tea. Miriam then leant into the larder and grabbed a packet of Jammy Dodgers: Nina's favourite. She also fished out a pack of chocolate digestives. She placed the biscuits in pretty pattern on a blue china plate, and they both walked into the living room with the biscuits and their teas.

'I could ask you the same question,' said Nina after she sat down on the sofa.

'What do you mean?' asked Miriam. She joined her on the sofa. 'Are you missing your dad still? I know how hard it is losing a parent. You know you can talk to me. I'm here for you. Always.'

'It's not that!' Nina snapped. Miriam was taken aback.

'Of course, I miss him,' said Nina, adopting a softer manner, 'but right now, that's not it.'

'Then what is it?'

Nina cast a wistful look at Miriam, who was unaccustomed to seeing her so quiet. Miriam wished she would just come out with whatever it was that was niggling at her, as was her usual style. This talking in riddles, in a piecemeal fashion, wasn't like her at all.

'I need to ask you something.'

Miriam looked at her blankly.

'Is everything okay?' Nina asked.

Miriam stared at Nina with a vacant expression. 'You've lost me.'

'With you and Zaf?'

'What do you mean?' Miriam asked, managing the tone of her voice very carefully.

'I mean, are *you* okay?'

Miriam now knee-jerked into answering back quickly. 'Well, of course I'm okay. Everything is absolutely fine, silly, fancy that, asking such a strange question.' She picked up the plate of biscuits and moved it towards Nina, who grabbed a Jammie Dodger, predictably. Miriam put the plate back down. She didn't fancy a chocolate digestive after all.

'I'm worried about you,' said Nina, obviously intent on not letting this go. 'The girls from uni say you don't have any contact with them anymore. Is that true?'

Miriam didn't answer, and instead, now, having changed her mind yet again, grabbed a digestive and started to bite into it, seeking some kind of a diversion from the uncomfortable conversation rather than wanting to eat it.

'They've all been concerned about you,' Nina persisted. 'They said you don't post anything on social media anymore, you never phone or text any of them. I have noticed myself that you hardly ever look at the messages in the what's app group. And I don't hear from you for weeks, sometimes months, on end. No messages, no phone calls. Nothing.'

Miriam looked at the part nibbled biscuit in front of her. 'I love these, they're so moreish. And of course, you can't go wrong with chocolate, can you? It always hits the spot.'

But Nina wasn't in the mood for any kind of a distraction, especially not one involving talking about the finer qualities of chocolate digestives. 'I have only seen you once since you got married, do you know that? Just one time. And it's not been for want of trying.'

Miriam finished her biscuit, put her mug of tea down on the table, and now started to pick at some fluff on her sleeve.

'Miriam!' Nina half shouted.

Miriam nearly jumped out of her skin, and she was grateful not to be holding her tea at the time. It was rare for Nina to use such an abrasive tone, or to raise her voice in such an explicit display of irritation. When she was her usual happy self, yes, Nina would talk loudly, trying to fit as many words into her sentence before she had to draw breath, and to this would be added plentiful amounts of timely screaming and laughter. Never had she before raised her voice in anger like this.

The inescapability of having to say something now struck Miriam. She carefully put on her best game face and spoke with a calm, unflustered voice. 'Honestly, you're such a worry pot. I'm just busy, that's all. We're not students anymore. And unlike the rest of you, I'm married now, and that means that I have responsibilities.'

'Like what?' demanded Nina.

'Like being a wife, like working hard in the family business, like looking after this huge house and garden.'

Nina rolled her eyes and let out a sigh of exasperation. 'Can't you see?' she asked. She was still persistent, but at least now her tone was less harsh.

'See what?' asked Miriam, back now to de-fluffing her sleeve.

'That everything in your life revolves around *him*. Where are you in all of this?' asked Nina.

'I don't know what you mean,' replied Miriam. She looked away, dismissively, and took a sip of her tea.

'Every time I contact you about meeting up, which is not that often considering I only come over from Dubai every three to four months, there is always some reason why we can't meet up. You never say yes or no straight away, you obviously check with

Zaf first, and then it's always a no anyway, apart from this time, which threw me to be honest.'

'Now you're just being melodramatic.'

'No. I'm not. You never seem to be able to make your own mind up about anything. And that's not the Miriam I know. You've changed a great deal. I'm right, aren't I?'

Miriam looked directly at her friend, but said nothing. Her mind ticked away, but she wasn't sure about how to respond.

'When I think back to our trip to London,' continued Nina, 'you were really hesitant initially about going down early, because you were stuck on the fact that Zaf was not expecting you to come until the day after.'

'What's wrong with checking with your husband first, or sticking to the plan that has already been made? That's how it should be, shouldn't it?'

'Maybe. But let me ask you this. Does he check with you first? Before he goes out, before he meets his friends, before he invites people to the house? And anyway, who usually makes these plans that need to always be stuck to, that should never be deviated from? You, or him?'

Silence ensued on Miriam's part. Nina placed her mug of tea onto the coffee table gently, and swivelled her body around, bringing one leg onto the sofa, twisting so that now she was facing Nina fully. She placed her left hand on Nina's right arm.

'Please don't take it the wrong way when I ask you this question,' said Nina.

'What, another one? Don't you think you've asked enough questions today?'

'Don't be like that. Just one more question, and after that, I'll drop it.'

'What?' What question?' Miriam turned her head to one side, and cast her gaze downwards.

'Is he controlling you?' asked Nina.

Miriam registered the words quickly, turned around to face Nina, and catapulted into reactionary mode. 'Where on earth have you got that idea from?' She almost snorted the words.

'*Is he*?' Nina raised her voice once again, demanding an answer.

Miriam said nothing, save from a tut which came out louder than she had intended. Nervous sweat gathered in her palms, which she clasped together. Her friend continued to look at her, her eyes searching for an answer in Miriam's, who now turned her head away once again from her friend's sharp glare. Miriam continued with the silence, and fortunately for her, she was saved by the doorbell. Just in the nick of time, thought a relieved Miriam.

'Oh, that must be the pizza delivery. Good, because I'm starving,' said Miriam with a sense of relief audible in every word; it was almost as though she breathed the words out, as opposed to simply speaking them. She walked off towards the front door.

They settled down with their respective hot veggie and margherita pizzas, with sides of cheesy garlic bread and spicy wedges. They watched Ocean's 8, as neither of them had managed to see it at the cinema when it was released last year. As they lounged on the sofa, each in turn giving her commentary about the acting and the plot so far, it began to feel like old times, the two of them back at university, watching romantic comedies or action movies, or just chilling, eating junk food and talking nonsense.

Before she married Zaf, Nina had loved going to the pictures; she used to go at least once or twice a month, and sometimes more frequently. She had become an avid cinema goer, going with as many or as few of her circle of friends that wanted to come and see whatever the movie of choice was. She loved the whole ritual; the girly banter on the way, buying the mixed up sweet and salty popcorn and colourful fizzy drinks, painstakingly choosing and shovelling their favourites from the vast array of pic-n-mix into pastel coloured striped paper bags, dissecting the film afterwards when they inevitably went for a bite to eat, often pizza, but sometimes tapas or burgers or curry. However, Miriam had not once ventured to a cinema since she had married and moved down. Zaf didn't enjoy going to the cinema. He considered it a huge bore and a laborious waste of time and money. That was all there was to it.

Once the pizza had arrived and they put the film on, to Miriam's relief, Nina had refrained from asking another twenty questions. Perhaps she thought better of flogging a dead horse. The tension slowly melted away, and Nina was soon back to her old self; funny, noisy, vivacious. Just how Miriam liked it. When Nina was herself, she was the perfect distraction from all the bad things that mired Miriam's mind.

The next morning, Miriam brought up two mugs of tea, and wandered into the guest bedroom with them.

'Here you are, sleepy head, a cuppa for you. Thought you could do with this first, before I make us a nice big brekkie.'

Nina stretched out, before shoving over a bit and sitting up in bed. 'Come on, jump in, let's have a proper girly catch up.'

Nina handed her one of the mugs, and put the other one down on the bedside table. She walked over to the window and opened the duck egg blue silk curtains to let in a soft golden stream of sunlight. Miriam always found it difficult to relax in a room when the curtains were drawn. She then walked back over to the bed, plumped up the pillow, positioned it against the headboard and got in. Before they could even start chatting, however, she heard her mobile phone ringing from her bedroom. 'I better see who it is, be right back.'

'Hi Zaf,' answered Miriam when she reached her mobile.

'Why did you take so long to answer the call?'

'Did I? It just took me a little while to actually get to the phone.'

'Why? Where were you?'

'I was in with Nina in the guest bedroom, and the phone is in our bedroom.'

'What were you doing in Nina's room?'

'Nothing really. We were both just chatting in bed—'

'What?!' he almost bellowed it down the phone. She could detect an impression of disdain which dripped from that one word as it poured from his mouth and into Miriam's ear. She couldn't see the disdain, but she could imagine it plastered all over his face, of course. However, she clearly heard it in his voice. It was in the tone; unmistakable, unforgiving.

Miriam held her breath, and could feel herself descending into a blind panic. *Think*, Miriam urged herself, *think. What have you done wrong? You must have done something wrong. Why else would he use that tone of voice? That awful tone.* She waited for him to tell her, for as sure as day followed night, he would tell her what it was that she was currently guilty of.

'You were in bed with another woman!'

'I...err...I don't know what you mean.'

'You are *disgusting*, do you know that?'

'It's not like that, you know it isn't.' She spoke as quietly as she could.

'What sort of a woman, a married one at that, gets into bed with another woman?'

'She's my friend. We're just friends, having a girly chat.'

'You *disgust* me,' he said, and then he cut the call. Miriam held the phone in her hand for a little while after he had gone, until she almost dropped it because of the irrepressible shaking of her hand. She put the mobile down on the bedside table, and allowed herself to drop down to sit on the bed. For the first time in a while, she could feel a panic attack coming on. *Calm down,* she told herself. *Nina can't see you like this.* She closed her eyes and tried to steady her breathing, and she stayed there for a few minutes, until she felt her breathing return to some sort of normality, until she felt able to get up and continue with her day.

Miriam walked back towards Nina's room. She paused at the doorway, knocked back the tears, took the deepest breath she had inhaled for a while, and let it out slowly. She put her smile back on and walked in.

'Who was that?'

'Oh, it was just Zaf.'

'Is everything alright?'

'Yeah, everything's fine.'

Nina looked at Miriam, perhaps expecting a bit more.

'He was just checking if we're okay for food,' added Miriam, 'or if we wanted some breakfast delivered to the house, but I told him that I went and bought plenty of croissants and pastries yesterday, or if you fancy a cooked breakfast then I have plenty of eggs and lots of stuff in the freezer, so we'll be fine.'

'Cool.'

Miriam picked up her mug of tea and walked over towards the dressing table, and sat on the velvet cushioned Italian stool which came with the Italian dressing table. She faced Nina and sipped her tea.

'Hey, what happened to chatting and chilling in bed.'

Zaf's words were still echoing around in her head, paining her ears; *you're disgusting.*

'My back is playing up at the moment, so I'm better off not slumping in bed,' Miriam assured her friend. 'But we can still have that girly chat, right? It really is so good to see you.'

21

Birmingham Crown Court
11 November 2019

'You are the family GP, is that right?' Ms Godfrey asks the middle-aged man who has now entered the witness box.

'Yes, that's right,' replies Dr David Murphy, after which he pushes his round brown rimmed glasses back up his nose with his right index finger. He is a short man, with square shoulders and a slightly bulging tummy. His face is quite red; some in the courtroom may be forgiven for assuming that he looks unwell, or they may think that the red patches on his face are an indication of his nervousness. However, this isn't the case at all. Miriam knows that he always looks like this, he always has a blotchy pink-red face.

'Dr Murphy. Can you tell us when was the last time you saw the deceased, Mr Zafar Hassan?'

'Yes. It was on the 24 March 2019.'

'At your surgery?'

'Yes.'

'And what was the reason for the visit?'

'Mr Hassan came to see me because he said he had been feeling very down and anxious recently.'

'Did he say why he had been feeling like this?'

'Yes, he did. He said he was having matrimonial problems.'

'Can you expand on that, please?'

'He told me that his wife had become increasingly verbally abusive and aggressive towards him in recent months. He informed me that it was affecting his mental health, and causing him a lot of stress and tension. I did tell him that what he was describing was actually domestic abuse, and that he perhaps should go to the police, but he said he wasn't sure about involving the police. I also gave him a helpline number to contact should he need to speak with someone about the difficulties he was experiencing.'

A few eyebrows are raised amongst the jurors; banker guy in particular is now looking at Miriam very sceptically. Marilyn whispers something to the hippy woman sat next to her, who shakes her head a little, although today she is minus the hoops, and instead she has long dangly earrings that look like they are made of papers clips.

'How did he seem to you?' asks Ms Godfrey.

Dr Murphy scratches the top of his balding head with his right middle finger before he answers. 'He seemed nervous; a bit jumpy. I told him that he was most likely suffering from depression. I ran through various options with him, and we agreed that he would start on a mild dose of an anti-depressant. I prescribed him a month's worth of medication, and told him to come back and see me in about three weeks' time to review how he was getting on, and we could adjust the dose if necessary.'

'Other than this, as his doctor, can you tell us, was the deceased in good health?'

'Yes, he was in very good health apart from this.'

22

17 August 2018

This evening was going to be a difficult evening, Miriam thought to herself. She could feel it in every bone of her aching body. From the moment he had walked in from work at 11 pm, she had sensed it. She always waited up for him in the evenings, and she always had the food ready for him. Sometimes he ate it, and other times he didn't. He never phoned ahead to say whether he would be eating at the restaurant, or eating at home. Therefore, she always cooked, to cover all eventualities; him eating, him bringing home with him unexpected guests that needed feeding, him asking what she had cooked and she being able to give an answer, even if he didn't eat it. She would be happy with beans of toast or a jacket potato or even nothing most nights.

Eighteen months into marriage, and she had now got the hang of most of things, or at least she hoped she had. There was a drill for any given scenario, which she had now pretty much rote learnt over the past year and a half. And there were many expectations of her. Always. Even when she was presented with a situation or predicament that she didn't have a precedent for,

for which she had no guidance or instructions, Zaf's expectations never abated.

'What have you cooked today?' asked Zaf, abruptly, as he walked into the kitchen, where he found Miriam robotically emptying out the clean crockery from the dishwasher and placing it into the cupboards. There was no hi, hello, *salaam*, how are you, how was your day.

'I've made *tarka daal*. And I've cooked some cumin rice; I can make some *rotis* as well if you want. I have some *atta* in the fridge.' She always had chapatti dough ready in the fridge. Any dough that she didn't end up using for them, she still rolled into chapattis and cooked, and then broke into pieces and fed to the birds.

'How old is the *atta*?' he asked.

'I made it fresh this morning.'

'Hmph. Which *daal* is it?' he asked, and then he walked out of the kitchen and into the living room before she could answer. Once in there, he flicked off his shoes, removed his tie, and then flopped onto the sofa.

'*Masoor*,' she said once she also arrived into the living room. She didn't bother to sit down until she knew either way whether he wanted her to prepare some food.

He stopped undoing the top button of his shirt, and he pointed a sharp angry glance towards her.

'How many times have I told you that I hate that f-ing *masoor daal*!'

Keep your mouth shut, Miriam. I know what you're thinking; he has never told you that, has he? Or has he? He probably did, you know. Whatever, he did or he didn't, regardless, keep your mouth shut.

She could tell that he had been drinking today, and he'd probably had a bit too much. She could smell it on him. He wreaked of that unmistakable odour that she disliked intensely. She couldn't understand how anyone could drink something that smelt so awful; for her, it was somewhere between the gassy smell of rotting fruit and the overpowering stench of sweat. Although not all alcohol made her feel like this. She always thought that the look of a creamy Bailey's was very inviting; smooth and velvety, and no unpleasant aroma, rather, it smelt like toffee or caramel.

Zaf only rarely touched alcohol, reserving it to those times when he deemed swigging liquor to be necessary and important enough to fit in with, or impress, whoever he may be meeting or entertaining, for whichever deal or contract that he considered to be crucial. He was by nature and at heart a chameleon. He could change his colours faster than the flick of a switch.

'Poor man's *daal*, that masoor *daal* is,' he started to rant. 'You think it's good enough for the likes of me!' Zaf's voice was gradually climbing in terms of its tempo and noise level. 'Rajpoots, me and my family, that's what we are. Rajpoots; sons of kings, do you understand?'

Silence. The best option at this moment in time, thought Miriam. She simply stood and listened, quietly, and allowed him free rein to blather on.

He now raised one hand which was loosely clenched as a fist, as though he was on a big stage rather than his living room, giving an important political speech as opposed to mindlessly drivelling away at his wife. 'You don't even know what bloody caste you are, do you? Your family are probably *Hajjams* or *Dhobis*, knowing you. Cutting people's hair or washing their dirty laundry is about all you lot would be good for. Bloody pant washers.'

And on that note, the speech was abruptly over, as he now decided he was going to bed; he started to climb the stairs, swaying unsteadily from side to side. She followed right behind him, holding onto his arm to steady him. She always went up at the same time as him. That was the ritual. He didn't like her coming upstairs after him. He claimed she was too noisy getting into bed and would wake him up. In addition, he liked to be suitably attended to before he slept. Today, it was his second favourite type of attending to that she was expected to perform.

'My legs are aching,' he moaned. 'Get the oil and start massaging,' he commanded, whilst he got comfortable on the bed.

Miriam imagined letting out a huge groan, a monumental sigh, telling him she's too tired today, for she *was* tired, wiped-out in fact, and she was simply longing to sleep. She dismissed the thought as swiftly as she could, and instead, she walked over to the window sill and grabbed the bottle of almond oil. She was about to pour some into the palm of her hand, when his next demand came.

'I want it warm. How many times do I have to tell you? Stop being so lazy.'

Miriam walked over to his bedside table, opened the top drawer and took out the thick white candle, the cigarette lighter, and a spoon. She lit the candle and placed some oil in the metal spoon and held it over the flame for a little while. She tested it with her finger, and once it was ready, she poured some into the palm of her hand, and started massaging his heavy, muscular legs with the warm slippery liquid. As she moved back and forth, her hands gliding smoothly with the aid of the oil, she closed her eyes for a while. She could feel herself swaying, like the branch of a tree moving back and forth to the tune of a warm breeze. She was so very exhausted. She could barely keep her eyes open, so she kept them closed, and she felt herself rocking back and forth, swinging side to side, as she massaged his lower limbs, which felt like wide trunks of jagged, stiff wood under her delicate skin.

'How many times do I have to say this to you; it's too soft, you need to be firmer, put some energy into it!' he whined.

'Yes,' she replied, suddenly opening her eyes again. She began to press and knead his rock like legs as hard as she could, pushing firmly with the svelte fingers on her small hands, which now ached. But still, she carried on, until he was satisfied, not necessarily pleased, but satisfied just enough for her to eventually be dismissed.

She finally got into her side of the bed, lay on the very edge, and within seconds of her head hitting the pillow, she was falling asleep. The day had knocked everything out of her. She just wanted to fall into an abyss of peaceful surrender; that bitter sweet place where your soul hangs between life and death. Sometimes she wished death would take her, and then she felt terrible for being so ungrateful, and asked Allah to forgive her. She had wished this far more often than she cared to recollect. No matter how bad things were after her mum died, how difficult life became after she became detached from her father, she had *never* wished herself dead. If anything, losing her mother taught her about the sanctity of life. She was therefore horrified with herself the first time she had thought death would be preferrable to living. She recalled the evening well. A few months into marriage, she was fast becoming acquainted with Zaf's unpredictable behaviour. On this occasion though, he had taken it to another level. She had held the fort for him at the office when the producer of a TV programme had come in for a meeting, and Zaf was running late. Rachel wasn't in for some reason either. So, it fell on Miriam to start the meeting; she and the producer had chatted in quite a relaxed manner about the business generally, and moved on to discussions about the possibility of the restaurant being part of a new reality TV series. The producer had told Miriam he would love for her to be the face of the show, and she hadn't known quite how to respond to that, apart from to be dismissive of the idea in a good-humoured way, and at that point Zaf returned and took over the meeting. Later

that the evening, Zaf had come home with that look on his face
and didn't waste any time in reminding her where her place was,
and it certainly wasn't in front of the camera in any future television project. 'So, what, you think you can be the face of *my*
restaurant? On prime-time TV? You? Hmph.' She had toyed
with not replying, but chose to put him straight. 'I didn't say
anything! It was his suggestion, and I said no'. 'You're getting
ideas above your station, you know that?' Zaf had proceeded to
pick up her plate of food (she'd prepared two plates of spicy
lamb chops with biryani, one of Zaf's favourite dishes). He threw
her plate onto the floor. He then grabbed her arm and pushed
her onto the cold kitchen floor where her last two hours of work
lay in a heap amidst the broken china plate, and hovering over
her, his breath on her face, his voice in her ear, he told her: '*this*
is where you belong, on the floor, under my feet'. Tears had
hurled out from her eyes like searing embers from a raging fire.
On that day, at that precise moment, on that kitchen floor, she
had wished to God that she was dead. Right now, feeling the
sting of those tears in her eyes once more, she sunk deeper into
her bed. She often felt as though her bed was the one loyal,
faithful presence in her life. Although this bed was the scene of
many uncomfortable moments with Zaf, it was also her refuge,
her place of rest, where she laid her head down and found
comfort. People let you down, she would think, but your bed is a
faithful servant, it is always there for you, night in, night out; it is
ready to catch you as you fall, to embrace your hurting body
when you lay it down, to let you drown in its softness, to allow
you to escape the day's exhaustion, to just let you be.

Only two hours later, however, she felt her peaceful slumber
being disrupted by something sharp jabbing her in the back. Zaf
elbowed her for a third time, this time hard enough to wake
Miriam from her deep sleep. She tried to open her eyes, but
sleep was still calling to her, like a lover whose locked embrace

you do not want to break free from, whose lips you do not want to detach your lips from, whose fragrance you want to stay close to, but her brain told her she must break free, she must wake up. She turned around to face Zaf, her eyelids still droopy and heavy with the desire for nothing else in the world apart from sleep.

'Finally,' he said. 'You sleep for England you do.'

'What's the matter?' she asked him, whilst she rubbed her weary eyes, and let out a yawn.

'Go make me some food.'

She tried to stifle a second yawn, without success. She used her hands to drag herself up to sit against the headboard. She stopped rubbing her eyes, and drank some water from the bottle by her bed, in a bid to try and wake herself up.

'And I don't want any of that *daal* muck you made either.'

'What do you want to eat then?' she asked him, now rubbing her eyes ferociously, for her eyes felt like they had little beads of sand trapped in them.

'Make me a spiced omelette, with thinly sliced onions and mushrooms, and a couple of slices of toast. And some *desi* tea.'

'Okay,' muttered Miriam, as she got out of bed and put on her slippers. She wondered if she had any of those little evaporated milk cans left in the larder. Zaf liked his traditional tea boiled up with evaporated milk only. He was very particular about it. There would be trouble if not.

She reached the bedroom door and heard his coarse voice again, like the spirit of doom which she could never escape. 'Make sure you get the spices right, and the onions and mushrooms better be thinly sliced, or you'll be making it all again.'

Silence.

She didn't reply. She walked downstairs and into the kitchen, eyes only half open, and got on with what she had been told to do.

23

Birmingham Crown Court
11 November 2019

'Do you recall, on the day in question when the deceased came to see you, did he say how long he had been suffering from this alleged abuse and subsequent depression?' Mr De Beaux asks his first question of the doctor as he commences on his cross-examination.

'He said it had been going on for some months,' replies Dr Murphy.

'Can you be a little more precise?'

'That's what he said to me.'

'You didn't ask him *precisely* how long it had been going on?'

'No. I don't think I did.'

'Therefore, it could have been going on for anything between 2 months and 11 months.'

Dr Murphy stares blankly at Mr De Beaux, until he finally realises that he is meant to say something in response. 'I suppose so,' he says.

'Did he give you any details of the alleged abuse?'

'He told me that his wife was verbally abusive, and aggressive in her nature towards him.'

'Did he give you particulars of any incidents?'

Dr Murphy scrunches his eyebrows together towards the middle of his face.

Mr De Beaux elaborates. 'Dates, times, what she allegedly said, where they were, if there were any witnesses, how it affected him?'

'No. Not really. But he did seem quite distressed. And, he also did say that he was scared of her.'

'Interesting. It is a fact that has been established in this court that Mr Hassan was about to embark on divorce proceedings; did he say anything about that to you when he came in for his appointment?'

'No. He never mentioned anything about getting divorced.'

'I see,' says Mr De Beaux. He silently taps his fingers on the desk, as he thinks for a few seconds, before continuing. 'Coming to the symptoms of the alleged depression. You said he seemed distressed, and agitated, and he told you that he was feeling anxious. Did he tell you about any other symptoms?'

'Not that I can recall.'

Miriam notices that the *hijabi* juror purses her lips and furrows her eyebrows now, as she listens carefully to the testimony of the doctor. She softly pushes back under her headscarf a strand of her dark brown hair that has managed to escape onto her forehead.

'Surely, he must have mentioned something else relating to the supposed depression, other than feeling anxious?' says Mr De Beaux, whilst referring to his notes.

'Well...' the solitary word from the doctor's mouth peters out, and is not joined by any others.

'For example, did he say anything such as: it was affecting his ability to concentrate on things, and to carry out his job,' Mr De Beaux asks, and continues swiftly, 'had he withdrawn from social engagements and become more isolated, was he having problems sleeping or having nightmares, was he eating properly, was he overeating, or had he lost his appetite, had he lost interest in doing anything for pleasure?' Mr De Beaux pauses for a well-earned breath. 'These are, I believe, just some of the very typical symptoms of depression, are they not?'

'They are, that is correct.'

'And he didn't mention any of these other symptoms to you?'

Hijabi woman is now shaking her head slightly. Miriam can discern that something in this testimony has got her goat.

'No. He didn't.'

Mr De Beaux now holds up a file of papers. 'I have a copy of Mr Hassan's diary here, Dr Murphy, and I have access to all of the deceased's social media activity as well. If we take the average length of time that he may have been supposedly depressed for, which would be 5 months, then in those 5 months before his death, you will see that the deceased in fact had a very full and active life. He was pressing ahead with new business projects as well as running his existing business which as you know consists of a national chain of very busy restaurants. He was managing staff, engaging in lots of social media, entertaining guests, hosting parties, trying out new recipes, travelling, and the list goes on. In one particular video interview on social media, he made a very bold joke about his wife.'

Mr De Beaux pauses and allows the jury to take it in.

'The interviewer asked Mr Hassan about his wife, to which he replied that he actually hadn't spoken to his wife in over three weeks, and when the interviewer asked him why that was the case, Mr Hassan replied, and I quote, "I didn't want to interrupt her"'.

Marilyn and the hippy woman throw each other a knowing

look. There is a little bit of noise from the public gallery which disappears as Mr De Beaux carries on.

'In your opinion, Dr Murphy, do you think that if he was as scared of his wife as he alleged, that would make such a joke about her in such a public way on a social media account that had thousands of followers?'

'I can't say, really. I can only tell you what he told me.'

'Well then. Let *me* tell *you*. The fact is that the deceased was about to embark on a divorce. He was going to allege unreasonable behaviour on the part of the defendant. What better evidence could there be to support his allegations than the independent testimony of a doctor that would back up his claims should this be required at any time during the court proceedings that would have followed.'

Dr Murphy places his right hand on his chin, as he looks at Mr De Beaux. He begins to pinch his chin with his thumb and index finger, as he continues to dwell on how to respond.

'Let me ask you this, then, Dr Murphy; do you think it is possible that the deceased was fabricating the details about the alleged abuse and his so-called depression?'

Dr Murphy now casts his gaze firmly towards Miriam. She is more petite than he remembers, and is now frail compared to when he had last seen her. She was never fat as he recalls, more what he would call a normal size, some may even use the word plump nowadays. However, she looks worse than thin right now, he thinks to himself. She looks malnourished in body, but more than that, she seems dejected in spirit.

'I don't know,' he replies eventually.

'I'm not asking you if you know for certain, Dr Murphy, I am asking you if you think it is *possible* that the deceased may have lied.'

'It is possible, yes.'

'Thank you. Consider this, then,' says Mr De Beaux; he pauses and turns towards the jury, ensuring he has the attention of all twelve of them before continuing. 'If this man was prepared to lie and cheat his way to a divorce—'

'Objection, my Lord, there is no evidence of this—' interrupts Ms Godfrey, but her interruption is short-lived as Mr De Beaux ploughs straight on like a bull in a china shop.

'—to lie and cheat his way to a divorce and treat his wife in such a shoddy manner, then imagine how he must have behaved towards his enemies.'

Mr De Beaux allows this thought to linger in the minds of the jurors for a few seconds, before he turns to the judge. 'No further questions, My Lord.'

There is no re-examination by the Crown, and Dr Murphy is released from the witness box, to be replaced immediately by another doctor.

Dr Heather Moore announces her name, and her occupation as a Forensic Pathologist.

'Dr Moore. You were responsible for examining the body of the deceased, and I have before me your report into the likely cause and time of death. Can you tell us about that briefly?' asks Ms Godfrey.

'Yes. The deceased had been stabbed by a weapon, which was confirmed to be a letter opener, in the abdomen, causing his spleen to rupture. When I was called to the scene of the crime to examine the body, I saw that the weapon was still lodged in the deceased's abdomen. The deceased had lost a lot of blood, which had pooled around his body where he lay on his back on the floor.'

'When first responders arrived at the scene, was he already dead?'

'Yes, he was.' Dr Moore locks her hands together in front of her whilst she waits for the next question, which she predicts accurately in her mind.

'Are you able to confirm the time of death?' asks Ms Godfrey.

'It is difficult to give an exact time, and he won't have died instantly. It is also hard to say exactly how long he might have bled out for before he did pass away, but I can narrow it down, and I can say that the time of death was almost definitely somewhere between 3pm and 4pm.'

'Thank you, Dr Moore. If you will just wait there for my colleague acting for the Defendant who will have a few questions for you.'

Dr Moore nods her head in anticipation. Mr De Beaux stands up and gives the witness a brief smile.

'Dr Moore. I don't have many questions for you if I'm honest. I do not dispute your report in any way in terms of the conclusions it draws as to how the deceased was killed. However, I would like you to answer this simple question for me. If the Defendant is telling the truth, and if she was indeed out of the house from 2pm and did not arrive back at the house until 4.15pm, am I right to assume that it was impossible that she could have killed her husband?'

'If what she is saying is true, then that is correct; as I said before, the time of death was almost certainly sometime after 3pm and definitely before 4pm, therefore, if she is being truthful, and she arrived home at quarter past four, then she cannot be the person who killed him.' A few mutterings surface around the courtroom. Dr Moore waits for a few moments until the noise filters away before adding, 'but as we all know, it is naturally for the court to decide on whether she is lying or telling the truth. I cannot in any way comment on the defendant's truthfulness or lack thereof, only as to the time of death.'

'Of course. Thank you. No further questions, my Lord.'

'Very well. Court is adjourned for the day,' announces the Judge.

'All rise!' squawks the Clerk, jerking Miriam up from her slumped posture into an upright position, after which she leaps up onto her feet like everybody else in the courtroom who have already beaten her to it.

24

---

19 April 2018

'It needs to be done today,' said Zaf. He placed the folder abruptly on Miriam's desk and headed in a hurry back to his own office. The folder contained a note with the mobile number of a Mr Granger, the man who Zaf wanted to arrange a meeting with for tomorrow. And it was Miriam's job to ensure that she arranged this meeting without fail. Zaf had been pretty clear about that.

She telephoned Mr Granger's office landline, and asked to speak with him, but was told that he was out of the office. She could try his mobile phone, she was told, although it was unlikely that she would get through as he was in back to back meetings.

'When will he be returning to the office?' asked Miriam.

'He will be back in from around quarter past four until five o'clock only today,' replied his Personal Assistant. 'Who is this calling?'

'I'm Miriam, I'm ringing from Zaf's Restaurant Group. Mr Zaf Hassan was told to get in touch to arrange a meeting with

Mr Granger. Would it be possible for me book that appointment through you?' she asked his PA.

'I'm afraid Mr Granger looks after his own diary, so you would need to speak with him if you wish to arrange an appointment.'

Not the answer Miriam wanted to hear. She ended the call.

Miriam then phoned Mr Granger's mobile phone, but there was no answer, as his PA had predicted, and worse still, the call didn't go through to voicemail, so she wasn't even able to leave a message. She buzzed through to Zaf and explained the situation. 'Can't we send him an email?' she asked Zaf.

'I've already tried that. It's coming up with a message to say he is currently not checking his emails, and to contact him on his mobile.'

'Oh.'

'Yeah. Oh. Miriam, if I'd wanted you to send him an email, I would have asked you to do that, wouldn't I? The only way is to get him on his mobile.' Miriam didn't retort. 'Just keep trying his mobile, I don't care if you have to redial constantly, just make sure you get through and get the appointment arranged.'

Miriam tried every five minutes, but with no success. At half past four, her mobile phone buzzed. She took it out of her bag which was resting by her feet, and looked at the screen. It was Nina, but she didn't get to it on time and she had already hung up. And then she noticed that there had been five missed calls from her, which was really unusual, and that meant there was something most definitely wrong. She phoned her back.

'Hi Nina. Sorry I missed your calls. It's completely mad at work. I haven't had a minute to myself today. Is everything okay?'

All Miriam could hear were huge sobs coming from Nina on the other end. She wouldn't talk, she just kept on crying, like monsoon rain on a tin roof that won't stop beating down. Miriam did her best just to be there, until Nina was ready to talk.

Miriam uttered timely, caring words "come on now...tell me what's wrong...I'm here for you...we can deal with it, whatever it is...please stop crying...you can talk to me about anything..."

Miriam patiently waited for her to start talking, and wondered what it could be. Nina could be a bit melodramatic at times, and in keeping with her noisy, overly flamboyant character, she would often make a really big deal out of something which wasn't *that* big a deal, and this would sometimes involve the shedding of big fat tears; like the time when one of her boyfriends of only two months, who she claimed she was madly in love with, and who she declared was the "one", dumped her and she wanted to kill him, or the tears that poured incessantly when she failed her driving test for the sixth time, or when she didn't leave her room for days because Oasis broke up.

Eventually the lingering sobs became little scraggly bits of weepiness, which became a broken, sad voice which began to speak.

'What's happened, bestie?' Miriam asked softly.

'It's my dad.'

'What's wrong with him?'

'He's dead.'

There was a gaping silence on Miriam's side, as she had just been completely floored by what she had just been told; she could barely take it in. She felt her friend's pain in every word that Nina just about managed to dislodge from her throat, where until now those words had been wedged, refusing to budge, not wanting to be said. Having lost a parent herself, Miriam knew all too well the agony, the sheer shock and the disbelief that Nina would be feeling in this brutal moment. So many possibilities that once were, and no longer are, would run through her mind; she would never again be able to talk to him, to hug him, to laugh at his dad dancing, to watch Coronation Street together, to cry on his shoulder, to make the Christmas dinner with him, to hear his terrible jokes, to tell him she loved him - Miriam knew Nina would be wishing that she had said that more often. She would also reproach herself for all those times that she hadn't got around to seeing him, or not appreciating those precious moments that they had spent together. He would never be able to give her away should she marry; never see her kids should she have any. Nina was inconsolable, and her best friend was the one person, the only person, that she could bare to speak to.

When Miriam finally got off the phone from a distraught Nina, it was gone 5 o'clock. *Shit!* She thought to herself. She telephoned Mr Granger's mobile once again, but no answer. She telephoned his office in the hope that he would still be there, but he had been and gone, and what's more, he was no longer contactable, as he had left for the airport for a business trip and wouldn't be back until next week. Miriam's heart sank into the pit of her stomach which churned fretfully.

Miriam got up from her desk and strode slowly towards Zaf's office; it felt like a walk of shame, a walk towards the inevitable derision and reprimand that would follow. He wasn't in his office though. She then went and popped her head around into Adam's room; he was just packing up to go home. They had never talked about the miscarriage since that terrible day, but that episode had changed their relationship. Neither of them overtly said or did anything to bring about this change, but there had been a shift as they shared a silent sort of a bond; one where they now understood each other better, felt as though they knew each other better, in a new light they had not seen previously. They looked out for each other in a way that they had never really done before that day. But all of this had come about quietly, with neither of them ever having to say even one word. A still and invisible meeting of minds that each recognised every time their eyes met.

'Do you know where Zaf is?' she asked Adam,

Adam could see the worry lines on Miriam's forehead. Her inner stresses always manifested in tiny thin creases on that part of her face.

'He's gone downstairs, there was some problem in the kitchen, he's speaking to some of the staff down there, saying he needs to sort it before evening service.'

There was a reasonably comfortable silence that filled the air, but one which Adam broke as the indentations on Miriam's forehead grew more prominent. 'Why don't you sit down.' Adam pointed to the chair, wondering what was bothering her. 'Are you okay? What's the matter? You look pale, Miriam. Shall I get you a drink?'

'I need to speak to Zaf,' she replied, and then started to nibble on the nail of her right thumb.

'What's wrong?'

'I've messed up, Adam. As usual.'

Adam was about to say something, but then he looked away from her and towards the corridor outside his room, and through the gap in the door he saw Zaf walk past.

'He's back, if you want to go in and see him. Do you?'

'I better had.' Miriam sighed almost achingly, and walked quietly out of Adam's office and into Zaf's. She didn't sit down, instead, she stood by his desk and told him straight away that she hadn't been able to get hold of Mr Granger, and she did her best to explain why.

'I gave you one job. Just one! I told you I *had* to have this meeting with him tomorrow,' Zaf reminded her.

'Well, that's impossible anyway, because he's flying out this evening for a business trip abroad somewhere,' she muttered.

'No, *that's* impossible, because I know the deadline for this meeting was tomorrow. I can't believe you could mess up such a simple task.'

Miriam was now close to tears, but she held them back as

soon as she heard a soft knock on the door, which was still open, after which Adam walked in.

'I'm sorry to interrupt, I couldn't help but hear as I was walking past. Is this about Granger?'

'Yes, it is,' said Zaf bluntly.

'Zaf, the deadline for the meeting with Granger wasn't tomorrow, it was a week ago, well, a week ago tomorrow.'

Zaf stared at Adam. Miriam could sense some tension, and the ensuing silence lasted for a little while. Perhaps Zaf wondered how Adam often seemed to be able to come to her rescue these days, because here he was, once again.

'Are you sure?' Zaf mumbled.

'It's in the diary; check it on your computer.'

Zaf pulled up the electronic diary for last week, and there it was, just as Adam had said. Miriam breathed out a quiet breath of relief. A difficult silence ensued between the three of them. which Adam decided to break. 'Hopefully you can re-arrange when Granger gets back. Right, I'm done for the day. So, I'll be off now.'

25

Birmingham Crown Court
12 November 2019

Now, it is the turn of the next witness, Mrs Pam Bains, to take her place in the witness box. She casts a vacant gaze towards Miriam, until she is addressed by Ms Godfrey, at which point she turns her attention away from the defendant's dock.

'Mrs Bains, I believe you live at number 2 Parkfield Close,' Ms Godfrey begins, whilst glancing down at her notes briefly.

'That's right. We live two doors from Miriam and... Zaf.'

'Their house is number 6?'

'That's correct.'

'Can you describe the road on which you live?'

'It's a secluded cul-de-sac, shaped like a sort of semi-circle. It's tucked away right down at the bottom of a lane that comes down off the main road. There are only five properties down on our road.'

'And it is quite near to the park.'

'Yes, there is a small entrance to the park just a stone's throw away.'

'Quite an exclusive road then?'

'Yes, it is I suppose. They are all very large, detached houses, number 6 being the biggest. Zaf had extended it quite a lot over the years. He had a ground floor extension built at the side, and a two-storey extension at the back. He had lots of extra features installed; a gym, a party room, and a cinema room, to mention a few,' Miriam is unsurprised to hear Mrs Bains continue in this vain with a mixture of envy and admiration that can be denoted in the superfluous detail that has just been volunteered by her.

'Mrs Bains, did you know the deceased and the defendant well?'

She raises her very thin, overplucked eyebrows for a few seconds. 'Not *really* well. They weren't close friends or anything like that, but we knew each other well enough as neighbours. We always said hello to each other if we were out on the road. We popped round to their house occasionally, and vice versa. As where we all live is off the beaten track a bit, so to speak, and there are only a handful of houses, we as neighbours do all know each other to a certain extent, as opposed to not knowing who our neighbours are at all, as is the case in some places, or so I've heard.'

'I want you to take your mind back to the afternoon of Sunday 31st March 2019. Tell me, with as much detail as you can, what you remember of that day,' Ms Godfrey asks.

Mrs Bains uses both her hands to push her grey streaked fringe out of her eyes, and the parting ends up looking like tied back curtains. She lets out a small cough, and begins her recollection.

'In the morning, at about 10 o'clock, I was walking out of the house to get in the car and go do the weekly shop. I like going at that time, as it's really quiet at the supermarket, although I have to say that I usually leave at around 9.30am, but I do remember I was running a bit late on that day. As I came out of my house and went to put my empty reusable shopping bags in the boot of my car, so much more environmentally friendly aren't they, as opposed to using those awful plastic ones that end up in the sea killing all the fish. Sorry, I've digressed. So, as I was saying, I was putting the bags for life into the car boot, when I saw Zaf standing by his front door, just down from their doorstep. It's a very large solid wood front door that they have. Quite decorative panelling on it as well. It is bespoke, I believe.'

'And what did you see, or hear, Mrs Bains?' asks Ms Godfrey quickly, before Mrs Bains can start rambling on about the door.

'I couldn't see Zaf's face, because he had his back to me. He was standing facing the front door, which was open. But I could see Miriam; she was stood in the doorway with the front door open behind her.'

'And how did the defendant seem to you?'

Mrs Bains looks over at Miriam once again, but Miriam does not raise her head which is stooped over.

Miriam is looking down towards her hands which are clutching her knees at present. She notices that so many of her fingernails have chipped. *I used to have lovely nails,* Miriam thinks to herself, *lovely hands, in fact. Soft hands, with strong, healthy round tipped nails, painted tea rose, or pale lavender, dusky pink or bold terracotta, depending on the season.* She inwardly frowns as she stares at her now bony hands which are dotted with small marks and cuts, and nails that are all different in size, and all of them jagged.

Mrs Bains turns her head back towards prosecuting counsel and replies. 'She looked angry. Upset.'

'Which one did she come across as more: angry or upset?'

'I would have to say she came across as both equally. She appeared to be very agitated. Zaf said something to her and she screamed something back at him, I don't know what was said by either of them. And then he fell backwards, although he didn't fall to the ground. He kind of stumbled a bit, and managed to stop himself from falling over completely.'

'I see. In your opinion, did Miriam push Zaf?'

'I think so.'

'Can you be more decisive, Mrs Bains?'

'It happened so quickly. It all looked very heated. But I would say, yes. Yes, she did. After the stumble a few more words were exchanged, I don't know what was said, and then he got into his car. An Audi R8. Which he had only just bought, brand new, on the 1st of March. Jet black—'

'And then what happened?' interrupts Ms Godfrey before Mrs Bains can give chapter and verse on the car.

'Well, he reversed out of the drive, and drove off quite fast.'

'And what about the defendant?'

'She stood there for a few seconds, as though she was in a trance or something. I don't think she noticed me at all. Then she went back inside the house and slammed the door shut, really loudly.'

'Were you surprised to witness such an exchange between them?'

'I was surprised, in a way, because I hadn't seen them argue before. Not publicly like that. Not at all, in fact. But on the other hand, I just thought it was a run of the mill domestic argument. All couples argue, I guess. I didn't think any more of it. I put it out of my mind and carried on with the day ahead.'

26

---

31 March 2019

Ahead of her today lay the prospect of a meeting which she had long lost hope of ever coming to fruition. Today seemed to have taken an eternity to arrive at, but now it was here, Miriam felt as though she could finally begin to visualise it, rather than to just anticipate it. She had waited for this day for far too long.

It was one week ago, at 10am, that she had received the call. 'Hello. Is that Miriam?' were the words he had uttered seven days ago, although it had felt like seven years since she had last heard him speak. She recognised her brother's voice with his heavy Bradfordian accent in an instant. She couldn't speak. He repeated the question. 'Yes. It's me, it's me,' she had replied back faintly, like an echo trying to reach back into time. 'It's been too long, sis.' She broke down. She couldn't control the tears. 'Don't cry,' he said, but his sweet voice brought the tears on even faster. 'Dad wants to see you. We all do. It's time, sis.'

She had busied herself with getting ready for the big day ahead; she was almost giddy with nervous excitement. Today, Zaf was going to take her up to her dad's house, back up north, back to Bradford, back home. Today, she was going to see her family again. She was going to see her dad and her brother after all these years. When they had parted ways, when she had left home, she had left with an obnoxious air of youthful defiance. But back then, she was completely unaware of how much she would come to miss them in the years that followed.

The death of her mother, when she was just 16 years old, had hit her hard. Harder that she had allowed herself to acknowledge at the time, harder than her family and friends had realised. From being told that her mum had advanced stage pancreatic cancer to finding her gone in under three months of the diagnosis was like being ran over by a bullet train she never saw coming. She had barely had time to understand the illness, let alone watch her mother deteriorate to a shell and then die within weeks of finding out about the illness. The agony of losing a loved one can of course manifest itself in a myriad of ways; in Miriam's case, overwhelming grief morphed into anger, and her anger then converted into an obstinate kind of revolt against everyone and everything. She pushed away those closest to her, those who deep down still cared for her; she cut off all emotional attachment with her nearest and dearest.

When she lost her mother, she lost not only a parent, but also her best friend, her security blanket, her confidant, her foundation, her compass. Her mother's unexpected death left a gaping big, dark hole. For Miriam, it was like looking at a brimming, bright blue sea that suddenly dries up leaving a vast, empty seabed which nothing else could ever fill. She lost her identity, she lost her way, and she lost herself. Nothing added up anymore. Most of the time, she walked about in a bubble of bewilderment, with no particular sense of direction. And without even realising how or when it happened, she went off the rails and simply refused to conform. She rebelled to an extent that her grieving father could not cope with. Most –

friends, relatives, members of their community - would say that her family ostracised her because of her wayward behaviour, staying out late, keeping dubious company, arguing with her father (which was the ultimate form of disrespect). But if she was honest, she had ostracised herself from her family the day that her mother had died. She had not understood then that her wayward behaviour was, on a basic level, simply a product of extreme grief. In the years that followed, many ifs and buts went through her mind; if only she had admitted to herself how bad she had felt, if only she had talked to one of her friends or teachers, if only she had told her father or brother, if only she had got help, counselling, psychotherapy, medication even, for she was surely going through some form of depression due to the bereavement - things might have turned out so very differently. If only, if only, if only...yet, despite the way in which her path in life had deviated away from her family, there was now a chance for their paths to converge once again. She had missed her family dearly. Misguided pride on both sides, and the inability to let go of hurtful things that were said and done, had prevented a reunion which was long overdue.

Miriam decided to don a light purple *salwar kameez* that was etched with flowery pink embroidery. It was the closest outfit she could find to the one that had been her favourite as a teenager, which her mother had lovingly stitched for her. She recalled it was the night before Eid, *chaand raat*, the night of the moon, when the sight of the full moon meant the festival would be celebrated the following day. This was the last Eid Miriam had spent with her mum before she passed away, and Miriam had um'd and ah'd about what she wanted to wear, from a choice of two ready to wear brand new outfits. Seeing her daughter's indecisiveness, her mother had marched Miriam to her own bedroom, and pulled out a huge brown suitcase from under her bed. She opened it, and in there were perhaps dozens of unstitched fabrics, some of which looked like they dated back to the seventies or eighties, and others with a more modern appearance about them. *Choose something from here, and I will sew it for you,* her mother had told her. Miriam had jovially rummaged through the layers of fabrics; reds greens blues pinks, some with heavy embroidery and shiny embellishments, others quite elegantly plain, some with flower power prints, or polka dots, or paisley patterns, or stripes. There were suits and scarves embellished with glittery sequins or skilfully embroidered borders with *zari* threadwork, tiny beads, and plush pearls, or panels of pale pastel organza. There were georgettes, silks, satins, nets, linens, cottons, chiffons, *banarsis*, velvets. A symphony of colours, patterns, and textures delighted her as she rifled through them one by one, until eventually her eye fell on the beautiful purple fabric with the delicate pink embroidery; she immediately fell in love with it. Her mother could cut and sew a suit from scratch within a few hours. On that occasion, she had stayed up until 2 am perfecting the outfit for her daughter. In the morning, Miriam was awakened by the unmistakable aroma of Eid; the smell of the mutton stock, a concoction of mutton bones, whole spices, pieces of onion and garlic, bubbling away on the stove, being prepared in readiness as an essential ingredient for the pilau rice. The fragrant tones of all the different spices - cassia cinnamon bark, black *elaichi*, cloves, bay leaves, black peppercorns, cumin and coriander seeds, and star anise - all infused into a unique and unmistakable scent, which wafted its way up to stir her from her sleep. And when she stepped into the kitchen, Miriam saw her mum cooking the other must make Eid dish; *saviyan*. Delicate strands of curly vermicelli were tossed around in melted ghee until they turned a russet golden brown. They were then simmered in a cardamom sugar syrup, finished off with slivered almonds, fat golden sultanas, and a few drops of *kewra* water. She had learnt over time that nothing else could ever replicate the inimitable floral fragrance and taste extracted from the flowers of the sweet-scented South Asian screwpine plant. Miriam couldn't believe that not only did her mother manage to cook a feast for Eid without batting an eyelid, but she had also finished stitching Miriam's clothes which when she wore them had fit her like a glove.

Miriam had left that favourite *salwar kameez* behind when she had left home, something she had always regretted, and now she hoped dearly that her father hadn't thrown or given it away. She wanted to hold those clothes again, to wear them again, to feel her mother's loving presence in every stitch of the fabric.

She was almost ready now. She was dressed, her makeup was on, her hair was done. She was putting on her second drop pearl earring when Zaf walked into the bedroom. He was sending a text, and once he was done, he put the phone in the back pocket of his Levi's jeans.

With her jewellery now on, Miriam turned around to look at Zaf, her eyes smiling, joy radiating from her face at the thought of seeing her family.

'You look happy today,' he remarked as he stood at the window and looked out over their street and into the park beyond. His phone buzzed and he took it out of his pocket to check it.

'I am,' Miriam replied.

'I have never seen you look this happy before.'

Miriam closed her jewellery box quietly. Zaf carried on, although she was hoping he wouldn't. *Let me just enjoy today, please, just this once.*

'You never seem this happy to see me or my family. If I'd known that seeing your family would improve your mood this much, I would have pushed for it myself ages ago.'

He turned around to look at her. And there it was. The look

of doom. Her heart began to sink, like a rock pushed off a cliff and deep into the sea; a big splash, and then a slow descent downwards. The all too familiar creepy feeling of nausea started to take hold somewhere in the bottommost region of her stomach. Miriam's smile disappeared quickly; eviscerated by the doom ridden look on his face, and that rock continued to sink, lower and lower.

'That's more like it. That's the sulky, sullen, unattractive, useless face I'm used to seeing every single day,' he said, turning just the right corner of his lips upwards.

She didn't respond. She had of course learnt, through bitter experience, not to rattle his cage - to let sleeping dogs lie, as the saying went. If she protested, she would incite a torrent of accusations; of how she loved to pick a fight, of how she was always ready and waiting to argue with him, of never knowing when to shut up, of being a disrespectful wife, of being incapable of just giving it a rest, of not leaving him in peace, of being a nag, of not doing as she was told – the list of claims against her could go on for some time. Silence was the best course of action right now.

He stared at her now more blankly than fiercely, perhaps a little surprised that his deliberately provocative comments had not secured any kind of a reaction. But this tame look only lasted a few seconds as Miriam witnessed the look on his face slowly change from a vacant expression to something more devious, more contrived, and after his next comment, she realised why. 'You're going to have to phone your brother and tell him we can't make it today.'

Miriam took a second to check if she had heard him right, then she stood up and walked away from the dressing table towards Zaf.

'What? Why?' she asked him.

He didn't answer her.

Miriam stopped in her tracks for a few moments, a brief

pause to get her head around this, a few seconds to think it through. *Keep quiet*, she told herself. *You have done it a thousand times before, why not today as well. Don't say anything. Just accept it and walk away. You know it's not worth it.* But today was different. Today, she couldn't keep quiet. Today she would protest. Today, she would speak up and he would have to listen. Today, he was not walking away from this, not walking away from her.

'You can't do this!' she said, surprising herself as soon as she uttered the words.

He looked at her and simply grunted, 'whatever.' He started to walk off to leave the bedroom and she went over and grabbed him by the arm.

'You know how much I have been looking forward to this. I haven't seen my family in years. I checked with you first before I agreed to today. I cleared it with you. You said today was fine. You're my husband, and you made me a promise; you promised to come with me.' Her eyes were filled with tears, but he noticed that they projected a look he had never quite seen before; a prickly, determined sort of a look.

'Let go of me, you stupid cow!' was his response as he force-fully removed her hand from his arm, and hurried on his way out of the room and down the stairs.

He grabbed his keys from the sideboard in the hallway and walked towards the front door. She followed him down the stairs, and then she followed him towards the front door. Today, for the first time perhaps since she married him, she allowed her long pent-up fury to completely boil over. Today she would not cower quietly, or hide in the corner, or bite her tongue, she would not just take it and let it be. Today, something had changed. *She* had changed. She had been like a slow burning, innocuous fire that had now had fuel thrown on it. A long stand-ing, long simmering fiery heat intensified inside her, it rumbled and growled as it tried to make its way out. She felt as though the fire may soon swell into blistering red-hot flames, flaring upwards, the black billowy smoke reaching high up to the sky, out of control.

They were on the doorstep now, she on the inside, he on the outside.

'Why can't you do this one thing for me, huh? I cook every day, and I clean this massive house, I work in the office doing mind numbing admin, I look after and entertain your parents when they come over and stay with us, I dress up for you, I dress down for you, I make appearances like a dolly bird on your arm, or I cover myself from head to toe like a nun, whatever you order me to do. I appear and disappear when you tell me to, I attend to your every desire. I am your wife cum servant, day in day out. Now, for the first time since I married you, I am asking something of you. Why are you doing this to me?'

'Stop being so bloody over-dramatic. Something's come up, that's all' he said, whilst still looking at his mobile phone, and managing to maintain a calm composure.

'Something, or someone?'

He looked up from his phone suddenly, and glared at what he now saw were her almost venom filled, icy cold eyes.

'You're going to see her, aren't you?' she screamed at him.

She had never raised her voice to him before. She had never dared to.

'You better stop this right now; do you hear me? I'm not listening to your nonsense anymore. I'm running late already. I need to go.'

To her own astonishment, she tried to lash out at him, to hurt him in some way. Whilst trying to dodge her wayward hand, he temporarily lost his footing, but managed to recover.

For a second, she didn't recognise herself. It was though someone else had taken over her mind and body. And in that same moment, she *hated* him like she had never hated anything or anyone in her entire life; she wished him harm, she wished him ill. She wished him dead.

She stared right at him, right into his miserable eyes; her next lot of tears forged hard, ready to descend onto her beautifully made-up face. Her reaction today was totally out of character, and it unnerved Zaf somewhat, but he soon took control - he made it clear that he didn't have time to deal with her right now. He would sort it out when he got back. She wouldn't be doing this again in a hurry; he would soon nip this absurdity in the bud. Whatever this sudden outburst was, it would not be happening again. He made that clear to her.

'Get back inside, I will deal with you later.'

'You can't do this!' she screamed at him, determined that her voice, lost for the past two years, which had now finally surfaced, would not fall on deaf ears.

'Just shut the fuck up!' he said through clenched teeth, in a stifled but firm voice. 'I will be back in the afternoon and I will talk to you then. Got it? Now stop making a fool of yourself out on the street like some fishwife cum banshee, and get back into the house.'

Zaf walked away and got into his car. He reversed out, and drove off at speed. Miriam's heavy tears now cascaded out, bringing down with them streams of what were supposed to be smudge proof black mascara and eyeliner, painting long charcoal grey stripes through her warm beige foundation and the peachy dustings of blusher. A few moments after he had sped off, it actually registered with her that he had gone, and so she went inside. She dragged herself back up to her bedroom, took her earrings out and placed them on her dressing table. Then she fell to the floor, resting her back against the side of the bed, the exact same place where she had started to miscarry. She tucked her knees under her chin and she cried and cried; she sobbed until her eyes were puffy red and they pounded with pain, until she felt as though there were specks of grit scratching away at their delicate surface. Once she had exhausted herself from her crying and she could cry no more, she phoned Zaf for one last ditch attempt to get him to change his mind, but she got nowhere with him, so she then phoned her brother.

'What time will you be arriving?' was her brother's first question, but he didn't wait for her to respond, and he continued talking before she could get a word in. 'Hey, you won't believe this, but dad has actually cooked for you,' he said, to Miriam's surprise. 'He was up at the crack of dawn. He's just popped out right now to get a bit more shopping. He's made your favourite – *achari* chicken. You always loved that pickled taste, didn't you? He blended the spices himself you know, from scratch. It *is* still your favourite, isn't it?'

'Yes, it is,' replied Miriam, with a lump in her throat as she thought of her father cooking for her. That really was quite something. She remembered how when she was younger, and her mum used to cook in the kitchen, for it was always her mother who had cooked, her father would go into the kitchen too, and make them both cups of tea. He would stay with her and keep her company, doing a few bits and pieces to help her along the way; washing a few dishes, putting the spices away, taking things in and out of the fridge, opening the can of tinned tomatoes, perhaps even stretching to chopping some fresh coriander, or peeling the garlic for her. However, he never actually cooked anything. Yet it seemed after all that he must have paid close attention to her mum whilst she had cooked, seeing as though he had managed to make the *achari* chicken.

'My wife has made fresh *ras malai*, which was always your favourite as well. I remember how you always used to nick my portion from the fridge! And we used to have the almightiest ding dongs about it. Come to think of it, you used to steal quite a bit of my food from the fridge, and mum used to have such a go at you! But then again, you always gave me your cakes and biscuits first whenever you had one of your baking days at school, so I guess you used to make up for it.'

The corners of her mouth and eyes curved upwards, as she thought back to happier days with her sibling.

'And my little one, he has been really excited about meeting you,' her brother continued. 'He has talked about it non-stop. He has even made you a card. He's drawn our family of stick people, and guess what? He's included you in it as well; he's drawn you with a very bright orange dress on, and really long hair down past your knees!'

Wow, she thought to herself. She had a nephew. A nephew she had never seen. She was an aunty and hadn't even known it until just a week ago. And she had a sister-in-law she had never met. It was in fact to her sister-in-law that that she owed her gratitude to for she was the one who had engineered the reunion. She had tracked Miriam down via social media. Miriam hadn't posted anything on her Facebook account for a long time. She had stopped engaging in any social media shortly after her marriage to Zaf, but she hadn't actually deactivated her Facebook account, and her sister-in-law had contacted her through Facebook Messenger. A woman's entry into their family had led to the facilitating of renewed contact between them. Miriam often wondered why more women weren't peacemakers on a global stage. They would be far better at it than the men, for women made peace between others, and for the sake of others, every day of their lives; at home, at work, between family members, their friends, their siblings, their colleagues, their in-laws, their squabbling kids. It was almost innate; to smooth things over, to talk things through, to listen to both sides, to reach a compromise, to make the peace.

She had to stop her brother now, before he said anything else that would only increase the level of disappointment when she told him she wasn't coming. She had waited so anxiously for this day to arrive, but the dream of seeing them all had been so cruelly snatched away by Zaf.

'Listen, the thing is, something really urgent has come up for Zaf at work, and we can't make it after all,' Miriam told her brother.

'Oh...okay, not to worry.' The disappointment in his voice was palpable.

'I'm really so sorry, you can't even begin to imagine how much I was looking forward to seeing you all. But next weekend we will definitely come up, and even if Zaf can't make it, although hopefully he will, but if he can't, I will definitely be there, I promise, *Insha'Allah*.' She quickly realised that she shouldn't have promised anything of the sort without checking with Zaf first. Going out of town alone without his permission was not something she would normally ever dare to do. Then again, she had to acknowledge that today was not normal. Today, normality had shifted into new, unfamiliar territory.

'It's alright, these things happen. We can always come down, if that's easier for you.'

'Of course, you're welcome to visit at any time,' she said reassuringly, but again, this statement was not one she would normally dish out without clearance, so she qualified it, 'but I really want to come home, you know, I guess you could say I want to come back to my roots.'

'I understand.' There was a brief pause before her brother continued to speak, his tone now less energetic, lacking the excitement that was evident previously; it was now softer, and more thoughtful. 'He's really proud of you, you know,' he said to his sister.

'What?' Miriam felt as though she hadn't heard him properly.

'Me too,' he added.

'Sorry?'

'Dad. He's really proud of the fact that you have sorted your life out. You're settled, happily married, working in the family business, supporting your husband.'

Miriam listened silently. Her eyebrows tensed up, making the familiar little wavy lines. She absentmindedly clenched her jaw hard.

'You are happy, aren't you?'

What does a girl like Miriam say to a question like that, to her, up until now, estranged brother? Where would she even begin.

'Of course,' was the only thing she could think to say.

'Like I said, he's chuffed, especially given...'

His voice trailed off, and perhaps he didn't want to rake up the past, but she didn't have the same qualms.

'Given the fact that I left home at 18 and never came back.'

'Listen, it's all ancient history. It's forgotten. Let's not go there.'

'It's okay. I have reconciled myself to the part I played in all of that. I was grieving, and I didn't know how to handle it. And so, I rebelled. But it wasn't really me, you know. Once I moved to Manchester, and I started university, this rebellion didn't really last all that long. It wasn't what I wanted. What I really wanted was my mum back, and as that wasn't possible, I wanted my dad, but he didn't know how to show me the love that I yearned for, or maybe I just pushed him away just a bit too far.'

'That's just dad. He doesn't do displays of affection. He's old school like that. And just because at that time he couldn't show his love to you didn't mean that that he didn't love you, or that he didn't care for you. You have to remember; he was grieving too.'

'He was grieving so much that he was thinking of re-marrying,' Miriam said, a hint of anger in her voice now tainting her words.

'What?'

'That's what did it for me. I could understand his disappointment at my stupid acts of attention-seeking and rebellion, I could deal with the arguments that would follow every time I kicked off. Most of that was my fault if I am honest. I was grief-stricken, but I couldn't find a way out of the spiral that the grief had sucked me into. I should have just talked to him, or to you, but things got so far down the line that talking seemed to have stopped being an option. Then, when I heard he was going to Pakistan to remarry, that was it for me. He didn't even ask me if I was okay with it, never mind ask me, he didn't even tell me. I decided I was going to uni and not coming back. No one could ever replace our mum, and I wasn't going to stick around to watch another woman try. But having said that, I have grown up a bit since then, you know. I promise I will be on my best behaviour for the step mum, although I see you haven't mentioned her yet. You don't need to try and spare my feelings; you *can* talk about her.'

'Where on earth did you get that idea from?'

'What?'

'About him remarrying?'

'The week before I was due to go away to uni, I heard him on the phone to his brother talking about marrying again. My Urdu is not great, but I got the gist of it. I also heard the both of you talking about it as well. I know he'd booked his ticket to Pakistan. He was all set to do it. He was ready to leave two week-ends after I left for university.'

'No! You got it all wrong, sis. Oh my goodness!'

'What? What do you mean?'

'You are right to some degree; his brother in Pakistan had suggested that he remarry, pestered him to do it in fact. They had many conversations about it. His brother had even found a suitable match for him. But you mustn't have got the full picture at the time, because although initially he had said he would come over and consider it, he actually changed his mind and, in the end, he did refuse. He told his brother that he wasn't ready to marry again, but more importantly, he told his brother that until *you* were older, and married and settled, he couldn't even entertain the idea. Dad and I did discuss the subject, but you must have taken what you heard out of context, or maybe you only heard part of the conversation.'

'But I don't understand. He had booked a flight to Pakistan. His brother had said he will arrange the marriage for him, and dad was set to go over.'

'Yes, he had booked a ticket, as his brother had asked him to come over, and he did go to Pakistan. But it was not to go over to definitely get married. That was an option presented to him which he declined. He actually went over to sort out some legal issues concerning the family land. That was the primary purpose of his visit.'

Miriam didn't know what to say.

'As it turned out,' continued her brother, 'he has not remarried. He's not that old, and I personally do think he should think about finding a companion for himself. But he says he's happy with the life he has, especially now he has a grandchild, and even more so now you are going to be back in his life. He always says he is happy with the memories of the most wonderful wife a man could ever have. In his words, the blessing of a truly loving spouse, who supports you one hundred per cent through all of life's ups and downs, is not something everyone gets to experience.'

They parted on this poignant but truthful note. Her parents had been devoted to each other, something that was rare indeed. Her brother said that her father would probably call her once he got back from the shops. He reiterated what a shame it was that she couldn't make it today, but that they were very much all looking forward to seeing her next week, and she echoed the same on her part.

After the call ended, Miriam sat in silence for a few moments. She exhaled a long breath that she had unconsciously been holding in. She got up and slowly walked over to the window, and looked out onto the road.

She couldn't believe how wrong she had got it all. All those years wasted, because of a complete misunderstanding. She cussed herself, but in the same heartbeat she had to acknowledge what a state she had been in back then; angry and sad, frightened and frightful, sensitive and pugnacious, and not really seeing the world as it was. When looked at in that light, perhaps it was not really all that surprising.

She could see now that the sky was a gloomy gunmetal grey, and the air was blustery. The tips of the silver birches swayed swiftly to the tune of the breeze. It was cold for the time of year. She must remember to wear her thicker raincoat, she thought to herself, the navy blue one with the fleecy lining, when she went out for her afternoon walk. Walking was something that she always loved to do.

27

Birmingham Crown Court
12 November 2019

'Do you remember seeing either of them again that day, Mrs Bains?' asks Ms Godfrey.

'I didn't see Zaf again, although I did notice that his car was back on his drive in the afternoon.'

'What about the defendant?'

'Yes, I did see Miriam again.'

'What time was that?'

'It was at around quarter past three in the afternoon. I saw Miriam returning back home from what I presumed was her walk. She usually goes for a walk on a Sunday afternoon.'

'Did you see her leave for her walk that day?'

'No, I didn't.'

'And where were you when you saw Miriam return?'

'I was upstairs in my bedroom at the time, which is at the front of the house. I had just started ironing, by the window which looks onto our road. I like to get things ironed and hung up for the week, you see. I'd been ironing for a few minutes and I saw her walk past.'

'Now, the next question I am going to ask you now is a very important one, so think carefully before answering: did you see anyone on your road matching the description of someone dressed in black joggers, white trainers, and a black hoodie, approaching or leaving number 6, at any point in the afternoon?'

Mrs Bains doesn't take any time at all to think about this very significant question, and replies brusquely. 'No. I didn't.'

'You are totally sure?'

'Yes, I would say if I did.'

'Very well.'

Miriam was hoping that her neighbour would have some memory of seeing this man too, and now feels deflated upon hearing her response. Why is it, she asks herself, that nobody else saw this man? She feels quietly infuriated.

Ms Godfrey shifts the papers around in front of her, a little too noisily and for a little too long for the Judge's liking; he peers at her over his half-moon glasses with disgruntled looking eyes. She pretends not to notice, although she does stop fidgeting, and continues with her examination in chief.

'The pathologist's report estimates the time of death to be between 3pm and 4pm. Now this next question is *extremely* important, Mrs Bains. I cannot stress that enough. You are most certain, aren't you, that you saw the defendant return home at 3.15pm?'

'Leading question, My Lord!' objects Mr De Beaux, clearly more alert than Ms Godfrey has given him credit for. Mrs Bains is left hanging with her mouth half open.

'You will rephrase that please,' orders the Judge. Mrs Bains looks on with some uncertainty as to what is actually happening.

'Very well,' replies Ms Godfrey, with a small bow of her head. 'Mrs Bains, are you certain that you saw Mrs Hassan return home at 3.15pm?'

'Yes. I am.'

'How can you be so sure?'

'Oh, that's easy. I know it was quarter past, because whilst I was ironing, I had the television on in the background. I like to listen to the news as I iron, and I heard the news presenter give the headlines at quarter past three, which was at the same time as I saw her walk past.'

'Thank you, Mrs Bains, that will be all for now.'

Mr De Beaux turns around and consults his solicitor briefly. There is a momentary tete-a-tete, after which he rises slowly to his feet.

'Mrs Bains. I must say, you have a remarkably good memory.'

'Thank you,' she replies. She can't help but break into a smug smile, delighted at having received what she considers to be a wonderful compliment from an experienced lawyer who must have seen hundreds, if not thousands of witnesses in his time, and for him to single her out in this way, well, that was quite something, she mused to herself.

'Now then, if you can turn your mind back once again to the events of the morning of 31 March 2019. Did you actually hear anything that was said during the alleged argument between the defendant and the deceased which took place on their doorstep?'

'I could hear that they were arguing.'

'Yes, I understand that, but that was not my question. What I am asking you is did you *hear* any of the specific words or phrases that either of them said that day?'

Mrs Bains shifts her gaze up and down as she thinks for a few seconds. 'No. I did not really hear any words, not that I can recall at any rate. It was just loud.'

'So, just to be clear, you essentially have no idea what this supposed argument was about?'

'No, I don't, but I could see that Miriam looked very angry. She was definitely screaming at him about something.'

'And the deceased? How did he look?'

'I couldn't see Zaf's face.'

'I would say, therefore, that you cannot possibly have a full picture of this incident, can you?'

'Erm, well...'

'You couldn't see the expression on Zaf's face, could you? Nor did you hear anything that was said by either party; therefore, you can't really tell us very much about this alleged argument at all, can you?'

'Well...I suppose...' On this rare occasion Mrs Bains doesn't manage to finish her sentence. Her pencil thin eyebrows gather together in confusion, and she starts to chew her bottom lip.

'Now, coming to the part of the day when you said you saw the defendant come home from her walk.'

'Yes?'

'You are quite adamant that it was quarter past three.'

'Oh yes. Quite sure,' she replies, quickly.

'Did you look at your watch?'

'No, I don't usually wear a watch. Which is a bit silly really, as I have two lovely watches sitting in the cupboard gathering dust. An Omega and –'

'How do you normally check the time?' interrupts Mr De Beaux, not interested in the least in what brand her watches are or how much they are worth.

'I usually check the time on my mobile phone if I need to,' she replies plainly, feeling a little wounded by his interruption. She supposed him to be a very nice man when he first started his questioning, but now she considers him to be quite a rude person. And arrogant to boot. Interrupting a lady mid-sentence. Not gentlemanly like behaviour at all, she thinks.

'Did you therefore check the time on your mobile phone?'

'No. I didn't. I think I had left my mobile phone downstairs on this particular day. That is something my husband complains about a lot, that I leave my phone lying around wherever, and so I often miss his calls. I sometimes leave it at home when I go shopping. Besides, as I have said before, I was ironing, so I didn't really have the time, or any spare hands, to be bothering with my phone.'

Mr De Beaux's eyebrows rise a tad. 'Okay. Just so we are absolutely certain. You were not wearing a watch, and you did not have your phone with you to be able to check the time on that. Correct?'

'Correct.'

'Did you, therefore, turn around and look at the television screen to check the time?' asks Mr De Beaux.

Mrs Bains curls up her left hand, and brings it up to her chin, as she thinks about the question carefully for a little while, her eyes squinting, the red apples of her cheeks rising, exposing prominently the crow's feet on either side.

'Did you see the actual time on the television screen displayed as 3.15pm?' Mr De Beaux presses her. 'Think *very carefully*.'

Mrs Bains takes her hand away from her face. She pauses for a few seconds further before answering. 'No. But I definitely remember that I heard the newsreader say "now the headlines at quarter past three" or something like that.'

'Hmmm. "Or something like that" you say.'

There is a short lull, timed to perfection, and then Mr De Beaux repeats, '" or something like that".'

The headteacher guy in the jury folds his arms and tilts his head to one side whilst he stares at Mrs Bains.

'Do you think, perhaps, the presenter might have said quarter past four?' asks Mr De Beaux

'No,' replies Mrs Bains, firmly, with an exaggerated lift of her head.

Mr De Beaux purses his lips together for a few seconds, whilst he thinks through his next bit of spiel.

'My client says she returned back home at about quarter past four. You were, by your own admission, busy ironing, and at the same time managing to look out of the window to notice the comings and goings of the day. Which means that you weren't completely focused on the television, were you?'

'Not completely I guess, no, as in, I wasn't watching it, but I could hear it.'

Mr De Beaux stands a little taller, and draws his shoulders back, as if he were trying to get his shoulder blades to touch. 'What was the main headline that day? When the newsreader said "now the headlines at quarter past three," what did he follow that with?'

Mrs Bains rolls her eyes upwards, and bats her eyelashes a few times, but says nothing.

'Okay, forget the main headline, do you remember *any* of the headlines?'

'I'm not sure to be honest, erm....'

The jury members wait pensively, and the whole courtroom is quietly focused on Mrs Bains, waiting to see what she will say next.

'If you don't remember what the main headline was, and nor do you remember the details of even one single news item that day, then how can you be so sure that you remember the time correctly?'

Mrs Bains scrunches her face up like a crinkled piece of paper. She glances towards the Judge, and then back at Mr De Beaux. She leans forward a little and clasps hold of the front edge of the witness box, feeling a little overwhelmed by the flurry of questions that she is now struggling to answer.

Mr De Beaux glimpses towards the jury, and clocks the looks on some of their faces; the headteacher guy still has his head tilted, only the tilt is on the other side now, and Marilyn is sitting rigidly with her arms folded, with a severe look on her face – the Kim Kardashian style sharp contour lines along her cheekbones, down the sides of her nose and at her hair and jaw lines seem at odds with the soft bouncy Marilyn hairdo.

'We know that the defendant was out of the house before 3pm, which is the earliest estimated time of death,' continues Mr De Beaux. 'We have an eye witness statement confirming sight of the defendant having coffee in the café at the local park at around 2.50pm. That is not in dispute. The only time that is the subject of disagreement is the time that she allegedly returned home. The defendant says she is certain about the time that she arrived back home, because she looked at her watch as she entered the house. She says, in her statement to the police, that it was just gone 4.15pm. She insists that when she got in, her husband was already dead, and she telephoned the police immediately.' Mr De Beaux now fixes his eyes firmly on Mrs Bains. 'I would ask you to think extremely carefully Mrs Bains. Are you absolutely, one hundred percent certain, without even a speck of doubt, that you saw the defendant return to her house at quarter past three?'

'Err, well, I—'

'Remember what is at stake here. I would ask you to have regard to the gravity of the matter before you, and the consequences for my client. Life imprisonment. You must be absolutely sure. There is no room for error.'

Mrs Bains' eyes wander around what now feels to her like an oppressively stuffy courtroom; sticky droplets of sweat seem to be clinging to her forehead and neck. Her gaze moves to settle on a very downcast looking Miriam, not looking at all like the Miriam she used to see up and down their road. Mrs Bains thinks that she looks akin to a wounded bird; so very fragile, and frightened. When Miriam catches her eye, Mrs Bains quickly averts her gaze and looks back towards the lawyers' benches.

'Is there any possibility that you could be wrong about the time, and it may in fact have been quarter past four?' Mr De Beaux pushes on, although he is now speaking very softly, and on another day and in another setting, once could say almost seductively.

'I suppose...I suppose it's possible...'

Chatter erupts around the court.

'May I remind you all for the need for silence in the court-room!' shouts the Judge.

'Thank you, Mrs Bains,' says Mr De Beaux.

Mrs Bains looks expectantly towards Mr De Beaux, secretly hoping that this will now be the end of what she considers to have been a bit of an ordeal.

'That will be all. No further questions, My Lord,' he says, and Mrs Bains feels a pang of relief.

Ms Godfrey tosses her pen onto her notes and lets out a sigh. Mr De Beaux stifles a wry smile as he looks back towards Miriam.

Miriam sits in her cell, with her hands clasped together in her lap, waiting for her legal team to arrive.

'How do you think it's going?' asks Miriam, impatiently, as soon as Mr De Beaux and Sara walk in through the door. 'What do you think so far?'

Mr De Beaux rubs his chin with one hand, as though he is stroking a non-existent stubbly beard. 'Okay. Let me level with you,' he says. 'As things stand, we are not anywhere near out of the woods. I have always said this, and I will say it again. It's entirely your decision as to whether or not you want to take the stand. But in my professional opinion, you *do* need to give evidence.'

Miriam looks back at Mr De Beaux quietly, her eyes thick with a mist of disappointment. From the very start, she has made it clear that she is very reluctant to give evidence. She was hoping to hear better news from her barrister.

Sara walks over and sits next to her on the bench. She gently places one hand on Miriam's arm. Sara has in fact become a great source of comfort to her, to Miriam's surprise. This is not something Miriam had expected; that her lawyer would actually care about her, really be bothered about what happened to her. And to some extent, she thinks this of Mr De Beaux too. Miriam is fully aware that at the end of the day, it is just a job for him, but he could well breeze through the case without demonstrating the touching level of kindness and humanity that she sees every day. He would manage to do his job perfectly well without opening up this compassionate side to her - get the case over with and move on to the next one. He could, but he doesn't, and Miriam appreciates that.

'Miriam, I know you're scared, and that is perfectly understandable,' says Sara. 'But if we are to have the best possible chance of keeping you out of prison, then you *must* give evidence.'

'She's absolutely right,' adds Mr De Beaux. 'If the jury don't hear what you have to say, they will come to a decision based on what they have heard so far from everyone else, and your refusal to give evidence could be seen as an indication of your guilt. Yes, the witness evidence of the Prosecution had a few kinks in it, but the forensic evidence is bang on. Your DNA was all over the murder weapon and the scene of the crime. Yours. *No one else's.*

Just yours. His blood was on *your* clothing. There is no categoric evidence that you arrived home after he was dead. It's your word against the neighbour's word. And the thing is this, if you don't testify, then it's more a case of it just being her word. We have no other witnesses who can confirm a sighting of the man you say you saw on that day. If you don't speak, the jury will never get to hear your side of what occurred that afternoon, because as far as your involvement in this murder goes, you are the only one who can tell the jury what *really* happened.'

'There's another detail that has come to me – I don't think it will be of any use.'

'Well, let us be the judge of that,' says Sara.

'When I was walking past our cul-de-sac on that day, towards the park, when I glanced over and saw the man in black, I also saw a red car parked at number 10 - that isn't their car.'

'Okay...but it's not in your statement...can you give us any more details...' Mr De Beaux waits for her to continue.

'Well, that's it. I don't recall anything else. It's just a small detail that came to me afterwards. And didn't think anything of it.'

'I'm not sure we can do anything with this information...'

'I know,' Miriam interrupts Mr De Beaux before he can finish his sentence. 'I don't know why, I just thought I would mention it.'

Miriam's forehead crinkles with little lines that gather together as her eyebrows tense up.

'You will have a think about what we have impressed upon you...about giving evidence,' says Sara.

But Miriam does not respond. She pulls her legs up onto the bench, and hugs her knees into her chest. She doesn't say anything further to either of them. She has now gone into her silent zone.

Sara and Mr De Beaux have got used to this. Sometimes they

can go for long periods of time without hearing a peep from Miriam. This is most definitely going to be one of those times. They know just from looking at her that they aren't going to get anything more out of her now. She is thinking. They know that she will speak to them when, and only when, she has thought things through and made up her mind.

'Sleep on it,' says Sara. 'We will have our usual meet up in the morning before court resumes, and you can let us have your decision then.'

Miriam gives a faint nod of the head; she doesn't really register the words that come out of Sara's mouth, but she can guess what they are, and she feels she may as well acknowledge that she has heard Sara speak. Miriam is exhausted. She does not have even an iota of energy to muster up any words in response. Although hard to believe, she longs to get back to her cell. Yes. It is a prison cell, but it is *her* prison cell, a cell that she occupies on her own currently. She thinks herself lucky for that at least. On the journey back to prison, in the back of the van, she soundlessly prays that it turns out to be a quiet night tonight, that there is no shouting or screaming or swearing, so that she can have the silence to think, for she has much to think about. It is time for her to decide whether she can rise to the biggest challenge of her entire life, bar none. Dare she take that stand. Dare she talk in front of everyone about what really happened on that day?

Dare she?

'She will be alright? Won't she?' asks Sara, hoping to hear some reassuring words from Mr De Beaux.

It is getting late, but she and Mr De Beaux have decided to grab a drink in town. There are bars and eateries aplenty within walking distance of the court. They have agreed upon a bar cum tapas type restaurant a few blocks away from the Crown Court, just across on the other side of the tramline.

They both take a seat and get comfortable, ready to discuss the case and make final preparations for tomorrow, although they cannot completely finalise their plan until Miriam decides whether she wants to take the stand. But, if nothing else, it is a good opportunity to try and iron out some of the creases in the case before tomorrow.

'I don't know,' is Mr De Beaux's frank response to Sara's question, accompanied by a tap of his right index finger on his lips.

They have chosen a quiet corner booth, with a large table that allows them to spread out some of their notes and documents.

'She didn't do it. I know she didn't. I can feel it.' Sara doesn't know if she is trying to convince him or endeavouring to persuade herself.

'She *says* she didn't kill him, and that's all there is to it as far as we are concerned,' reflects Mr De Beaux. 'That said, we do have some serious issues with our case, as you well know.'

Sara opens her mouth to speak but then she pauses whilst the waiter pops the drinks down on the table for them, together with the tapas selection; golden crispy fried cod, patatas bravas, spinach and halloumi croquettes, sweetcorn and goats cheese fritters, hummus, olives and bread.

'What's bothering you?' asks Sara when the waiter leaves.

Mr De Beaux puckers his lips for a moment whilst he thinks. He pops a piece of cod in his mouth, and deliberates whilst he savours it. 'There's the time issue, obviously. Her word against the Bains woman. God that woman can talk. Convincing the jury about the exact time that Miriam got back home is the crux of it, hence she needs to give evidence. There's no two ways

about that. I hope to God she makes the right decision. But...'
His voice trails off, and he picks up his glass and has a sip.

'But what?' asks Sara.

'It's this story about the mystery man.'

'What about it?'

'Well, that's just it; it *sounds* like a story. It *sounds* made up.
She didn't mention it in her first police interview, did she?'

'No. She didn't...' Sara's voice trails off.

'And now she's thrown in some red car parked at one of the
neigbour's driveways, which is neither use nor ornament to us,
and if she testifies it's best she doesn't mention it as it's going to
sound like yet another detail she forgot to mention before.
Devil's advocate now: this is a small but quite tightly-knit road
where neighbours are friendly and someone always seems to
notice the comings and goings. It's tucked all the way down a
lane, well out of the way, so you would rarely get strangers
walking down there, and if there was a stranger lurking around,
then someone would notice them. Hell, that annoying Bains
woman would notice them, even if no one else did. But no one
saw the mystery man. No one, except Miriam, that is. And she
initially didn't even recall that she'd seen this mystery person.
She divulged this information later down the line. Which all
sounds very convenient.'

'So, you think she's lying?' asks Sara, as she nibbles her way
through a fritter.

'There's the conundrum.' Mr De Beaux sighs wistfully.

'How do you mean?'

'I can't believe that she saw such a man, it doesn't sound
plausible, but by the same token, I also don't believe that she's
lying, and that, I know, Sara, doesn't make sense.'

Sara just smiles at him, a soft, "I understand" sort of a smile,
after which she chips in with her own puzzling thought. 'There
is something that I can't get my head around.'

'What's that then?'

'What I don't understand is the disparity of her reactions.'

'Disparity?'

'I get that she would be upset with him on that day of his murder, because he broke a promise, and she had been looking forward to seeing her family, but she wasn't just upset, she was very angry, livid in fact. So, her reaction was quite extreme. But compare that to when she saw in him bed with another woman. She walked off and never even mentioned it to him, or anyone else, not even her best friend. If that was me, and I found my husband in bed with a hussy, not that I have a husband, but if I did have a husband, and like I said, if I found him in bed with some tart, I would rip his bloody head off, and one or two other things as well!'

'Whoa! Steady on!' Mr De Beaux lets out a laugh, and Sara joins him. 'Remind me, never to get on the wrong side of you!'

'But you see what I'm saying, don't you? If there is ever a time for a woman to be pushed over the edge, I would say that would be it,' says Sara quite adamantly, with a few heavy taps of her index finger on the red folder that is placed on the table in front of her.

'I know, it is another bit of the jigsaw that doesn't quite fit.'

'Hmmm.'

'I have to say, she's definitely one of my more unusual and interesting clients,' says Mr De Beaux.

'You and me both.'

'Honestly, it's hard to imagine that she could even think of killing him, let alone actually do it, but then, if she didn't, who did?'

Sara raises her pristinely threaded and shaped eyebrows. 'That's not our problem,' she says.

'Damn right it's not. Our only problem is making sure that she doesn't go down for this. She's a good person by nature, anyone can see that, but as we both know, even good people are capable of murder if they're pushed far enough. But whether she killed him or not,' adds Mr De Beaux, with a faint grimace that one rarely sees on his face, 'that bastard bloody well deserved it! I just hope she *does* give evidence, and it goes her way on the day.'

28

Birmingham Crown Court
13 November 2019

Day after day whilst on remand she has thought about what it would be like if she did give evidence, but she just couldn't picture it. And now, to her own surprise, here she is, standing lifelessly in the witness box, poised to do just that.

She almost never made it, so determined was she to not give evidence. But memories can do strange things, and it was a memory of her late mother that made her mind up for her. Whilst drifting off to sleep in her cell a couple of nights ago, she recalled a conversation with her mum one cold winter's evening, more specifically some advice that her mother gave her which now resonated after all these years - "whatever difficulty you might come across in life, don't *ever* expect anyone else to come and rescue you – you must rescue yourself".

If not now, when?

She feels limp, like a ragged doll that is barely hanging on at the end of a marionette string. In fact, she is reminded of her favourite battered doll that she carried around constantly when she was little. The words that she has just uttered, to tell the whole truth and nothing but the truth, are already beginning to weigh heavily on Miriam's conscience, before she has faced even a single question; she feels deflated, but she is also aware of a heavy, invisible force that is pulling down inside her. She must fight them both; the desire to wilt on the spot, and the urge to allow the boulder like force to take her down.

She stands up a bit straighter now, as though someone has finally tugged at that marionette string, ready for the performance that is about to resume. Puppets and audience all in place, Miriam looks across at the dock. *So, this is what it looks like from the other side. The other side.* She tries to imagine herself sitting in there. She looks across at herself now. She can see herself, her eyes cast down towards the ground, looking forlorn, feeling small and powerless. Scared, as well. She wonders how the onlookers in the courtroom see her, and how the members of the jury view her. They most likely don't detect the fear that permeates her, the despair that lives inside her, the darkness that troubles her - every waking hour of every day. They can, or at least they eventually will, only see one of two possibilities; guilty, or not guilty.

Mr De Beaux and Sara both look towards Miriam, and she senses that they are almost as nervous as she is; their demeanour is upbeat and positive, but the eyes give it away. Miriam is well aware why their eyes portray a sense of unease. Will she come through? That is probably what they are asking themselves. God knows how they have shown so much patience with her throughout this whole ordeal, she wonders. At the start, getting her to say anything had been like pulling teeth. It took time, but gradually, Miriam had started to confide in them, which was promising. However, the only problem for them had been that although she did eventually start to speak, none of it had made any sense; it was like trying to untangle dozens of large solid knots in the longest of hair, but they persevered. Combing out the knots hurts like crazy at first, but it soon gets better, and after a while, you have long tangle-free tresses through which the comb glides smoothly, save for the odd little knot that snags here or there. Not one person in her legal team, not Sara, not Mr De Beaux, not any of their juniors or assistants, ever gave up on Miriam. Getting Miriam to talk has been one half of the battle only, but convincing her to give evidence has been much harder for them. All Miriam has been able to think about was the humiliation for herself were she to take the stand, and so she had not allowed herself to imagine being in this box. Standing in this tiny square space, in front of her family, her friends, her former work colleagues, strangers, reporters, lawyers; spilling her guts. Feeling nothing but degradation. The shame that she felt, and still feels, is the reason she has refused to see her father and brother when they have tried to visit her in prison whilst she has been on remand. How can she see them? How can she face them, sit opposite them and talk about all of this? By the same token, how can she stand up in court and tell all and sundry about what had happened in her marriage? How can she allow such scrutiny, such examination of every minutiae detail of her relationship with Zaf? These questions had previously steered her away from agreeing to give evidence. But the blunt reality has been driven home hard to her by her lawyers; speak up and *maybe* go to prison, stay quiet and almost *definitely* go to prison. Their message has in the end triumphed, and here she is today, ready to bare all, ready to unearth the shame that she feels, to say it out loud and clear for all to hear. But she has come to realise one thing; if she doesn't fight for herself, no one else will.

Mr De Beaux stands up tall and gives Miriam a slight smile of encouragement which helps her to feel at ease, a little.

'Mrs Hassan. I am going to ask you to cast your mind back to the day that your husband died. We have heard evidence previously from witnesses who saw or heard you and the deceased arguing on the morning of 31 March. Can you explain to the court what happened on that day? If there was such a disagreement, then what was this disagreement about?' asks Mr De Beaux.

Miriam swallows hard, and takes a deep breath. *You can do this.*

'I hadn't seen my family for many years, since the age of 18. We had recently been back in touch, and Zaf and I were supposed to go up to Bradford to visit them that day.' She looks over at her father and brother who have so far attended every day of the trial, and her bottom lip starts quivering. She bites on to it with her top two front teeth.

'Why had you and your family become estranged?'

Just be yourself, just tell the truth. Miriam reminds herself of Mr De Beaux's words.

'There's no one single reason to be honest. It was a series of difficult events, hurt feelings and misunderstandings. When my mother passed away when I was a teenager, I suppose I couldn't deal with it. And I don't think my father could find a way to help me. I started to rebel against pretty much everything. I became argumentative, troublesome, and I don't think my father knew how to handle me just as much as I didn't know how to handle my mother's death. When I left Bradford to go to university in Manchester, I told him I was never coming back. And true to my word, I didn't return home after that.'

'Did you ever try to make contact?'

'No.'

'Why not?'

'I thought *he,* my father, that is, didn't care, and I now feel that he must have thought that *I* didn't care. Things became very entrenched in a way. And sadly, the longer we were out of touch, the harder it became to get back in touch. For my part, I think I always feared rejection.'

'Thank you for providing that background regarding your family. Turning now to the 31st March of this year, what happened during the argument between yourself and your husband on the day in question?'

'As I said, we had planned to go up to Bradford that day to see my family. It was all arranged. To say I was excited would have been an understatement. Zaf knew exactly how much I had been looking forward to it. But without warning, or any kind of justification, he told me that something important had come up and we couldn't go. He didn't give my any details about what this supposedly urgent matter was. He ordered me to telephone my family and let them know.'

'He *ordered* you?'

Hippy woman in the jury sits up straighter upon hearing this, her eyes wide and alert, her lips drawn together tightly.

'Yes. Zaf always ordered, or instructed me to do things. He never asked me, or consulted me, or sought my opinion. He just told me.'

'And how did you feel when he let you down in this way?'

Miriam sighs. 'I was really very, very upset. Distraught, in fact. I never asked much of Zaf. And he knew this was really important to me. Hence the argument on the doorstep.'

'Why do you think he had changed his mind?'

'I had no absolutely no idea, and even now I still honestly couldn't tell you. Zaf was a law unto himself.'

Miriam pauses, and hesitation begins to slowly encroach into the corners of her mind.

'Can you describe to the court what you mean by that?'

He's not here anymore. You can say whatever you want! Just tell them!

'Zaf did whatever Zaf wanted to do, and to hell with

everyone else, that was Zaf all over. But this time, I couldn't let it go. This time, I was angry, and I accused him of going to see Rachel, though I didn't know that for sure. I knew they were having an affair. I had known for a while. But this was the first time I had said it out aloud and I think it surprised him a little.'

'Mrs Hassan. Did you try to hit your husband?'

Miriam's scrunches up her eyebrows, and her forehead crumples with the threadlike wavy lines that Mr De Beaux is now so accustomed to seeing, signalling a sense of her increasing anxiety.

'I lashed out at him, yes, out of sheer frustration. It was more a pathetic attempt to push him rather than to actually hit him. It was in a moment of anger. I was infuriated with the way he was treating me. There is no way I could or would ever have actually hurt him. And besides, he was physically much stronger than me, not to mention the fact that I was ordinarily very scared of him. I actually surprised myself when I reacted towards him in that way because it was totally out of character for me.'

'Did you make any threats to kill or hurt your husband?'

'No. Never.'

'What did you say?'

'I said something like "you are now dead to me"'

'And what exactly did you mean by that?'

'I meant it in the sense that he no longer meant anything to me, or as if to say I didn't care about him anymore. I don't even know where I had found the courage to say that in the first place, because like I said, it wasn't like me. But I certainly did not threaten to kill him.'

'What happened after that?'

'He drove off in a hurry, and I went back inside. I sat and cried, and then I phoned him a little while later, as a final attempt to try and persuade him to change his mind, but it was no good. He wasn't having any of it. In fact, the whole conversation was really odd.'

'What do you mean by that? In what way was it odd?'

'It's kind of hard to explain, but basically, his responses on the phone didn't seem to match up with the questions that I had asked him. I remember asking him if he would please reconsider, because it wasn't too late, and he answered back with "stop threatening me" or words to that effect. But I wasn't threatening him in the least. It was bizarre. I soon realised there wasn't much point in continuing the conversation, so I ended the call.'

'What did you do after that?'

'I then telephoned my brother to say I was sorry but we couldn't make it.'

'What did you tell your brother, as to why you would not be coming?'

'I told him it was because an urgent work matter had cropped up for Zaf.'

'Mrs Hassan, you didn't actually know *why* Zaf had cancelled, did you?'

'No.'

'I'm sure this is something the Prosecution will ask you, so tell me, why did you lie?'

The Asian guy in the jury, the Zaf lookalike, is subtly but repetitively nodding his head, a bit like the dog in the back of the car in the insurance advert. She can see him in the corner of her eye, but she does her best to ignore him.

'Because I was embarrassed. Because I didn't want them to know that I had a husband who didn't care one jot about my feelings. Because I didn't want them to know I was in an unhappy, abusive marriage.'

'When you say "abusive", what do you mean, Mrs Hassan?'

There is a sensation which feels like tiny bits of hair standing up on the back of her neck, causing a spiky feeling, as though someone has literally just breathed cold air onto her skin. Miriam tries to focus on Mr De Beaux's advice that she shouldn't hold back with the details about the abuse. *But wouldn't that give the jury reason to believe I had motive to kill him?* she had asked him. *Possibly*, had been his response, however, he had told her that he also needed them to have sympathy for her, and as far as possible they needed to see Zaf in his true light, as the villain that he was. The more sympathy they had for her and the more they believed she was incapable of committing such a gruesome act, she recalled him telling her, and the more they began to dislike Zaf as a person, the more this may consciously or subconsciously help to lead them to a not guilty verdict.

Miriam takes a deep breath before she replies, trying to stifle the tremble in her voice. 'If you are asking me whether he hit me, beat me, or punched me, or tried to strangle me, then the answer is no. But he was very controlling, and emotionally abusive.'

'I know this is extremely difficult for you, Mrs Hassan, but can you describe to the court in as much detail as possible how your late husband was controlling and abusive.'

You have to tell them Miriam, you have to!

Miriam inhales deep and long before she speaks.

'In so many ways. He was the one who told me I had to work in the family business and could no longer pursue my teaching career. He dictated what I should wear, when I could go out, who I could meet with, if at all, who I could invite to the house, again, if at all, what I had to cook, what to spend my money on, what to say even. Appearances were everything to him. In the eyes of the world, I was to be a dutiful, respectful wife, and above all else, I was to do as I was told by him. Always do as I was told.' Miriam's eyes start to fill up, but she raises her head, determined not to fall to pieces. 'He treated me like a child really. But unlike a parent who is *there* for his or her child, he

was never there for me. Even during the most traumatic experience of my life, when he knew I was miscarrying, he wasn't there
for me. I don't think at the time that I realised it was abuse,
when it was happening, or perhaps I did realise it on some
subconscious level but I didn't want to acknowledge it. My many
months in prison have given me time to reflect, and I have come
to know that I was in fact emotionally neglected and abused in
equal measure.'

Mr De Beaux notices a few of the members of the jury look
moved by Miriam's testimony so far. He hesitates a little before
his next question; he takes his time to soften the tone of his
voice right down.

'Was there sexual abuse?' he asks.

Miriam feels wretched upon hearing this question; as
though someone is tying her insides in knots, and wringing
them out mercilessly. Her face reddens; intense shame engulfs
her at the thought of having to discuss this topic in front of
anyone, let alone her father and brother. She is spared, in part at
least, for she catches a glimpse of her father walking out of the
courtroom. She exhales a pent-up sigh. She knows she must
answer the question. *She knows that the show must go on.*

'I was made to have sex when I didn't want to. Many, many
times. Wherever he chose, whenever he demanded it, and...
however he wanted it. If that is what you are referring to as
sexual abuse, then the answer is yes.'

'Did you realise that what you were being subjected to was
in fact marital rape?'

'Objection, My Lord!' declares Ms Godfrey. 'This is a slur on
the good character of the deceased, and there is no evidence that
Mr Hassan was committing such abuse.'

'My Lord, I must be allowed to explore the background to
this relationship so that the jury is in possession of all the facts
of my client's case,' Mr De Beaux responds.

'Overruled. The witness is under oath, and I daresay this is quite a difficult matter for her to talk about in any event. Continue, Mr De Beaux,' announces the Judge.

'I'm obliged, My Lord,' says Mr De Beaux, and he then turns to Miriam. 'I had just asked you if you realised that what you had been subjected to had been marital rape.'

Most of the members of the jury look perturbed. A couple stand out more than the others; Marilyn is shaking her head, hippy woman's face is a bit contorted due to a clenched jaw, and the *hijabi* woman looks close to tears.

The filled courtroom waits keenly for the next part of this story to unfold; no sound escapes anyone's lips, nor does anyone move a muscle. Pin drop silence.

'I didn't see it like that at the time, although I do see it now. He told me it was my duty as his wife to provide sex, basically on tap. I just did as I was told. Me doing as I was told was the most important thing to him. After a while I became like a robot. There was no love or affection. It was something I had to do; a demand to fulfil, an instruction to follow, a request to comply with, and I did it. It was something I detested. It made every part of my skin crawl, it made me feel physically sick, and sometimes, I was actually sick afterwards, quietly in the bathroom, whilst he slept. And though I hated it with every fibre of my body, I did it all the same, because I didn't see that I had any other choice.'

'What did all this emotional abuse and controlling behaviour on the part of Mr Hassan do to you? How did it make you feel?'

One lonely tear escapes Miriam's right eye. She blinks slowly to try and turn away the other tears that are ready to drop.

'The sex...the rape...it made me feel dirty, and cheap, like a whore or something. I felt...dehumanised. Worthless. And on a more general level, all the emotional abuse just made me feel like a useless human being; as though I could never do anything right. Whatever I did, somehow or other, it always seemed to be wrong. And he never hesitated in pointing out my flaws to me. Worse than that, he would completely mess with my head; he would say things that didn't make sense, he would distort the truth, or out and out lie, and then he would convince me that it was me who had got it all wrong, me who was a bit crazy.'

'Did you ever confront him about these matters?'

'I was never brave enough to challenge him. Never.'

'Can you tell us what kind of an impact all of this had on you?'

'It knocked my confidence to a point where I barely recognised myself. I had zero self-esteem, and that hasn't changed if I'm honest. I felt stranded, and lonely. As I explained before, I had no communication with my family, and what's more, he didn't let me see or speak to my friends. Added to all that, I was completely financially dependent on him. Within weeks of marrying him, I went from being an outgoing, educated, financially independent, career driven woman, to a neurotic, needy, helpless person without even a crumb of self-belief.'

Most of the jury members, although not all, still seem to be visually and emotionally affected my Miriam's words. Their grave faces indicate that, on some level at least, Miriam's testimony so far has moved them. The Asian Zaf lookalike guy doesn't appear to be affected by it, and a couple of others seem a little ambivalent, but the rest look visibly stirred as a result of what they have just heard.

'You say in your statement to the police that you left the house at around 2pm on the 31 March?' asks Mr De Beaux.

'Yes, that's right.'

'Can you tell the court about your movements that day, and tell us exactly what happened from the moment when you left the house, until the time that you returned?'

Miriam takes a few seconds to gather her thoughts before answering. 'Yes. I left the house as you said at around 2 o'clock. Zaf was still out at that time. He hadn't told me where he was going or what time he would be back. I decided to go for my usual Sunday afternoon walk in the park. This was one of the few things Zaf didn't mind me doing.'

'Why do you think that was? As you said, he was very controlling otherwise?'

'For a while this puzzled me too. But then I figured it was because he was usually home on Sundays, and I think he didn't mind getting me out of the way for a while, so to speak, in fact he welcomed it. A bit like getting a child out from under your feet. He did always treat me like a child.'

'I see. When you left home, did you go straight to the park?'

'No. On this occasion I didn't go straight to the park. I had a letter to post, so I decided to walk up to the High Street and post it first, and then come back down for my walk to the park. At the other end of our cul-de-sac, it's right to go to the park, and left to go up towards the High Street. So, I turned left. It's about a ten-minute walk to get up to the main road. There are no other houses along that ten-minute walk up to the High Street. I say High Street, but it's just a few shops really. It's about another ten-minute walk to the post box once you reach the High Street. I posted the letter, and then walked back down.'

'Did you notice anything unusual?'

'It seemed so insignificant at the time, that I initially forgot about it, but as I walked back down the lane towards the park entrance, I caught sight of someone in the corner of my eye, on the other side of the lane walking into our cul de sac.'

'Can you describe this person?'

'I'm pretty sure it was a man, but it was such a fleeting glimpse to be honest. He was, I think, wearing a black woolly hat, a black hoodie, black joggers and white trainers.'

'Did you get a look at his face?'

Miriam shook her head gently. 'No. I didn't. I have thought about this a thousand times. I had no idea that my brief sighting of this person would turn out to be so significant. I only caught a quick look, and like I said, it was more of a cursory glance rather than me turning my head and getting a proper look. I wish to God I had been more observant.'

'And you think this may be the person who killed your husband?'

'Yes, I do, because I cannot think of any other plausible explanation. Zaf did have some enemies, as the court has already been told.'

'Talk us through what happened after you caught the brief glimpse of this person. What did you do next?'

'I thought nothing of it, and I continued walking towards the park. After I entered the park, I pretty much headed straight to the park café and sat and had a drink.'

'What time was it when you sat down to have a drink?'

'It was around ten minutes to three.'

'How long did you stay there?'

'I think it was around 25 minutes, perhaps half an hour.'

'What did you do after that?'

'I then went for a walk around the top part of the park, which is away from the lake and the children's play area. It's the quieter bit of the park. A good place to think. That's where I usually go.'

'Was the park busy?'

'No, it wasn't. It was a cold, overcast day, and it looked like it might rain, so there weren't many people about. Of those that were there, most were by the lakeside or with their children in the play area.'

'Did you see anybody you recognised on this walk?'

'No, I didn't. As I said before, I was well away from the busier parts, other than my visit to the café.'

'What time did you leave the park?'

'I can't remember exactly, but I was home for quarter past four.'

'How can you be so sure that you arrived home at 4.15 pm?'

'Because I looked at my watch when I got in.'

'Why?'

'Sorry?' Miriam asks, perplexed by Mr De Beaux's question.

'What I mean is, was there any specific reason that you checked your watch? Were you checking the time for anything in particular?'

'Oh, I see. Yes. I checked it because I had been thinking about the fact that I needed to make dinner, and I looked at my watch to see how long I had before I had to make a start on the food. Zaf was very particular about what time his food had to be ready on Sundays when he was home.'

'Did you have your mobile phone with you?'

'No. I didn't have my phone with me when I went out. I left it at home. Upstairs in the bedroom.'

'Why did you leave your phone at home? Is this something you normally did?'

'No, I usually have my phone with me when I go out. But my brother had mentioned that my dad might call, and I really didn't feel able to speak to him just yet. I was too upset, and I feared I might start crying down the phone. I left the phone at home so I could have a peaceful walk, to give me time to think about everything that had happened, and if there was a missed call when I returned, I could phone back.'

'Your neighbour, Mrs Bains, has said that she believes you returned home at 3.15 pm. What do you say to that?'

'For whatever reason, that is obviously what she thinks. She has to say what she believes to be true, but she is mistaken. I know that I was home at quarter past four.'

'What happened when you did return home?'

'As I turned into our road, I noticed Zaf's car was in the drive, so obviously he was back, which filled me with dread if I'm honest. When I got inside the house, I took off my coat and bag in the hallway, then I walked into the kitchen, filled the kettle and switched it on. I figured he must be in his study, and I went in to ask him if he wanted any tea...and...'

'And then what happened?'

Miriam can feel a suffocating lump gathering in her throat. She coughs it away gently. 'When I walked into the study, that was when I saw...'

'What did you see, Mrs Hassan?'

'I saw Zaf, lying on the floor, with a pool of blood around him. He'd been stabbed. The letter opener was poking out of his stomach.'

Mr De Beaux leans forward and places his hands flat on the table in front of him, his eyes transfixed on his client. 'Mrs Hassan, did you kill your husband?'

'No,' replies Miriam, firmly.

'Did you plunge the letter opener into his abdomen, causing his death.'

'No.'

'How do you explain the fact that your fingerprints were all over the letter opener, and his blood was on your clothes?'

Miriam brings her hands together, folds her fingers over, and presses her palms, one into the other, firmly, as if in prayer. She takes a measured breath, in, and out. 'I use the letter opener quite often, so I guess it would be covered in my fingerprints. And when I found him, I knelt down beside him, which would explain the blood on my clothes. It was just a natural reaction. I didn't think about it. I saw him lying there and I went over to him. Any human being would. I would do that with a stranger, and he was my husband.'

'The husband which the prosecution alleges that you stabbed to death.'

'No! I did not stab him. I did not kill him. He was killed by someone else. It wasn't me.'

For the first time, Miriam becomes visibly emotional, whereas before now she has managed to keep her emotions rumbling inside of her. She grips onto the witness box, her knuckles shining on her otherwise dull and dry hands. Her breathing has become rapid and cumbersome, and so she closes her eyes and tries to breathe deeper and slower, tries to regain some calmness in the movement of her breath.

'Would you like a glass of water, Mrs Hassan,' asks the Judge.

'Yes. Please,' replies Miriam, as she gazes at the judge with grateful eyes.

She sips the water slowly, and once she finishes drinking Mr De Beaux continues.

'What did you do after that, Mrs Hassan?'

'I got back up; I walked over to his desk and I telephoned the emergency services from the landline phone.'

'What did you say when you got through to the police?'

'I can't remember word for word, but I know I told them who I was, and where I was calling from. I said I came home and found my husband lying on the floor. I said he'd been attacked and that I thought he was dead.'

'I have no doubt that the Prosecution will mention this next point, so I may as well address this now. You were very calm on the call to the police. Perhaps one might expect you to have been more emotional, hysterical even, having come home and found your husband dead on the floor of his study. Can you tell the jury how you were able to remain so composed in the circumstances?'

'This may sound strange, but even though it was a huge shock to see him like that, I didn't really feel anything beyond this. I didn't feel any emotions, and I wasn't tearful, or, as you said, hysterical. I only felt numb. That's it. Numb.'

'Thank you, Mrs Hassan.'

Ms Godfrey rises to her feet, but as it is nearly four o'clock, she has a feeling she knows what is coming.

'Given the time, Ms Godfrey, perhaps you can commence your cross-examination in the morning,' requests the judge.

Ms Godfrey was hoping he wouldn't say that. Mr De Beaux looks pleased and Ms Godfrey feels short changed. Sometimes, in those last few minutes of the day, when the witness is weary, it is much easier to catch the witness out. A little like when a new batsman comes onto the cricket pitch as the night watchman with only ten minutes left. He's thinking, only ten minutes to survive, should be a doddle. And yet so often, he doesn't survive. Perhaps the spin bowler picks up one or even two quick wickets in a row, perhaps with a doosra or a flipper, or the fast bowler bowls an unplayable yorker, all in that small window of time. Ms Godfrey was similarly hoping she would be given half an hour or so to make a start, to be allowed the chance to induce Miriam to trip up, thus leaving the jury with those thoughts uppermost in their mind as they retire for the day. But it was not to be.

'As you wish, My Lord,' replies Ms Godfrey, resentfully, through clenched teeth.

'All rise,' announces the Clerk in a voice that is far too grating for any time of the day, let alone the end of a long one.

Miriam rises to her feet, and wonders what tomorrow will be like. Most certainly, the cross-examination will be the hardest part yet in this miserable journey she is on. Of that she is almost certainly sure.

29

---

1 March 2019

'Sure, Zaf, I'll be ready.'

After Miriam finished listening to Zaf's instructions, she ran upstairs to find a suitable *salwar kameez* to wear. *And a long cardigan*, she thought to herself, yes, *don't forget a cardigan with good coverage, considering they're very traditional people, or so Zaf said. There must be no lumps or bumps on show.*

She had thought that she would be having a quiet day at home. She had planned to get all the housework done and out of the way, and then enjoy some baking in the afternoon. She always found baking to be very therapeutic; the joy of creating a lemon drizzle cake, or a Victoria sponge, or a salted caramel cheesecake, or rosy pink buttercream topped cupcakes, all gave her much pleasure. The magic of turning flour sugar eggs and butter into a creation that not only looked pretty but tasted delicious was the reason she enjoyed it so much; it satisfied the creative side of her which she did not otherwise have a chance to indulge herself in, not to mention it satisfied her sweet tooth. However, Zaf had just put pay to that thought of a relaxing afternoon of baking. He telephoned from the office to tell her that his relative (an uncle type figure) had recently passed away in Pakistan. The late uncle's son (cousin of some sort to Zaf) lived down in Slough, and he had returned from Pakistan yesterday. Zaf said he was coming home to pick her up so they could both go down and pay their respects to the family.

Miriam had never met these Slough relatives before, but when she and Zaf arrived at their relatively modest terraced house, these relatives of his were certainly very welcoming; more so towards Zaf, who they were very pleased to see, and cordial towards Miriam, who they now met for the first time. The cousin and his wife were much older than Zaf, at least in their fifties. They talked about how Zaf's visit was long overdue, as he was visiting them after what was apparently many years.

The wife was very chatty, and some would say outright nosey; she asked Miriam question after question and gave matrimonial advice in bucketloads: 'do you get to visit your family much...when is the first baby coming....you mustn't leave it too long, you know, or you will have problems conceiving...I know you girls love to think about your figure these days, but you shouldn't delay motherhood...what does Zaf like you to cook for him...when are your in-laws next coming over to England?' Her conviviality was now turning into an attempt towards over-familiarity, which Miriam did not feel very comfortable with. The only respite Miriam had from her non-stop chatter was when the woman left her to go to the kitchen for a few minutes to check how her daughter-in-law was getting on with the cooking. When she came back from the kitchen, she announced that the meal was ready.

All four of them shifted to the dining room, sat at the table, and started to dish up the food onto their plates. His relatives had put on a good spread; kebabs, pilau rice, chicken *jalfrezi*, *karahi* lamb, *rotis*. She was about to reach over for a kebab

when what Zaf was doing caught her eye; Miriam looked at
him with absolute incredulity. Her mouth almost dropped
open, as she wondered if she was seeing properly, when she
witnessed Zaf pile the *masoor daal* high onto his plate on top of
some of the rice, and get stuck into it, as though he was raven-
ously hungry, and he had never seen or been fed this *daal*
before.

'You like *masoor daal*, then, I see!' said the wife.

'Oh, I love it,' he said, in between mouthfuls, 'I know some
people call it the poor man's *daal*, but I think it's the tastiest lentil
of all. And, by the way, this is very delicious, *Baji*!'

He ate it like he had never had homemade *masoor daal* in his
life. If Miriam was completely honest, it was embarrassing, but
also, it was remarkably hurtful.

'Well, that is a compliment indeed coming from you Zafar,'
said the wife. No one ever called him Zafar. 'It's good to see you
are still humble despite your fame and fortune. And that you
know your roots. I saw you on the television on one of those
Saturday morning cookery shows only a few weeks back!
Looking quite the celebrity! But I am so glad that really you have
remained modest. And I have to agree with you. Cooked with a
traditional *tarka,* and made with *ghee*, you can't beat a good old
masoor daal. Of course, in Pakistan we would use the fresh home
made buffalo milk ghee. Pure and organic. But still, the ghee in
the shops here is not so bad, although I prefer to make it at
home myself from good quality butter. I can give you my recipe
for the *daal* if you like, Miriam.'

Miriam gave her a faint smile.

'I ought to send her down to stay with you for a week, to
learn all your cooking secrets!' declared Zaf. 'And steal some of
your recipes for my restaurant menu!'

'Oh, you're too kind!' she replied, with a brimming smile that
displayed a chipped front tooth. The grin was accompanied by a

casual wave of her hand; her explicit attempt to display some degree of humility, which she did not quite manage.

'Or I can send my wife up to stay with you and teach Miriam; you can have her with pleasure!' said the husband, and the three of them started laughing at the supposed joke.

'We will come up to see you when the pitter patter of tiny feet arrives soon no doubt, *Insha'Allah*,' added the wife.

The constant references to her producing a baby riled Miriam inside, but she stayed quiet. She simply, silently observed it all from the periphery, as though she wasn't really there, more like a bystander looking in through misty, stain speckled glass. Her outer calm composure belied her inner rumbling contempt. She wanted to scream at them all, and select a few choice words for the woman in particular. *You probably didn't even make this daal, it was probably your daughter-in-law, who is still slaving away in the kitchen right now. She has cooked all this food, because you were too busy asking me fifty questions and doling out your useless advice. But you don't consider your daughter-in-law important enough to come and take a seat at the table with your rich cousin who you see once in a blue moon when he deigns to visit you.*

Miriam's internal rage continued on the way back in the car. It wasn't the first time she had been made to feel inadequate for not yet being on the road to motherhood. Zaf had not hidden his disappointment to her at the news delivered by the doctors about her probable infertility, but more upsetting had been his lack of care of how Miriam had been emotionally impacted by it all. He continued to busy himself with his work, and they largely avoided the elephant in the room. But she knew her value in the eyes of this society, and she feared in the eyes of her husband and his family, would remain at rock bottom as she was unable to produce an heir to the Hassan clan. Unless she produced a child, she was worthless. That's how it felt to Miriam.

30

Birmingham Crown Court
14 November 2019

Miriam feels that it is very cold in the courtroom today. Perhaps there is a problem with the heating, she thinks. Or perhaps the tiny goosebumps on her skin are a natural consequence of her nerves. She wraps her long black cardigan securely around her waist and hugs her arms around herself tightly.

Her discomfort only increases when Ms Godfrey stands up, looking eager and ready to cross-examine her, almost like a wolf that has just caught sight of its prey. Miriam concentrates on her breathing, and manages to bring her heartrate down a tad. She steels herself for what she knows will be a monumental character assassination. *Sparks will fly*, she thinks; *great entertainment for the audience, especially as you don't have any way of avoiding them. Stand firm as best you can, and hope there isn't too much damage. Let's see.*

'If we can firstly turn to the matters you alluded to previously, concerning your family. Mrs Hassan. You say you had not seen your family for a number of years, and that you had become "entrenched" in your position. Would you say you are stubborn person?' asks Ms Godfrey.

'Not necessarily stubborn,' replies Miriam.

Ms Godfrey folds her arms and waits for Miriam to expand further.

'Proud, perhaps,' adds Miriam

'You are used to getting your own way, though, aren't you? And on the 31 March, you were angry about not getting your own way for once, when your husband told you that he couldn't make it to the family get together that you had planned.'

'I wasn't angry about not getting my own way.'

'No. Then what were you angry about?'

'I was angry about being let down, about him putting others before me, just like he always did.'

'And so, you decided to stand up to him?'

'I suppose so.'

'And yet, you claimed, when questioned by Mr De Beaux, that you were, and I quote, "genuinely scared of him".'

'I *was* scared of him.'

'Erm...how does someone who is supposedly so very frightened of her husband manage to shout at him, and what's more, manage to attack him, outdoors, in broad daylight, for any of the neighbours to see?'

Miriam didn't answer.

'Those don't sound like the actions of someone who is "genuinely scared" of that person, do they?' Ms Godfrey stretches her eyebrows way up high as she waits for an answer.

'I *really was* scared of him, I have always been scared of him, but on that day, something inside me just snapped.'

'Ah! Yes, quite.'

Miriam looks over at the jury. She can see that their minds are ticking away. The Asian Zaf lookalike is sitting with one eyebrow raised. The banker man is resting his chin on the palm of his right hand with his eyebrows tied together in the middle. The hippy woman on the other hand is looking very wide-eyed today.

'We have had witness evidence which has confirmed that you threatened your husband during this argument on the doorstep.'

'I didn't threaten him.'

'You said he was dead to you, or words to that effect.'

'But I've explained what I meant by that.'

'Yes, I have heard your explanation, but I have to ask, why choose *those* words? Why not pick other words to denote what you really meant, Mrs Hassan. Why not, for example, say "I never want to speak to you again" or "don't talk to me" or "go away I don't want to see you"?'

Miriam shuffles around on the spot for a few seconds. 'I don't know. The words just came out of my mouth. I didn't plan them.'

'Well, I would have to say that, in my humble experience, the words that just trip out of one's mouth spontaneously are usually the most truthful.'

'But...'

'Not content with shouting at, attacking and threatening your husband on the doorstep, you later telephoned him to threaten him once again.'

'No. I did no such thing.'

'Why would your husband say "stop threatening me" unless you *were* threatening him?'

'I don't know. Perhaps so that Adam could hear him saying it, so he could put me in a bad light, so he could use it against me. He was a clever man, you know, he was always way ahead of me.'

'I see. Well, as he is not here to contradict you, we only have your word for that, Mrs Hassan, don't we?'

There is a small period of silence, just five or six seconds, as the two women lock eyes.

'Moving on,' continues Ms Godfrey.

Miriam holds her breath for a few moments, as she waits to hear what she will be subjected to next. What justification will she have to give now? What will she have to explain to everyone who is sat gawping at her? It is as though all these dozens of eyes are penetrating her all at once, trying to stare right into her very soul.

'You claim to have been emotionally abused and neglected by your husband throughout your marriage.'

'Yes. I was.'

'Did you tell anyone about this abuse?'

'No.'

'Why not?' asks Ms Godfrey, her eyes fixed on Miriam's.

'Objection My Lord,' says Mr De Beaux, springing quickly to his feet. 'It is a well-known fact that victims of abuse are quite often too scared to disclose their abuse to others.'

The Judge nods his head slightly as he ways things up in his mind. 'Overruled,' he responds, finally, 'for now. Continue, Ms Godfrey, but tread carefully,' he warns her. Mr De Beaux sits back down.

'Thank you, My Lord,' says Ms Godfrey, with a small bow of her head, and then she turns to address Miriam. 'Why did you never tell anyone about the emotional abuse that you were allegedly suffering?'

'Because as I have said before, I was scared.'

'Of him?'

'Yes. Scared of him, scared of the implications.'

'Can you explain what you mean by that?'

'It's hard to explain.'

'Do try,' says Ms Godfrey. Her tone comes across as sarcastic, even if the words aren't meant to be.

Miriam speaks slowly. 'I didn't know at the beginning that it was abuse. I didn't really know what was happening. Initially I used to think that the bad things that happened to me happened for all kinds of reasons.'

'Such as what? What reasons?'

Miriam is stroking her forehead with the fingers of her right hand. She can feel that her forehead has crinkled. She smooths down the little ridges with a circular motion, and also hopes that the headache she now feels brewing doesn't actually materialise. She brings her right hand back down by her side and begins her response. 'At the beginning, I used to think that he was in a bad mood with me because he was tired, or he was stressed about work, but over time, I began to believe that he was angry, or frustrated, or short-tempered, because I must have done something wrong, because he always made me feel that I just couldn't do anything right. So, it wasn't his fault, was it? It was my fault. That's what I thought. Every time. I was to blame. That's what he always said or implied. Over time, it became normal, but saying that, somewhere deep down, I started to realise that it *wasn't* normal. Every time someone told me about their married life, their relationship with their husband, what they did together, every time I saw how other couples interacted with each other, how they spoke to each other, how they supported and respected each other, I realised, I knew, our relationship wasn't normal. But what I didn't know was what to do about it. The thought of doing anything about it became harder and harder over time. The longer I left it, the higher the mountain in front of me became. I did think, sometimes, just sometimes, that I should tell someone.' Miriam looks down now, and closes her eyes for a couple of seconds, whilst she draws a deep breath.

'Why didn't you?' asks Ms Godfrey.

Miriam raises her head, and speaks softly. 'Because the

moment you tell someone, you have to do something about it, don't you?'

'Do something? Like what?'

'Like face up to it, like tell the police, like leave him, like leave the house, like no longer have a home to live in or a place to work at, or a family, or any money. And all this knowing that if I did try to leave him, I wouldn't succeed because I would not be allowed to leave if that was not what he had decided; I would be emotionally blackmailed and bullied into staying because of his pride and so-called family honour. And yet, even if I somehow managed to leave him, it was all so very hopeless. Can't you see?'

'See what, Mrs Hassan? You will have to elaborate.'

'I was estranged from my family and I had no friends nearby. The only people I knew were *his* friends, or the people at work who were employed by *him*. It was as though I wasn't *me* anymore. I was just a part of *him,* or an extension of *him*. Nothing about *me* was actually *me*. Not any longer. My identity and my autonomy vanished the day I married him. I belonged to *him* in every single way. I didn't even have possession of my own passport, or driver's licence; he had them. And he had complete access to my only bank account, into which *he* paid my salary. Where would I go? What would I do? What would I live on? My self-esteem was as low down as it could possibly have been. I couldn't see a way out.'

Ms Godfrey taps the tip of her pen on her notes for a few moments, gathering her thoughts, before continuing. 'You could have contacted a domestic violence charity, you could have moved into a refuge, you could have received benefits until you found a job, gone back to teaching perhaps. So, I ask you again; if you were, as you allege, having such a terrible time at the hands of your husband, then why didn't you do anything about it?'

'Because I didn't have the courage!' Miriam shouts back, and then puts her hand over her mouth having realised the extent to which she raised her voice. She looks towards the Judge, expecting some sort of a reprimand.

'Please go on,' says the Judge, with a gentle nod of his wigged head.

'Every time I thought about telling someone,' she continues, now having lowered her voice, 'every time I went through these questions in my head, at the end of it all, I didn't have the courage to face the consequences of such an action. I didn't have the courage to tell anyone, or do anything about it, okay.'

'But you managed to find the courage somehow to plunge a weapon into him on the 31 March, didn't y–'

'No!' Miriam bats back her response to Ms Godfrey immediately, cutting off prosecuting counsel before she can quite finish her question.

'Objection, My Lord!' says Mr De Beaux who has now leapt to his feet once again.

'You found the courage to murder him before he could make a will to exclude you?' Ms Godfrey hurtles on, ignoring Mr De Beaux's protestations.

'I said no!' cries Miriam, tears now toppling out of her strained eyes.

'I think that is quite enough Ms Godfrey,' the Judge orders, which she acknowledges with the nod of her head. He looks at his watch, and then looks towards Miriam. She is not looking back; she is looking down. She's had enough, he thinks, and so has he. 'That will be all for today,' announces the Judge, to everyone's surprise, as he has not before finished this early. 'Court is adjourned.'

'All rise,' announces the Clerk.

Miriam feels a sense of relief. She closes her eyes and no longer wants to think.

31

30 April 2018

'Think it's time for a cuppa. Do you want one, Rachel?' asked Miriam, as she stood by Rachel's desk and collected her empty mug as well.

'No time for that!' said Zaf who had suddenly appeared from behind her, making Miriam jump.

'God, you frightened me!' she said to him, and placed the two empty mugs down on Rachel's desk.

'Well, it doesn't take much to scare you, does it?' he replied.

'What's up?' asked Rachel.

'As though we're not busy enough, that Hilton guy from London has been in touch. He's asked me to move the meeting forward.'

'It shouldn't be a problem. Move it to when exactly?' asked Rachel.

'Today,' replied Zaf.

'Today! What?' shrieked Rachel.

As was normally the case, Miriam was in the dark about the finer details of their conversation. But she did know that this

Hilton man was important, as there was most likely a deal in the offing for Zaf's Restaurant Group to secure the contract for the catering for all of Hilton Hotels *desi* wedding bookings requiring South Asian food on the menu, in all their hotels in the Midlands and the South of England. This had been Zaf's latest expansion; moving into high end wedding catering on a grand scale. He was hoping to go national with it eventually, and to make a move on other hotel chains as well.

'Why today?' asked Rachel.

'He called me to say he is up in Birmingham today. His parents live here, and he thought that as he is in the city anyway, why not meet up, if it was possible. He apologised for the short notice, but said that as he was around, he thought it would be a good opportunity to see our operation up here. So, of course, I said yes, and I told him to bring his parents along for a meal they won't forget.'

'Okay then. What's the plan?' asked Rachel, as she opened up the file on the computer screen.

'Well, we have three hours until they arrive. Rachel, you spend that time getting the presentation ready. All the figures, the projections, the latest brochure, the different menus, and also the reviews, testimonies, and all that jazz. Can you do two physical copies as well as the computer presentation? I can bring him up to the meeting room if he insists on seeing everything on a screen, but he might be okay with the physical copy.'

He then shifted his attention towards Miriam, who was still standing nearby, listening to their conversation, but not having felt any urge to join in. 'Miriam. I need you to go to town and get presents for all three of them.'

Miriam's eyes widened. 'But I have a doctor's appointment. I need to leave in an hour.'

'I'll be back in a minute,' said Rachel, as she took the empty mugs from the desk and headed towards the staff kitchen.

Zaf looked at Miriam with disbelief smattered all over his face.

'You know how long it takes to get an appointment at the surgery,' Miriam added, hoping it may make a difference.

'And what exactly is wrong with you?' he asked.

She thought Rachel may walk back in at any minute, so it wasn't worth going into it all right now. So, she kept it simple. 'I've just not been feeling well.'

'Well, that doesn't sound like any great emergency. You'll have to rearrange it. This is way more urgent. This deal is worth a lot of money for the business.'

The business, of course. 'Okay,' she said, as she, predictably, acquiesced. 'By the way, what presents do you want me to get?' Miriam asked Zaf.

'For God's sake, do you need to be spoon fed everything!' His voiced had gone up a notch, and Miriam knew it was best not to respond.

Rachel walked in, carrying two mugs brimming with freshly brewed tea.

'Miriam was wondering what gifts she should get. Any ideas, Rachel?' asked Zaf, calm as you like.

'Let's look online together, Miriam; we can choose the items and check availability, and then you can go and collect the gifts from town.'

'Here's the money.' Zaf handed Miriam a wad of cash. 'Buy yourself something nice too; maybe that new Dior perfume you've had your eye on, eh?' She had not once mentioned any such perfume, but then she knew the dance by now. Her dance. His tune.

Zaf then promptly turned his attention towards Rachel, leaning over on the desk to say his final few words. 'Thank you, I really appreciate this, Rachel,' he said, and then he left the room.

The waiting room was almost empty. Miriam had rushed around like a blue arsed fly getting the presents, then sped to the doctor's surgery before it shut. She wasn't needed at the meeting, and knew she wouldn't be missed. She had made it within five minutes of it closing.

'Do you have an appointment?' asked the receptionist after Miriam announced her name. She was busy twirling one of her strands of long blond hair around her left index finger and thumb.

'Well, I did have an appointment. I'm sorry, I am a bit late.'

'What's the name and date of birth?'

Miriam waited patiently after giving the details.

'A bit late? You were supposed to be here hours ago,' the receptionist said, frowning. Miriam could really have done without the scolding from a receptionist who only looked about 15 years old. She didn't much like her acrid tone, and her strong Brummie accent probably didn't help with that. But she was only doing her job, Miriam told herself; she thought it best to keep on the right side of her if she was going to have any chance of seeing the doctor.

'Yes, I'm so sorry,' Miriam told the receptionist, 'something really urgent came up.' *Everything that Zaf needed doing was always more urgent.* 'I've been trying to get through on the telephone, but the line is always engaged. I received a call a few days ago asking me to come in to see the doctor about some results that couldn't be discussed over the telephone. And I'm here now. Can you please see if the doctor can fit me in?'

'Okay, take a seat in the waiting room. I will see if we can squeeze you in.'

A few minutes later Miriam walked into the doctor's room. She hadn't seen this one before. He was a youngish doctor, in his late twenties or maybe early thirties at the most, and not the usual, older male GP that she normally saw. He looked a bit like Idris Elba, she thought, although a less rugged version perhaps.

'Take a seat please, Mrs Hassan.' She complied and sat on the navy chair which was to the other side of his very neat and tidy desk. He continued to scroll through some notes on his computer screen and Miriam felt a little tenseness in the air. The silence, albeit for probably less than a minute, was uncomfortable.

'Mrs Hassan. We have received the results of the tests we carried out after your miscarriage, and I'm afraid I have some bad news.'

Miriam didn't speak, she preferred it if the doctor just came out with it.

'You will recall that you had the D&C procedure carried out. All surgery carries risk, and the dilation and curettage procedure is no exception. Whilst the operation itself was a success, it has unfortunately left some scarring in the uterus.'

'Scarring? So, what does that mean?' she asked.

'Well, I'm afraid, that it means that you may find it difficult to conceive again.'

Miriam wasn't sure if she had heard him correctly.

'Are you saying I will never be able to have a baby.'

He didn't respond for a few seconds, as though he was carefully measuring up in his mind each word's suitability before he blurted it out. 'What I am saying is that the results show that you have scarring on your uterus which may affect your ability to get pregnant again.'

Miriam sat in a daze as he continued to explain what happened to her in more technical terms, the more he spoke, the more his words faded out towards the edges of the room. She hadn't even thought about what may be said to her today at what she thought was a routine follow-up after routine tests after her routine miscarriage. She had not expected this. Something like this hadn't even crossed her mind. She had felt a mountain of pressure from everyone pretty much since the day they married to produce an heir to the Hassan clan; Zaf talked about having a son to take over the empire just as he had done from his father, parents-in-law talked incessantly about the day they would become *daadi daada*, the Urdu titles given to paternal grandmothers and grandfathers which all their peers had become, so the race was on.

She walked out of the surgery, down the corridor, got into her car and drove home with one thought in her mind; how was Zaf going to take it?

32

Birmingham Crown Court
15 November 2019

It is a warmer day in the courtroom today. Perhaps the heating is working again, thinks Miriam. She takes her place in the witness box once more, and steadies herself for the deluge of questions that are inescapably going to follow.

'If we can come to the mystery person that you claim to have seen on the day of your husband's death,' begins Ms Godfrey.

I did see him. Miriam refrains, however, from saying it out aloud, for now.

'You said you caught sight of someone, and I quote, "in the corner of my eye".'

'Yes. That's right.'

'You didn't see this person's face?'

'No.'

'But you did manage to see that this person was wearing, now let me see,' Ms Godfrey pauses and rolls her eyes upwards for a few seconds, 'ah yes, a black woolly hat, a black hoodie, black joggers, and white trainers.'

'Yes.'

'It sounds very much like the man in the Milk Tray ad to me, minus the white footwear of course.' There are a few giggles from some of the older people in court.

'Sorry? What advert?' asks Miriam, genuinely bemused.

Mr De Beaux directs a cold, sideways stare at Ms Godfrey.

'Don't worry about it, before your time, I think. But just so that I know I am understanding this correctly,' says Ms Godfrey, now deliberately dragging her words, 'you saw someone from the corner of your eye, you did not see this person's face, however, you can recall with a great degree of clarity what this person was wearing.'

'That sounds correct.'

'How convenient. You remember everything else, apart from the person's face.'

'That's because I didn't see his face.'

'And neither did anyone else, apparently. None of your neighbours saw anyone matching the description of this mystery person on or near your street that day.'

Ms Godfrey pauses, to give Miriam a chance to chip in if she wants to, but Miriam stays quiet. 'Do you get many people walking down that quiet lane down towards your road, or to that particular entrance to the park which is close to your home?'

'No, we don't. That's why I noticed him. The only people who would be walking down that end by our road, or going into the park by that small entrance, which most people don't even know about, are the people who live on our cul de sac. Visitors to our houses would normally come and go by car. So that's why he stood out to me.'

'Either that, or he is a figment of your imagination.'

'No. That's not true. I did see him.'

'I daresay that, considering there are no other witnesses who can confirm seeing this person, he is most likely a fictitious red herring thrown in by you to deflect us all away from yourself.'

'No!' Miriam realises that she has been slowly crinkling her eyebrows and now makes a concerted effort to relax them, and ease away the lines that have congregated on her forehead.

'Turning now towards your return home from the park. Clearly, we have a dispute as to when you arrived home. You say 4.15pm and your neighbour Mrs Bains is certain it was 3.15pm. The jury will have to decide who they believe, whose version of events is more plausible, who they think is more likely to be telling the truth. If we move past that point of contention for now, and look back to your evidence-in-chief, you said that you went into his study to ask him if he wanted a cup of tea.'

'Yes, I did.'

'Why?' asks Ms Godfrey, her palms upturned, her face donning an exaggerated look of bewilderment.

Miriam creases her eyebrows once again, but doesn't answer the question.

'You will have to help me out here, Mrs Hassan,' says Ms Godfrey. 'Earlier that morning, you argued with him, lashed out at him, and wished him dead. By your own admission you were extremely upset about being let down by him. However, you expect us to believe that when you came back from your walk, you calmly and lovingly went into his study to ask him if he wanted some tea. Tea. As if nothing had happened.'

Miriam opens her mouth but struggles to find any words in response.

'You expect us to believe that when you got back from your walk, you were going to go about your day as normal, as though there had been no disagreement between you and your husband at all. You expect us to accept that you were going to play happy families with tea and biscuits.'

Miriam notices that most of the members of the jury are very alert. They are sitting in anticipation, perhaps wondering when prosecuting counsel will be getting to the actual moment of Zaf's death, perhaps wondering how Miriam will cope with the questions, wondering what she will say.

'I'm telling you the truth. I did go in to ask him if he wanted to have tea,' says Miriam.

Marilyn lets out a quiet sigh, the *hijabi* woman looks sombre, and the Zaf lookalike Asian guy rolls his eyes upon hearing Miriam's response.

'You weren't annoyed with him anymore?' asks Ms Godfrey.

'I'm not saying I wasn't annoyed with him anymore. But whatever had happened, I was still his wife, I still lived in that house with him, and I had to try to push what passed between us in the morning to the back of my mind and try and resume some sort of normality. Tea is normality. It was just tea!'

'Hell hath no fury like a woman scorned,' declares Ms Godfrey, theatrically, with a swish of her cloak. 'Without wishing to be unfair to my own sex, I would say that women do not forgive and forget so very easily. In fact, generally speaking, women do not move on until they have had the chance to talk about whatever it is that has happened; women like to dissect every word, examine every phrase, to have a post-mortem, so to speak, if you would forgive my choice of phrase. Would you say that's true?'

'May be. It depends on the woman.' Miriam now sighs heavily, for she is tired, in body and in spirit, she is so very tired.

'You see, here's what I think happened.' Ms Godfrey takes her time, speaking slowly, teasing and dragging her words out. And she is speaking quietly. Not so quietly that people in the courtroom cannot hear her, but not really as loudly as one would expect. They can make out what she is saying, but they have to concentrate, and listen carefully. Miriam was taught this technique during her teacher training. Shouting in the classroom is not effective, she was told. Speak quietly and the children will automatically pay attention to you. They will be desperate to know what it is you are saying, and therefore, they will be forced to listen carefully. And it is the same in the court-room right now. 'When you came home and saw that he was back, you went into the study to confront him,' continues Ms Godfrey. 'You wanted to get some answers about why he had, as you called it, let you down. Understandably perhaps. You wanted to find out where he had been. He knew how signifi-cant that day was for you, so you needed to know what had been more important for him. You went in there, and you asked him where he had been, who he had been to see and why.'

'No,' says Miriam, shaking her head.

'Things became very heated, and he told you that he was going to write you out of his will.'

'That's not true!'

'And what's more, to add insult to injury, he told you he was going to divorce you.'

'No, you're wrong!'

'Am I? Really?'

'Yes! Really. He was lying in a pool of blood on the floor when I walked in.'

'Then after he relayed these shocking decisions of his, to leave you out of his will and to file for divorce, the argument between the two of you became much fiercer, and in a fit of rage - which I would say was an extension of your anger from the morning which had now bubbled over completely having heard what your husband had just told you – in a fit of rage, you grabbed the letter opener and without another thought you deliberately and violently plunged it into him.'

'No, I didn't touch him.'

'Perhaps, it was self-defence? Perhaps he goaded you?

Perhaps he mocked you? And something inside you, as you said before, just snapped?'

'No!'

'And you killed him.'

'No...no...no...' Miriam's words fade away as her tears begin to emerge. The two slowly melt into one. She has nothing more to give, nothing else that she can dig out from anywhere, no other words that she can find to say.

A short time later, when Miriam is settled back in the dock, flanked either side by the prison guards, Mr De Beaux stands up, and pulls firmly at either side of his black gown. He is standing now with a sense of focused determination fixed in his eyes as he looks towards the jury and begins his closing speech.

'Ladies and gentlemen of the jury. You have now heard the case for the prosecution, and the case for the defence. You have been presented with all of the evidence, you have heard from a number of witnesses, and you have heard very conflicting testimonies.'

Mr De Beaux tries his best not to become distracted by some sort of activity that is going on somewhere behind him, which at first, he only hears, but which he also catches a glimpse of when he steals a quick look.

The court usher has dashed into the courtroom. She whispers something in Sara's ear, who then whispers something back to the usher.

'The simple fact is,' continues Mr De Beaux, undeterred as far as possible by the commotion, 'that the defendant is innocent until proven guilty. And in order for guilt to be proven, you must be certain, beyond any reasonable doubt, that my client murdered her husband. If you have any doubt whatsoever, even the tiniest uncertainty, then it's quite simple: you - must - acquit.'

Mr De Beaux suddenly feels Sara's hand brush against his

arm, and then she tugs at his sleeve; he swivels around a little and she hands him a note.

She nods her head in a most strange, frantic manner, and pops her eyes out at him, as if to say, *read the note, now!*

'If you will just excuse me for one moment, ladies and gentleman,' says Mr De Beaux to the members of the jury. In the next breath he says to the Judge, who now has one eyebrow severely raised, 'I do apologise, your Lordship, if you will give me just a few seconds.' Mr De Beaux then quickly scans the note; both his eyebrows rise slowly as he tries to finish reading the note as quickly as he can, but he has to read it again, just to be sure that he has not misread it. He has a peculiar look on his face, the sort of look when it is difficult to tell if the person has read something that has surprised him in a good sort of a way, or a bad sort a of a way. The only certainty that can be deduced from the expression on his face is the fact that whatever that note contains, it is something he wasn't expecting.

Ms Godfrey leans over a little, and peers across, but in vain, as she cannot see the contents of the note from where she is sitting.

Mr De Beaux finally looks up from the note to address the slightly irritated Judge.

'My Lord. A matter of the utmost importance has just come to my knowledge, and I would be grateful if you would allow me to bring this to your attention in private.'

The judge does not look amused. His cumbersome sigh is matched with a disgruntled noise of some kind, after which he speaks more audibly. 'This better be good,' he says, and then turns towards the jury. 'Ladies and gentlemen, you will shortly be taken out of the courtroom so that certain legal issues may be discussed, issues which you do not need to be privy to. Clear the public gallery also,' instructs the judge, and slowly the courtroom is emptied of everyone apart from the judge, the legal teams and the court clerk.

'Now then, Mr De Beaux, what is so very urgent that you had to abandon your closing speech mid-way and have me clear the court?' asks the judge.

'My Lord, I have just been notified that a new witness has come forward. He is here right now, waiting outside this very courtroom. He claims that he witnessed something of signifi-cance on the date of Mr Hassan's death, and wishes to give evidence on behalf of the Defence.'

'I strongly object, My Lord. This is outrageous!' claims Ms Godfrey. 'All the evidence was agreed at the outset of this trial, none of the usual protocol has been followed with regards to the late submission of evidence, therefore any application now, at this eleventh hour, to bring forward any new evidence should not be allowed.'

'My Lord, I appreciate that this is the first that the prosecu-tion is hearing of this new witness, but it is also the first that we are hearing of it. I understand from this brief note that the witness in question has been abroad and was unaware of these proceedings until he returned yesterday and was informed of what had happened.'

'The allowing of such late evidence, without disclosure and without the chance for us to examine it is potentially very damaging for the prosecution case, my Lord,' argues Ms Godfrey.

'And not allowing it is detrimental to my client,' retorts Mr De Beaux, 'and I contend that it would serve the interests of justice better if the witness was allowed to testify. I admit that this is very late in the day, but I would also contend that if my application to the court to allow new evidence is denied, then in the event of a guilty verdict we would most definitely lodge an appeal immediately, and that is not a good use of taxpayers' money, nor does it serve the interests of justice.'

The judge sighs again. He looks at his watch, then rests his chin on the palm of his right hand, and chews things over in his mind for a few seconds.

'Well then,' says the Judge; all eyes and ears are on him, as everyone waits for him to announce his decision. 'Given the seriousness of the charge and the potential sentence of life imprisonment, given the fact that neither the defence nor the prosecution have had a chance to see this evidence previously and as such are both are more or less on an equal footing, and in light of my duty to act in the interests of justice, I will allow the witness to give evidence. Mr De Beaux, you have thirty minutes to speak with the witness, and a further thirty minutes to produce a brief written statement with copies for the prosecution and myself to have sight of, after which I want everyone back in court.'

'Thank you, My Lord,' Mr De Beaux says, and he then lets out a quietly exuberant "yes" under his breath. He is now eager to get cracking with this, to speak to this witness and get hold of this new evidence. Even though he has been doing this job for far longer than he cares to remember, these unexpected twists and turns, these bolts out of the blue which have the potential to flip the case on its head, never ever fail to excite him, and for that moment in time, he feels like a junior barrister all over again.

An hour and a half later, there is much chatter in court as everyone tries to second guess what the mysterious adjournment was all about.

'All rise!' announces the clerk, and the judge enters the courtroom and takes his seat once again. He then promptly explains to the jury what is about to happen.

The court calls Harry Rushton to take the witness stand. He takes his oath, and looks to Mr De Beaux for the first question.

'Mr Rushton, can you tell the court why you are here. What is your connection with this court case, and why you have come forward at such a late stage in the proceedings in order to give evidence on behalf of the defence?'

'Erm, yes, I can explain. Tom Lester lives at number 10 on the same road as that lady.'

'I take it you are referring to the defendant?'

'Yes. That's right. Tom and I were at university together until we graduated a couple of years back. On the 31 March of this year, I was visiting Tom at their house. His parents were out at the time. We just chilled on the PlayStation for a bit.'

'What time was this?'

'I was there from around quarter past two, and I left around quarter to three.'

'Why has it taken you this long to come forward?'

'I didn't know about the murder until yesterday evening. My girlfriend and I have been abroad, backpacking around the Far East. I got back a couple of days ago, and I met up with Tom and a few other mates at a bar in town last night. I don't know how we got onto talking about this murder, but when he mentioned the date, and details about the case, I realised I may have seen something that might be significant, and I saw it as my duty to come down here and let the court know before it was too late.'

'We are obliged to you for that,' says Mr De Beaux, quite genuinely. 'Can you tell the court what you saw on the 31 March.'

'As I said, I left Tom's house around 2.45pm. I was in my car coming out of their drive, my car was facing forward so I didn't need to reverse. As I started to drive off, I briefly looked towards number 6, which is the defendant's house. I saw a man open the door. I believe that was her husband, as I had seen him before once or twice when I had visited. And he had opened the door to let another man in. The other man was entering the house as I drove off. I didn't think anything of it until the conversation at the bar last night.'

'Can you describe anything you remember about the man who entered the house.'

'He had dark, sporty clothes on, and a black woolly hat.'

'Did you see his face?'

'No. He had his back to me,' Harry Rushton nodded.

'And you are certain of this.'

'One hundred per cent.'

'Thank you, Mr Rushton. The prosecution will have some questions for you now.'

'Mr Rushton. Quite some time has elapsed since this murder occurred, therefore, how can you be so certain of the date and time? It might have been a different day that you are thinking about,' says Ms Godfrey.

'No, it was 31 March for sure, because I left the UK that very day with my girlfriend. We flew out of Birmingham airport that evening. I had gone over to say bye to Tom, and also to pick up a couple of spare adapter plugs that he said I could have. I know I left around 3 o'clock, because I had to drive over to the retail park and grab a few more last-minute things, and it closes at 4 o'clock, so I remember looking at my mobile phone and thinking it I've got loads to do so I better hurry.'

'Even so, a lot of time has elapsed since you left the country; you must have spoken to Tom or messaged him since that day?'

'Yes, we did stay in touch, but as we were backpacking the communication was quite infrequent. It was just more like touching base to check the other was okay. He never mentioned the murder. It wasn't something that cropped up until the conversation in the bar last night. And once Tom told me what had happened, I couldn't stay quiet about what I'd seen, in case it was important.'

Miriam looks over at this young man, and her eyes silently thank him for coming and saying what he has said. She doesn't know how much of a difference it will make, but she is more grateful than he will ever know.

After the surprise witness' brief time in court, Mr De Beaux manages to finish his closing speech. The judge delivers a well-balanced summing up to the jury, and the members of the jury then filter out of the courtroom to go away and deliberate.

Miriam walks out of the dock, and down the cold steps that lead to the cell. She knows her entire future now hangs by the slenderest of threads. And not just any thread. It is like that marionette string that is holding her up is spun with mere *kachay dhagay*, an Urdu phrase meaning raw thread; so brittle, so fragile, one touch and its fractured, then broken forever.

She sits in the cold cell and wraps her arms around herself securely. Since her incarceration, she has slowly been thinking about what kind of change she needs to cultivate going forward. She has thought long and hard about this. She pulls her knees up and encloses them with her arms. She rests her chin on her knees and in this very moment, she makes herself a promise. If she survives this, if she receives another shot at life, she swears by everything she holds dear, she will do whatever it takes to make herself strong. She will weave her life back together again, but not with *kachay dhagay*. No. This time it will be put back together with the strongest, most durable, most resilient rope possible. Never, ever again will she allow another person to break her.

33

Birmingham Crown Court
19 November 2019

Her waiting continues, as one day rolls into the next, and still nothing from the jury. Each day is insufferably long, and Miriam thinks this waiting is an even worse kind of hell than prison. The not knowing is what is killing her, and the questions that no one can answer roam around in her head like demons running wild, intent on ruining her every conscious moment; when will they reach a verdict? What verdict will they reach?

At the end of the second day of deliberation with no word from the twelve men and women, the judge decides to call them all back into the courtroom. The jury reports that after two full days, it still cannot reach a unanimous verdict.

'Very well,' says the judge, 'you may now go back and deliberate to see if you can reach a majority verdict.'

The jury leaves the room, and Miriam wonders how much longer this agony will last.

That night in her prison cell, Miriam encounters a strange dream. It is in fact the continuation of a previous dream.

Even thinking about her dreams carries with it such thorny memories that make her shudder. Not long after marriage, she had to learn not to mention her dreams to Zaf. She recalled the first time she had done this quite innocently, not realising that this was another thing he would find fault with. It had been on her part an attempt at a simple conversation about a dream she'd had.

'Will you please stop banging on about your dreams. You're not some prophet, you know. Your dreams aren't important. In fact, they're meaningless. The average person's dreams are a load of nonsense, and you know I don't like to be bothered with nonsense. I've got far more important things to think about.'

The first of the two dreams her mind was now preoccupied with had occurred the night before Zaf's death. She dreamt that her mother had visited their house. Her mother had walked over to Miriam, and kissed her on the forehead. Miriam had been so pleased to see her, and as she was about to talk to her, her mother walked past her and into the lounge, and straight over to the mantelpiece. Miriam followed behind her. Her mother gazed at Miriam and Zaf's gold-plated framed wedding photograph for a few seconds, after which she picked the photo up, and she left the house, taking the photograph with her. Miriam was left standing, just watching her mum walk away.

Last night, in her dream, her mum came to visit her at the house again. She walked through the front door, and over to Miriam who was stood in the hallway. Her mother was carrying a beautiful, white rose. It was not yet in full bloom; its powdery snowy leaves were snuggled together tightly, but its heady perfume permeated the air around them, infusing the atmosphere with a soothing, mellow ambience. She placed the rose in her daughter's palm, and on top of it she placed a small photograph of Miriam. The photo had been taken on the last Eid before her mum died. In this image, Miriam was wearing the purple and pink salwar kameez that her mum had stitched for her. Miriam's face was alight with the widest smile possible, a grin that stretched from ear to ear. As she stared at the photo, Miriam realised that she could not remember the last time that she had smiled like that. So abandonly, freely, deliriously almost. And there, the dream ended.

Miriam wonders if she will ever smile like that again.

Birmingham Crown Court
21 November 2019

Again, the waiting is unbearable, but two long days later, at a few minutes to half past three in the afternoon, the jury returns to the court and declares that it has reached a majority verdict.

The courtroom is tense. Zaf's parents are waiting, poised at the edges of their seats, with sombre faces, his mother wiping away a stray tear, both of them hoping for a guilty verdict to be announced.

Miriam's father and brother are sitting diagonally opposite Zaf's parents. Her father is staring straight ahead, perhaps at the court clock. Her brother is sitting tensely; he has both of his palms pressing down firmly on his thighs, in an effort to stop his legs from shaking. Nina is in court too, her arms are folded, her face serious and still.

The work colleagues who have followed the trial consistently are all also seated. This does not include Rachel. She did not return after she gave evidence.

The reporters inside in the courtroom are poised and waiting. The journalists outside are getting in their places, positioning their cameras, attaching their microphones.

The foreman of the jury is asked to stand. It is the head-teacher man; predicted correctly by Mr De Beaux who suspected right from the start that he would be chosen as foreman.

Miriam is also told to stand. This is it; she thinks. The show is nearly over. This is now the grand finale. The story is nearing its end, the final curtain in nigh, although none but the jury know the ending.

The foreman stands with his hands clasped in front of him and listens carefully to the questions that follow from the clerk.

'Have you reached a verdict upon which at least ten of you are agreed?'

'We have,' replies the foreman.

A few tense seconds pass before the next question is asked.

'Of the crime of murder, how do you find the defendant?' asks the clerk. 'Guilty, or not guilty?'

The suspense is palpable. Nobody in the public gallery utters a noise. None of the lawyers dare move. Miriam can scarcely breathe.

The foreman opens his mouth.

It has probably only been three seconds since the question was asked, but Miriam's perception of time is not the same as everyone else's. Hers is a mere distortion, because those three seconds are passing very differently for her. For her, the walls feel like they are closing in, suffocating her, stifling her breath, moving menacingly towards her, as though they will soon crush her into tiny little pieces. Everything around her is dark and sinister, and her thoughts are like two different sides of a battered old coin; she wants this moment to stay forever, so she never finds out what the jury has decided, but then, no, no, she just wants him to spurt it out so that this dreaded moment can be over with as rapidly and painlessly as possible.

The foreman takes a breath.

Miriam is catapulted back savagely into the here and now. The walls have shifted back to where they were before, the room is lit up painfully brightly, and she can see clearly that the foreman's lips are now moving. She has no option but to hear what he and his fellow jury members have decided. Slowly, the words emerge.

'Not guilty,' he says.

The heat rises in Miriam's face, and around her neck. She swallows hard, but there is nothing to swallow, her throat is as dry as a desert.

'And as to the alternative count of manslaughter, how do you find the defendant; guilty or not guilty?'

Miriam's forehead is now smothered in sweat, and she clasps her hands together tightly to stop them from shaking. She rubs her palms together as she waits. Her legs have now turned to jelly. She sees the foreman's mouth open once again. And now he speaks.

'Not guilty.'

Miriam's legs give way and she falls to the floor. She tries to catch her breath, and she ends up having a coughing fit whilst she sits in a heap on the floor, desperately trying to get her breath back.

The courtroom erupts with noise, like a sleeping volcano suddenly let loose. Mr De Beaux turns around to see the prison guards helping Miriam back up to her feet.

'Mrs Hassan,' says the judge, ignoring the racket around the courtroom and instead looking straight at Miriam, once she is upright again, propped up by one of the guards, 'you are free to go.'

Sara now takes over from the guard, and holds on to her as Miriam comes out of the dock, and she immediately whisks her off to a consultation room. Mr De Beaux follows behind. They need a few moments to take stock before going out and facing the cameras.

Miriam sits down, and rests her palms face down on the table, one on top of the other, and then places her still sweaty forehead on top, and closes her eyes. She needs a moment. Her legal team know that. She needs this little bit of time before they go out and face the media barrage.

A few minutes later, Miriam lifts her head up, opens her eyes, and sits upright in her chair. She exhales loudly.

'How are you feeling?' asks Mr De Beaux.

'Confused.'

'Confused?' asks Sara. 'Why?'

Miriam sighs, once again, loudly this time. She nods her head. 'I hadn't prepared myself for this. I was going down, in my head, that's what I believed. That's what I had readied myself for. Being sent to prison. For a very long time. That was going to be my future. It was the only future I had imagined, and now I've been given a different future, I feel lost. What am I going to do with it?'

'One step at a time, eh,' says Mr De Beaux. 'You are a free woman, and you can do exactly as you please, whatever you want, but baby steps.'

Miriam looks at them, one by one, her head turning from one side of the room to the other in quick succession.

'Thank you. Both of you. So, so much. I will be eternally grateful.'

'Hey, we were just doing our jobs,' says Sara.

Miriam allows a little smile escape onto her lips. This is the first time Sara and Mr De Beaux have seen her smile.

'I think we all know you went way above and beyond, and I know what a mardy cow I was at times. I was uncooperative, and stubborn, and I am sorry for that.'

'Nonsense. You were a fantastic client,' Mr De Beaux reassures her. Miriam smiles a bit more. 'That's better,' he adds. 'You have a beautiful smile, you know; you need to show it off more often.'

When they do eventually step out, there is a wall of press

and cameramen that greets them. Mr De Beaux addresses those waiting very briefly.

'My client has been through a most traumatic experience, but in the end, justice has been done. Whilst the correct verdict has been delivered, my client has endured a great deal of suffering, not only because of this trial, but also as a result of the emotional and psychological abuse that she endured throughout this marriage, abuse that we sometimes refer to as gaslighting. I would urge the legislators and politicians to think again about how we can better protect the victims of such crimes. I have nothing more do add except to ask that you now please allow Mrs Hassan her privacy so that she can start rebuilding her life. Thank you. That will be all.'

34

31 March 2019
Miriam

All that I wanted was to see my family again. I've waited a long time for this, but the chances of it happening today have now vanished, I know that. There will be other days, other weekends when we can go and see them, and yet, I am fixated with it being today. It was supposed to be today. It *should* have been *today.*

Sometimes, I think Zaf really enjoys this. No. Not sometimes. Most, if not all of the time. He takes some morbid pleasure in grinding me down until I am reduced to the lowest, most pitiful state, not that he ever does actually take pity on me. He dangles me precariously from a long, frayed, string, and watches my panic-stricken face fill with fear. Sometimes he builds up my hopes, only to let me down, as only he knows how. These thoughts pester me as I get ready to leave the house. I glance at my watch; it is two o'clock.

I do up the zip on my coat and walk out of the house. Our road is quiet; there is no one around. The sky is threatening a deluge which has not yet materialised, and I wonder if I should have brought my brolly.

When I reach the bottom of our road, instead of going directly to the park, I turn left and walk up towards the high street. Zaf handed me a letter on Thursday evening and told me to post it as soon as possible, and not wait until I was next in the office on Tuesday. That was what I would normally do. Any post from home that needed sending out, I took with me to the office and it went out at the end of the day along with all the other letters and packages. But I must post it today, not leave it until Tuesday, because I know I need to say it's done if he asks me about it later on. And he will. Of course, he could take it with him to the office on Monday and stick it in with the rest of the post. But that was not something Zaf would do. Mundane tasks like posting letters were not his thing.

After I have posted the letter, I head back.

When I get towards the bottom of the lane, before I carry on towards the park entrance, I notice what I assume to be a man, judging by his height and build, turning into our cul-de-sac.

I catch a glimpse of him from behind; he is a sporty looking type with black joggers and a black hoodie, and white trainers that have shiny stripes on the side. He is wearing a black woolly hat too, which is not surprising given how cold it is. I don't see his face. But I notice him because I rarely see people walking down this end, and I wonder who he is visiting. My father always said that even as a child I had a photographic memory; I would see something once and recall it with highly accurate detail. I think that's how I managed to do well in my 'A' levels, despite the ridiculously unsettled life I was leading at the time; grieving over my dead mother, rebelling against everything I could possibly rebel against, arguing with my dad, shouting and screaming like a banshee at times. None of this had left me with much time for revision, other than the very last-minute sort, and yet, it all came good in the end. The photographic memory came through. But that was then. Now, I often doubt myself. It's as though the old, seemingly intelligent Miriam has disappeared, and this new Miriam is very different. I now usually get even the simplest of things wrong; I dither, and constantly question my own judgement. I even feel scared of my own shadow sometimes. I don't seem to know how to make a decision anymore, how to stand up for myself, nor can I recall what it feels like to be worth something, anything.

Whilst I am walking past our cul-de-sac, I also notice, during my brief glance, a car parked at number 10 that isn't one of their cars - such a non-consequential detail, I think nothing of it. I carry on and head down towards the park. As I walk through the tiny entrance, I look up and notice that the leaden overcast sky has now grown darker, and a downpour seems even more likely, so I turn towards the park café. It's the usual girl, Mary, behind the counter. She has large baby blue eyes and a heavily bronzed and contoured face; the blue and the brown seem like they would be a mismatch, but she pulls it off. I notice that the clock on the wall behind her says 2.50pm. I grab my flat white and sit away from the counter, in a section of the café that's tucked to one side and usually much quieter. I pick up the newspaper and read the headline, "Furious Tory MPs tell May: we'll block snap Brexit election". I tut quietly, and put the paper back. I, and everyone else I know, is sick of Brexit, and yet, no one talks of anything else these days. People yak on about Brexit anywhere and everywhere you go; on the news, on the radio, at work, at the doctor's surgery, at the supermarket. I don't want to read about it as well. I sit and drink my coffee quietly, looking at the continually threatening steely sky.

35

31 March 2019
The Visitor

Both of their cars are parked on the drive, but I sincerely hope and pray that Miriam isn't in. I need to have this discussion with him alone. I have no option but to have it out with him. If she is in, I will keep it brief, and arrange a time and place with him where we can talk privately. I don't want her to be around for this meeting.

I ring the bell and pull my mobile phone out of my pocket whilst I wait, and when I turn it to silent mode, I notice that it is about quarter to three. Zaf comes to the door, and immediately raises an eyebrow upon seeing my face, followed by a miserly smile.

'Well, this is a surprise.'

'I'm sure it is. Is Miriam in?'

'Miriam? No, she's not.'

'Good. We need to talk. Can I come in?'

Whist I stand there and wait for his answer, I hear the noise of a car starting up from one of the neighbour's drives, but I don't bother looking back. I am on a mission; I only have one point of focus at this present time, and he is standing right in front of me.

'Yes, I guess you better had come in.'

He leads me to his study. Most studies are small rooms, usually the smallest room in the house, you know, the room you can't do much else with. The tiny box room that's not big enough to use as the extra bedroom, or the little cubby hole under the stairs or to the side of the kitchen which was maybe a pantry in years gone by, that would be better suited to conversion to fulfil the modern day need of being able to work from home. But not Zaf's study. His study is huge, and most definitely not the smallest room in his mansion like house. There are luxury fittings from top to bottom; an indulgently crafted grand wooden desk, a most comfortable looking high backed dark brown leather swivel chair, wall to ceiling dark wooden bookshelves, and two smart black filing cabinets. There is even a racing car green leather two-seater sofa and hardwood side coffee table. There are also expensive memorabilia of previous global travels, dotted around the pristine walls, and precisely placed in the sparkling glass display cabinet, which houses a number of costly looking model cars; a Ferrari Spider in black, and a red vintage Alfa Romeo both catch my eye.

Zaf doesn't walk around to sit down on his expensive chair, instead he stays on my side of the desk and leans casually back onto it, his hands down by his sides resting on the wood, his ankles crossed on the ground. Even though the study is quite warm, I leave my hat and gloves on. I don't intend to stay for long.

'What do you want?' asks Zaf.

He astounds me. He is so cocky, it is almost laughable, and it would be if he wasn't such a powerful bastard.

'You know what I want.'

'If it's about the contract, like I told you, it's nothing personal, I've just decided—'

'I'm not here about the contract. Sod the contract. I couldn't care less about it.'

Zaf's eyes widen, but they don't show any fear or anxiety, quite the opposite; he looks more as though he is excited, thrilled even, at the prospect of what is coming next. You are one warped individual; I think to myself.

'So, she told you already?' he asks, with a slight nod of his head.

'Yes. She has.'

'That's that, then,' he says, the presumptuous, condescending swine that he is.

'No, not quite,' I tell him.

'Oh? Really?'

He is trying to goad me. I just need to stick to the plan. Tell him what's what. 'You listen carefully.'

'I'm all ears,' he says, with an arrogant smirk splashed right across his arrogant little face.

'I want you to leave my wife and my son alone.'

He leans forward a tad, his unblinking eyes penetrating mine. 'Don't you mean *my* son.'

There. He's said it. The verbal blow that I knew was coming, heard by me for just the second time now.

'Whatever you and Sheree say, let me tell you this. *I'm* his father dammit, and he is *my* son! I have raised him. I have loved him. I'm all he's known as a father for the seven years that he has existed! He's my little boy, and I'm his dad.' I am determined not to let my emotions get the better of me. I keep my voice at a moderate level, and I look at him coolly, waiting for his response.

'But you're not though, are you? Biologically, I mean. Biologically, and legally, I'm his father,' says Zaf, indignation pouring out of each word that he emits from his poisonous mouth.

'Why are you doing this to me? Isn't it bad enough you had an affair with Sheree all those years ago when she was already married to me? Right under my nose? Something that you both kept from me. Now you want to take away *everything* I have. Why? Just because you've suddenly discovered he's your biological son? You think you can just waltz in and take him away, and by doing so take my whole life away with you.'

'That's where you are mistaken, my friend.'

With great difficulty, I ignore his reference to me as his "friend", although I want to spit in his face for even daring to refer to me as that. 'What do you mean?' I ask him, as I genuinely have no clue as to what he is talking about.

Zaf displays a smile so smug, that I feel sick just looking at him. 'What I mean is that I haven't suddenly discovered that he is my son. I've always known.'

'What?' I blurt out this question straight away event though his words have not quite registered properly. Once I acknowledge to myself what I have just heard, I feel a tremor that rocks me to my core. My heart begins to hammer against my ribcage, and my legs begin to waver.

'I'm a true businessman in every respect of my life. I make it my job to know everything. As soon as she had the baby, I had a test done. I've always known he's mine. That's why I've always contributed financially, although I do believe the money goes into an account you don't know about, and it'll be a nice tidy sum for him when he's older.'

'Why now? Why didn't the pair of you just have the guts to come clean at the time? Huh?'

Zaf lets out only a small laugh, having stifled what seem like a much larger one that had threatened to escape.

'Shall I be frank?'

'Are you ever anything else?'

'It didn't really suit me. I was busy growing the business, but also going out a lot, you know, partying, travelling, living my best life, cars, girls, the lot. I didn't want to suddenly become some boring, family man lumbered with a wife and kid, singing at bath time, going to boring school performances, or reading bedtime stories. Plus, there was the added complication of our personal and family ties. I persuaded Sheree that us getting together would bring shame on her parents, so it was best to let this secret lie. She's always been putty in my hands, you know; she was back then, and she is again now. But if it's any consolation, we didn't see each after she got pregnant, until recently, that is.'

'Why? After all these years. Why now?'

'Things are different now. I'm not the same person anymore. My wild days are behind me. I think I'm ready to settle down now.'

'You are already married and settled, for God's sake. What about Miriam, what are you going to say to her?'

'Whatever the hell I want. She'll be served with divorce papers soon enough, as will you, and you will both have to accept it.'

'No way!' I tell him, 'Sheree doesn't love you, she loves me, as does my son!'

'What rubbish. Your marriage has been on the rocks for ages, she told me everything. And how many times do I have to say it, he's *my* son.'

My face feels red hot, like someone has pushed my head into a fire pit. But even that image can't do justice to the rage that I feel inside of me.

'How long have you been seeing each other again?' I ask

him, forcing my hands to stay at my sides, my fists balling up, me pushing them downwards, resisting the overwhelming urge to strike him. I can now feel a rampant fire erupting inside me, one that needs putting out, but I don't know how that's going to happen the way things are going.

'Not that long,' he replies.

I give him the coldest stare he has probably ever received.

'Don't look at me like that, as though it's something seedy,' he continues. 'It's not a fling. This time, it's for real. For good. So that we can be together as a family. The three of us.'

'Over my dead body are you taking my son and wife from me.'

'You don't get it, do you? You were always second best. I've always had the power to do this at any time I wanted. All I had to do was click my fingers and Sheree would come running. I just chose not to do it until now. She's besotted with me, well, with whatever version of me that's stuck in her head, that is. It's a done deal, mate.'

'I'm not your mate!' He has the audacity to just coolly stare at me. 'I don't care what lies you've fed her, I don't care what Sheree has or hasn't done, I will never let this happen.'

'You don't have a choice my friend. Pretty soon, Miriam will be gone, and then Sheree and my son are going to leave you and move into this house with me. I do kind of feel sorry for you; you will just have to watch and weep.'

He's right. I know he's right. He has all the power. He has all the money to pay for expensive lawyers, and in my wife, he has a woman who is obsessively in love with him, like some school girl, displaying child-like adulation, someone who appears to have lost hold of her senses. The level of her infatuation was evident when she gave me the two worst blows that I've ever received in my life; that the little boy I've loved for seven years is not mine, and that she is leaving me for Zaf. But I don't care what the biology says, where his genes come from, what his DNA profile is, that little boy is my son and I am his father. I was the first person to hold him, to read the *azaan* in his ear within seconds of him entering this world, I gave him his night feeds, rocked him to sleep, comforted him whenever he was upset, applauded at the end of his first school nativity when he played one of the wise men, kissed him better whenever he scraped his knee, taught him to swim and play football and ride his bike, and to play Scrabble, and lately I have been teaching him how to play chess. I don't care what any test says. He is my son. But I also know this; Zaf *will* take my son from me unless I stop him.

Zaf is now smirking at me, his teeth shining like bright white lights that hurt my eyes, his eyes revelling in what he most likely sees as his moment of triumph, a marked silent pause in time that seems to be signalling the onset of his victory over me. His evil eyes do not betray his evil intentions. He is now laughing at me, in a *I am going to ruin your life and there is sweet f-all you can do about it!* kind of a way. I have never caused this man even one speck of harm in his entire life. But his smile tells me that doesn't matter one little bit, for he will soon ruthlessly destroy me, cruelly snatch away everything I have loved and worked hard for. I know he won't stop until my life is shattered into tiny smithereens, never to mend back together again.

In what I can only describe as a split-second moment of pure terror, a panicked kind of madness, akin to the feeling of fight or flight, in an instant when the immediate and acute desperation for self-preservation takes hold, I grab the letter opener that is sitting on the desk right next to him, and without a further single thought, I thrust it into him with force. Zaf's breath catches in this throat as the blade goes in; he doesn't even see it coming. A coarse bark-like cry trips out of mouth, after which he staggers forward a couple of steps. He then falls with a thud to one side, the force of which sends him onto his back. He stares at me, as he holds his stomach, trying to contain the tide of blood. He calls out to me in a faint voice.

'Raza...Please...Raza...help me...'

He's not so cocky now, I think to myself. The enormity of what I have just done should absolutely floor me, but I don't seem to feel a thing. I should feel some remorse, maybe I should be in shock, perhaps I should be shaking with fear about the consequences of my actions. I think about what would be the right thing to do. I don't have to think for long, because I already know what that is. I should phone for an ambulance, and notify the police, and I should face those consequences. What about Miriam? I can't leave her to face the consequences of my actions, can I? What if she comes back and finds him dead? How will she feel? Perhaps I will have done her a favour. Who needs a husband like that? Perhaps I will spare her from the misery of a divorce. But that isn't the right thing to. I should do the right thing. I have done the right thing all my life. I have never so much as short changed anyone by even a penny, I have been a devoted husband and a doting father, I have worked myself crazy to provide everything that my family could need or want. I have always gone the extra mile to try and be one of the good guys. I am the type that will always put the trolley back in the trolley bay and not just shove it to one side like so many others, because that will make the life of the man at the supermarket who collects the trolleys much easier. I will carry litter around with me all day if I have to, but I won't put it anywhere but in a bin. I will always give my seat up for the elderly man, or pregnant woman. I will not just walk past someone who is in any kind of trouble. I will always help. I have been one of the good guys all my life, but seriously, where has that actually got me.

I look down at his pathetic face, his body squirming on the

floor, his eyes pleading for help, and still, I do not feel a thing. He may live or he may die. But I have to get out of here. I will let God decide both our fates.

I turn around, and I do not look back. I head towards the door, and just keep on walking.

36

31 March 2019
Miriam

Walking is what I have come to the park for, so I finish my coffee, and leave the café after just 15 minutes. I am restless, and I feel the need to move my legs. I walk along the lakeside, and notice the park is quiet today. There aren't many people around, and there aren't even the usual groups of pearly white swans who like to glide around the water majestically, or the greyish brown striped ducks that like to meander through, leading their ducklings in a neat regimented row behind them, quacking noisily as they go. The cold, grey weather is obviously keeping everyone away. I don't know why, but I decide to just head back home. I thought I wanted to walk, but as soon as I start to, I'm not in the mood anymore. I don't want to take a long walk after all, because I don't want to think and deliberate and analyse and ponder. The day has been bad enough without dissecting it all in my mind.

As I approach the house, I notice that Zaf's car is back on the drive. I feel annoyed that I have to face him so soon. If he couldn't be bothered to take me up to Bradford, then he could at least have stayed away from the house a bit longer.

I look at my watch as I enter the house, as I'm thinking about how long I have got until I need to make a start on dinner. I see that it is quarter past three. I start to walk up the stairs to go and get my phone to see if there are any messages or missed calls, but I change my mind, and decide to go and make some tea first, so I walk into the kitchen, fill the kettle half way with fresh water, and flick the switch on.

I look into the fridge to see what there is for to me to rustle up for dinner tonight. I spy a pack of lamb mince, and some aubergines. I check the freezer, and see that we have frozen peas. So, I'm thinking *keema mattar*, with *bengan aloo* and fresh *rotis*. I have enough chapatti dough left over from yesterday. And I can whip up a quick mint chutney and a green salad on the side.

I hear the kettle boil up and switch off, and I wonder if it might be a good idea to break the ice with Zaf by asking him if he wants a cup of tea as well. I am still very angry, but I know that I have to carry on as best I can. I'm still his wife, I still have to live here, I still have to work with him. None of that has changed. And no doubt my anger will subside with time. It's just a cup of tea. A gesture. To try and clear the air. Even though I am not at fault, but since when has that ever mattered. It is always down to me to smooth out the creases, to break the silence, to resume the dialogue, to apologise profusely, to beg forgiveness. I am pathetic, I know that. Pathetic for the way in which I long for his approval, his forgiveness, his smile, his attention, his love, his praise. This is all I have ever wanted, and yet, it has always eluded me. I don't feel that I can try any harder than I have done for the past two years. There is a certain amount of rage that festers inside me, because I have done everything I could possibly have done for this man; personally, practically, emotionally, physically, sexually. And yet, all those things that I yearn for from him will, I know in the bottom of my heart, continue to be withheld from me. I will forever be starved of his love and affection, deprived of his validation, and by the same token denied any autonomy.

My insides hurt with the pain of the past two years. I feel pain from the knots which bear witness to the emotional struggles I have lived through, from the kinks left by the physical exertions I have endured, from the humiliation I have felt from having to endure unwanted sex, from the fatigue caused by my endlessly futile attempts to please him. I feel hollowed out by all of the hurt. I am like a dead tree trunk that it is still standing, but only just; lacking any inner vigour, foundation or support, which may blow over at any moment if hit with the slightest gust of wind. And yet, despite all of this, I will still go into his study and ask him if he wants a cup of tea, as though nothing has happened, in my usual wretched attempt to paper over the cracks. I will say sorry and make him tea and cook his dinner and convince myself that the wounds are no longer there now that I have put a plaster over them. There we are. All gone. Nothing to see.

I open the door and walk in, and notice that he isn't at this desk. I start to spin back around to leave, suspecting he must be upstairs, as I can't hear the television from the lounge, but and as soon as I turn my head, I see him. He is lying on the floor. His vintage dagger style brass letter opener is stuck in his tummy, and there is a swirl of blood that has gathered around him.

He is looking straight at me and I freeze in the spot I'm in.

He struggles to speak but I can hear him.

'H-h-elp m-me, M-iri-am. H-elp...'

I don't speak. I don't do as he says. I do not react. I stay where I am, for now, rooted to the spot, by the door.

'C-c-all the am-bu-lance..'

He can hardly get his words out.

I suddenly feel so very dizzy, so I walk past him, over to the sofa, and sit down. I sit on the sofa and I think.

Think.

What shall I do?

Think. Miriam.

Quickly.

He is about three feet away from where I am sitting. His eyes open and close and he continues to bleed.

Think!

If I call the ambulance and he survives, then what?

If I don't call the ambulance, and he dies, then what?

Which life is better? For me?

This one, or that one?

This prison, or that prison?

This life, or that life?

But I didn't kill him!

I didn't do this!

So what?

Like anyone will believe you?

I close my eyes and sit back. I can no longer watch him. I need to think. I need to hear myself better. I think better with my eyes closed. Thoughts spark up and run around in my head like dragonflies. The lights come on and then they go off. Indecisiveness creeps in and my mind feels overwhelmed.

Why?

That is the word that keeps cropping up in my head.

Why have I been put in this position?

Why me?

I open my eyes, and stare at him. I don't move. I don't speak. I just watch him. And then I close my eyes once again, and lean right back. My body is very still. I feel cold and rigid, like a mummy in a sarcophagus. I zone out. Thinking, thinking, thinking...

When I open my eyes, I rub them violently, and then look down at the floor; he is still there. It wasn't a dream. He is still lying on the ground, and the crimson pool of blood has now spread bigger and wider than before.

His eyes are now closed. I stand up with a shudder and lightly walk the couple of steps over to where he lies. I kneel down beside his motionless body; his blood immediately stains my grey jeans. My hands are trembling. I try my best to steady them, and then I check his neck for a pulse. Nothing. I feel again. And again. Nothing. I check his wrist. Nothing. There is no beat, there is no sound, there is no breath.

Dead.

He's dead.

I walk over to the desk, pick up the telephone and call for an ambulance. My hands still shake, but my speech does not waver. I speak clearly and coherently. Then I place the receiver back down, walk back over to the sofa and sit down. And I listen to the voice in my head.

I didn't stab him.

That's a fact.

But I let him die.

That is also a fact.

Does that make me a killer?

Someone else came here and did this.

Someone else killed him.

But I allowed him to die.

Does letting him die make me just as bad as the person who stabbed him?

Does letting him die make me a killer? Make me guilty of murder? You decide.

ACKNOWLEDGMENTS

I would like to give huge heartfelt thanks to those who have helped me in the journey of bringing this book to life.

Firstly, my family. My children Bilal, Aminah, Hajrah, Mustafa and Suleman for their continued love and unstinting support, my gorgeous grandsons Yusuf, Musa, Danny and Zach who bring joy to my heart, and my husband Simon, my biggest cheerleader, for his unwavering love, constant support and endless encouragement.

Gratitude to my editor Elizabeth Garner who has once again so deftly worked her magic, to Stuart Leasor at Chiselbury Publishing for believing in this story, and to Indra Murugiah for the striking cover.

Thank you to my brilliant first readers, my niece Rehana and my husband Simon, whose insightful feedback and words of assurance inspired me greatly!

Finally, to the readers of this story, without whom none of this would matter - thank you so much for choosing this book!

ABOUT THE AUTHOR

Abda Khan is a lawyer turned writer and author of the novels 'Stained' (2016) and 'Razia' (2019) and her poetry collection 'Losing Battles Winning Wars' (2023). She is currently working on her first historical book inspired by her late father's service in World War II as part of the Punjab Regiment who fought alongside British soldiers in Burma. Her work has also featured in various anthologies and publications. She writes commissioned pieces (short stories, scripts, poetry), delivers creative writing courses, and produces and directs her own creative community projects.

Abda often writes about difficult themes, such as the topic of 'gaslighting' in her novel 'That Which May Destroy You', and is passionate about using fiction as a vehicle to amplify unheard voices and shine a spotlight on challenging social issues.

She was Highly Commended as a finalist in Arts and Culture category of the Nat West Asian Women of Achievement Awards in 2017 and she won British Muslim Woman of the Year in 2019.

ALSO BY ABDA KHAN

Stained

Selina, a beautiful, British-born Pakistani young woman recently lost her father, and finds herself struggling to cope with life, in particular with some aspects of her studies. Matters go from bad to worse, when a trusted family friend from the mosque offers to tutor her, and rapes her instead. With the threat of dishonour to her family at her back, Selina goes to extreme lengths to avoid scandal, and prevent shame being brought to her widowed mother's door. It will take all the strength and courage Selina can muster when her life travels down a dangerous path, from which there may be no return...

Razia

Farah is a young lawyer living and working in London. She's just ended a long relationship, and her parents are looking for a husband - whether Farah wants one or not. So far, so normal. But at a work dinner, hosted by a dangerously powerful man, she comes across a young woman called Razia, who Farah soon realises is being kept as a domestic slave. We follow Farah's daring investigations from the law courts of London to the brick kilns of Lahore, as she begins to uncover the traps that keep generation after generation enslaved. Everywhere she turns there is deep-rooted oppression and corruption, and when the authorities finally intervene, their actions have dire consequences. Farah teams up with a human rights lawyer, Ali, and the two become close... but can she trust him; can they help Razia and others like her; and will they ever discover the explosive secret behind these tragic events?